KID-NAPPED IN CARTAGENA

A Casey Clark YA Mystery
(Book #2)

by

Michael Balkind

TELEMACHUS PRESS

Cover Designed by Michael Balkind

Published by Telemachus Press, LLC
7652 Sawmill Road
Suite 304
Dublin, Ohio 43016
http://www.telemachuspress.com

ISBN 978-1-965121-08-5 (eBook)
ISBN 978-1-965121-07-8 (Paperback)
ISBN: 978-1-965121-17-7 (Hardcover)

Version 2024.12.19

What Readers Are Saying About
Kid-Napped in Cartagena

"An excellent follow-up to Balkind's "Gold Medal Threat". Casey and Johnny are back, this time in Colombia, to rescue the abducted families of two top soccer stars. International intrigue, snappy dialogue and rich settings combine to make *Kid-napped In Cartagena* your next best read. Get yours today and enjoy the adventure!"
— **Nicky Testaforte**, Adult & Children's book author

"A fun, action packed novel that reads like a combination of The Hardy Boys and Nancy Drew mysteries of yesteryear, with a current day theme. It's perfect for older children, teens, and adults."
— **David Barnes**

"Another brilliant Balkind nail-biter featuring his young sleuths. Vivid depictions of the excitement of the World Cup mixed with an epic story featuring life and the underworld in South America and the passion of sports. "
— **Kerry Lawrence**

"I really enjoyed this book. It is so kid relatable and the language is exactly how adolescents communicate. The story held my attention; and it is so wonderful to read a story that doesn't involve fighting aliens and bad monsters who want to destroy Earth."
— **JoAnn Ferrigno**, Founder of Camp Summerset, a Reading & Creative Writing Camp

"Kid-Napped in Cartagena is a nonstop action story with some humor sprinkled in. Young readers are sure to enjoy the character development and will surely relate to the interactions between their peers and the adult characters. I found it hard to put down as I remembered my days as a youth."
— **Michael Rooney**

"I loved *Kidnapped in Cartagena*. Great characters. Very enjoyable read. Another winner by Michael Balkind."
— **Brian Summer**

"Having grown up in the 50s and 60s I always felt badly that my children did not have mysteries like the Hardy Boys and Nancy Drew to read and enjoy. Michael Balkind has changed that with a series that young adults, adults and kids of all ages will enjoy. The stories have a group of young adults that work together to resolve criminal cases and use all of today's social media and electronics so everyone will enjoy reading them."
— **Steven Peltz**

"I loved *Kid-Napped in Cartagena*. It's an incredible and wonderful read!"
— **Harrison Mellor**

"A captivating mystery about a group of teenagers who travel to Colombia to watch the World Cup. While there, the teenage friends embark on an adventure to solve a crime involving the players. If you want an author to capture your attention and have you guessing, yet trying to put the pieces together, then you want to read this book by Michael Balkind. This has everything that I look for in a book…a great plot, interesting characters, and grabs your interest right away. Although written for young adults, it is a must read for mystery and suspense fans of all ages!"

— **Jennifer Jenkins, M.Ed.**, Elementary/middle school special educator (and regular educator). And, also a superfan of thriller/mystery/suspense!!!

Dedication

I would like to dedicate this novel to my cousin's son, Teddy Balkind, a 16-year-old boy who lost his life while playing in a high school hockey game. Teddy was a smart, funny, and independent kid who loved life and everything it had to offer. Always with a huge smile, he was kind, thoughtful and lived and played with heart. He was an outstanding human being who always thought of others and always tried to do the right thing. He will forever remain in my family's heart and in all those who knew him. His life, while short, had an incredible, positive impact on those around him...something we should all strive for.

Kid-Napped in
Cartagena

Chapter 1

"OH MAN, I can't sleep," Johnny Rebah groaned as he rolled over and flung the twisted bed sheet off his wiry body.

Barely conscious, Casey Clark opened one eye just enough to see the red digits on the bedside clock and muttered, "Shut up. It's 3:30 in the morning."

"No, I mean it. This happens like every time we travel. I don't know whether it's the time change or because I'm not in my own bed, but I can't sleep."

"Time change?"

"Yeah. You know, like the jet lag that kept us up when we went to Australia."

"We're in Colombia, dude."

"So?"

"So, there is no time difference between New York and Colombia."

"Are you kidding me? The flight took eight hours. Of course, there's a time difference."

"Oh, I don't believe this. Just be quiet for now and I'll explain it in the morning?"

"Fine!"

After two minutes of silence, Johnny whispered, "Casey?"

No response.

"Hey, wake up." Johnny's voice was annoyingly louder.

Casey moaned, "What now?"

"I'm trying to sleep. Really I am, but this is driving me nuts."

"What is?" Casey slurred.

"When we flew to Australia, you said it was like we were flying into the future. The flight was about twenty hours, but since Sydney is like sixteen hours ahead of New York time, when we landed, it was only about four hours different than when we took off. "

"Yeah, so?"

"So, why is the time here the same as in New York?"

"Johnny, I'm too tired to explain it now. Either wait till the morning or Google it."

"Fine," Johnny said, reaching for his phone.

After another few minutes, Johnny whispered, "Hey."

Again, Casey didn't respond.

Johnny raised his voice, "I still don't get it."

"Oh my God, Johnny," Casey moaned. "You're driving me crazy. Australia is in a different time zone than New York. Colombia is in the same time zone as New York. I'll show you on a map in the morning. Now please, let me sleep."

"Okay, okay. You don't have to be so grumpy about it."

"Really? Just shut up already."

"Fine!"

A minute later, the room brightened, and the TV's volume blasted as Johnny fumbled with the remote. He glanced at Casey.

"Are you kidding me?" Lying on his side, Casey glared at Johnny with his elbow on the pillow and his head propped on his fist.

"What?" Johnny said.

"Don't give me that innocent tone of yours. I know what's going on here."

"What do you mean?"

"I mean, if you can't sleep, then I shouldn't either, right?"

"Well?"

"You're incredible," Casey said as he reached for a second pillow and stuffed it under his head. "Just find something good, and I'll watch with you for a while."

Johnny smiled and began surfing channels. "Thanks."

"Whatever," Casey said quietly, shaking his head in resignation.

"Sports or a movie?"

"I don't care."

"Spanish or English?"

"Really?" Casey looked at him in wonder. "Why would we watch a show in Spanish if we don't understand it?"

"Well, we're going to be here for a week, it would be good if we knew some Spanish. Maybe watching a movie in Spanish will help."

Casey's head slumped. "You really are unbelievable sometimes. Put on whatever you want."

Johnny clicked past a few channels, then stopped. "How about this?"

Casey watched for a second as Harry Potter spoke to Hermione in Spanish. Johnny laughed.

"What now?" Casey asked.

"It's funny. Their lips aren't in sync with their voices, and I can't understand a word they're saying."

"Duh!"

Johnny shrugged as he changed channels. "Okay, I'll find something in English, or we'll just watch some sports."

"Great."

"Here we go. How about some UFC?" Johnny stopped on an Ultimate Fighting Championship fight.

"Sure, that's fine. But, I thought Conor McGregor retired?"

"Me too, but who cares? He's sick!" Johnny said.

"Yeah, he is."

They watched for a few minutes. The crowd roared when McGregor won the round.

"Lower the volume a little," Casey said, staring at the screen.

When the volume didn't change, he looked over at Johnny. His eyes were closed, and his lips fluttered with a quiet snore.

"Unbelievable," Casey said as he tossed the light blanket off his thin, muscular legs and climbed out of bed. After gently removing the remote from Johnny's hand, Casey got back into bed, glanced at his sleeping friend, and grinned. Wide awake now, he watched the rest of the fight, doing all he could to refrain from cheering as McGregor pummeled his opponent. He looked at Johnny once more and chuckled before shutting off the TV and closing his eyes.

***

A warm, gentle breeze cascaded over Casey as he slowly awoke. The room was bright, and the delectable smell of bacon lured a loud growl from his stomach. Staring at the wall adjacent to his bed, his eyes meandered to a painting of a tropical beach scene. He squinted, thinking, *Where am I? Where's the poster of Johnny, Chelsea, Samantha, and me standing in front of the Olympic flag?* Baffled, he thought, *Wait, is today a holiday? Mom only cooks bacon on special occasions.*

He rolled over and saw Johnny sitting at the table in their hotel room. Reality gradually sank back in—*Oh yeah, we're in Colombia for the World Cup.* He sat up, rubbed the sleep from his eyes, and dragged himself out of bed. Still groggy, he trudged, zombie-like, toward the bathroom.

"I didn't know if you'd want eggs or pancakes, so I ordered you both from room service," Johnny mumbled through a mouthful of food.

"Thanks."

Casey left the bathroom door ajar as he stood in front of the toilet.

"I think I got the time zone thing down, but I want you to explain it anyway."

"Can you at least wait till I'm done in here?"

"Oh, sure, sorry. I wasn't paying attention."

"Shocking," Casey said quietly with an eye roll as he walked into the room. He grinned at the sight of food-warming domes on the table. He lifted one, revealing a single pancake and a few scattered specks of hash browns.

"They only give you one pancake in an order?"

"I ate two. Sorry."

"That's okay, I'll eat the eggs." He lifted the second cover to see a small pile of scrambled eggs and half a slice of bacon. "You ate the bacon too?"

Johnny's pale face squished into pitiful remorse. "Sorry, but you just kept sleeping, and I was still hungry after my omelet."

"Wait. You mean you already ate your breakfast, and then you had mine too?"

"I left you the eggs, didn't I?"

"How generous."

"Oh, come on. I tried not to eat yours, but it smelled so good. Since when do you sleep this late, anyway?"

"Only when somebody wakes me up in the middle of the night and won't let me go back to sleep."

"What are you talking about?"

"You don't remember? You woke me from a deep sleep. Then, you turned on the McGregor fight and made sure I'd watch it with you. Then, you fell back to sleep."

"Sorry."

"Whatever."

"How many rounds did it go?"

"All the way. It was so amazing! I can't believe McGregor lost again."

"What? He lost? Holy cow! Why didn't you wake me?"

"Wake you to watch him lose? That's ridiculous."

"No, it's not. I can't believe he lost!"

"Yeah, well, don't."

Johnny squinted. "Huh?"

Casey smiled.

"Wait, you're messing with me, aren't you? McGregor won, didn't he?"

Casey grinned and nodded.

"I knew it. He's insane!"

"Yup," Casey agreed.

"Oh here, I almost forgot," he lifted another plate and removed the cover as he handed it to Casey. "I saved you some sausages."

"How nice of you," Casey said, rolling his eyes again.

"What?"

"You hate sausages."

"Hmm, I guess you got me."

"It's alright," Casey said, taking a bite. "I appreciate that you at least attempted to be nice."

"Attempted? That hurts. Maybe I shouldn't give you this." He lifted yet another plate from the crowded cart.

"What's that? Half-eaten toast?"

"Take the lid off, jerk."

Casey removed the cover, and the tantalizing aroma of cinnamon wafted from the hot, gooey, spiraled roll. "Wow. I love cinnamon rolls."

"I know," Johnny said.

"Dude, you're awesome." Casey took a bite. His eyes closed, and his lips curled blissfully.

It was Johnny's turn to smile.

"This is so good. As soon as I finish, I'll explain the time zones. It's much easier to understand when you look at a map."

"Show me later. I forgot to tell you, my dad texted. They're waiting for us at the pool. I told him we'd come down as soon as you woke up."

"Okay, I'll go put on my shorts."

Johnny didn't respond. He was already completely engrossed with a game on his cellphone.

Casey rummaged through his suitcase and grabbed his blue Quicksilver boardshorts. He picked up the remote and turned on the TV as he slowly walked toward the bathroom. A local Cartagena news announcer was reporting the day's headlines.

Casey stopped and increased the volume. "Johnny, look."

Johnny looked up. "So, it's Erminio Marrese and Leonardo Sauro. Of course, they're on the tube. They're Italy's best players."

"I know who they are. Just keep watching."

The newscast changed back to the previous part of the story showing a slow-motion, black and white video of two men being shot in a café, and then two women and two children being aggressively led from the café at gunpoint. The story continued in Spanish.

"I wonder who they are?" Casey said.

Johnny's thumbs raced across his phone's screen at lightning speed. "Marrese's and Sauro's wives and kids. They were taken from that restaurant yesterday. It's right here in Cartagena. The police don't know much yet, but they're saying it's probably a cartel thing."

"Wow, that stinks," Casey said. "I wonder who the guys that got shot were? They didn't look like Marrese or Sauro."

"It says they were their bodyguards. Erminio and Leonardo were training with the team at the time."

"You think all the players have bodyguards?"

"I don't know," Johnny said.

"I wonder why they took the wives and kids?"

"Maybe they expected the men would be at the restaurant too."

"Hm, maybe?"

"It doesn't matter anyway. It's not like there's anything we can do about it. Go get changed. Let's go to the pool."

"Yeah, I guess you're right." Casey stepped into the bathroom and closed the door.

Chapter 2

"WELL, LOOK WHO finally decided to wake up and join us," Casey's mom, Shane, said as he walked toward his parents' poolside chaise chairs.

"Yeah, well, someone in my room had a problem getting to sleep and decided it was a good idea to keep me up half the night."

"Again?" Johnny's dad, Joel said. "What's with you and hotels, son? The beds are comfortable, aren't they?"

"My bed's fine. I think it's the time change thing again."

"Time change?" Johnny's mom, Cindy, asked.

"You know, like when we went to Australia. The jet lag thing that we had to get used to."

"I explained that we're in the same time zone as New York," Casey said. "It's easier to understand when you're looking at a map. I'll show him later."

The smiles and nods were hard to miss.

"Okay, everyone. Please don't make fun of me. It's my vacation too."

"Nobody's making fun of you," Cindy said.

"Right. Call it what you want, just please stop."

As Casey and Johnny gave their parents quick hugs, Casey said, "Did you guys hear about Erminio Marrese's and Leonardo Sauro's wives and kids?"

"What about them?" Joel asked.

"They were taken yesterday," Johnny said.

"What do you mean, taken?" Reid Clark, Casey's father, asked.

"They were having lunch at a café near here, and a couple of guys shot their bodyguards and took the women and kids."

"Oh my God," Shane said. "That's awful."

"They think it's a cartel thing," Casey said. "But they're not sure yet."

"What a shame," Joel began.

"Yeah, I hope they're okay," agreed Cindy.

"I can't stand that organized crime has infiltrated the world of high-level sports. Between Peter Buckar's abduction at the Winter Olympics, the assassins you boys stopped at the Olympics in Australia, Bob Thomas' murder at AllSport, Reid's death threats, and now this, it's gotten way out of hand."

"Well, at least you didn't have anything to do with it this time," Shane said, looking at the boys.

"Mom!" Casey snapped. "You make it sound like we were involved."

"Well, you were."

"But we were on the right side of the law."

"Of course you were. I'm just glad you're not tangled up in it this time."

"Me too," Cindy agreed. "I'd prefer this vacation to be nice and relaxing. And besides, you boys are only fourteen, you should be having fun instead of trying to stop criminals. You can save the world when you get a little older."

The adults chuckled.

Casey and Johnny looked at each other and shrugged. They removed their sunglasses and World Cup hats, slathered themselves with sunscreen, and stretched out on lounges, side by side, between both sets of parents.

Within minutes both boys were fast asleep. Shortly after, they were awakened by a spray of cold water on their legs.

"Stop it, Johnny," Casey mumbled with his eyes shut.

"Me? You stop it!"

After another squirt hit them both, Johnny reached over and smacked Casey's leg. "I said, cut it out!"

"Ow. That's not funny, you idiot."

One more squirt made them both sit up, fists clenched, ready to pounce on each other.

Loud laughs from two girls in the pool got the boys to look. Samantha and Chelsea, their friends from Australia, were both holding water guns.

"Holy cow," Johnny yelled, jumping up from his chaise. He ran toward the pool with Casey close behind. Both boys leaped in and proceeded to dunk the girls in retaliation.

"Easy, mate," Samantha said, pushing aside her long, curly, auburn hair. "I am a girl, you know."

"You sure are," Johnny said with a big smile, not trying to hide the fact that even after two years, he still had a crush on her.

"Wow." Samantha looked up at Johnny. "You guys must have grown about ten centimeters since the last time we saw you."

"No. Only about four inches," Johnny said.

Samantha, Chelsea, and Casey smiled.

"What?" Johnny asked. "Same thing, huh?"

"Not exactly," Casey said.

"Whatever. You both look great," Johnny said.

"Yeah. And that's so cool," Casey said to Chelsea, tapping the side of his nose in the same spot where she had an emerald stud. "It matches your eyes."

"Thanks, mate," she answered, pushing away a blond lock that had escaped the tightly coiled bun her hair was tied in.

"I can't believe you guys are here," Casey said.

"Yeah, pretty cool, huh? Your mom and dad made all the arrangements with our parents. They wanted to surprise you both." Chelsea rubbed the water from her big eyes, then reached for the edge of the pool.

"Well, it worked." Casey gave his parents a thumbs up, then asked the girls, "How'd they know how to find you?"

"Your mom sent me a private message on Instagram about a month ago," Samantha said.

"Cool!" Casey said, flinching as a soccer ball splashed down, just missing his head.

"Whoa! Where did that come from?" He reached for the ball.

"Lo siento," a boy said as he swam toward them.

Casey handed the ball over with a smile.

"Gracias," the boy said.

"De nada," Casey answered, noticing that the boy had winked at the girls just before swimming away. He was good-looking and more muscular than Casey and Johnny. His skin tone and accent were similar to the local Colombians Casey had met at the hotel and airport. Casey glanced coyly at the girls wondering, *did they smile back when he winked?* He looked at Johnny, who returned a raised brow and shrug.

"Wow! Look!" Chelsea exclaimed. "How cool!"

They all turned to see the boy approaching his friends, who were standing chest-deep in a circle near the other end of the pool, heading a soccer ball back and forth across the circle.

Casey began keeping count each time the ball left a kid's head. On sixteen, the ball splashed down, far outside the circle. He watched as a kid retrieved the ball. Casey squinted, then rubbed the water from his eyes and blinked a few times. Yup, the kid was a girl in a bikini. After a few additional eye-clearing blinks, he thought, *Whoa, she's pretty!*

"They're so good," Samantha said.

"Good? They're amazing!" Johnny exclaimed.

"Let's go closer and watch," Chelsea said.

They began swimming toward the shallow end. The sky was cloudless, and the sun was bright. The temperature was rapidly climbing, and while the large pool wasn't overly crowded, there were many small groups throughout the deep and shallow ends. Casey listened as he slowly breast-stroked, weaving his way around clusters of hotel guests enjoying the water. He heard five conversations, each in a different language. Testing himself as he went by, he knew the first was French and the second was Italian. The third language sounded Scandinavian. The fourth was Asian, but he couldn't pinpoint its specific country. Then, he had to listen harder as he was passing three men who were speaking so quietly Casey couldn't hear a word. They looked to Casey like South or Central Americans, but, of course, he couldn't be sure.

Slowing to the pace of a drifting seahorse, he did his best to keep his surveillance inconspicuous.

"Moverlo chico!" one of the men said loudly, glaring at Casey.

Casey nervously looked toward the man and their eyes locked for an intimidating moment. Thick, wet, black hair and a bushy moustache were plastered against his dark brown scalp and upper lip. A twitch of the man's left eye caused Casey's body to stiffen. With a flick of his wrist, the guy waved Casey on. While Casey's comprehension of Spanish was sketchy, there was no mistaking what the man meant.

Quickening his pace with his eyes fixed on the guy, Casey swam into someone.

"I'm so sorry," he said, flustered and overly apologetic.

"It's okay, mate. It's only me." Samantha placed her hand calmingly on his shoulder.

"Oh, thank God."

"What was that all about?" she asked, tipping her head subtly in the angry man's direction.

"I don't know. I passed them really slowly. I guess he thought I was eavesdropping."

"Were you?"

"Kind of," he said with a grin.

"Why?"

"I was counting how many languages I could identify as I swam by different groups. I didn't mean to upset anyone."

"You never do."

"What's that supposed to mean?"

"Oh, I don't know," she said with a chuckle. "It seems to me that you and Johnny are like magnets when it comes to trouble."

"What? No way."

"Well, maybe trouble is the wrong word, but you sure manage to get into some interesting situations."

"Okay." Casey shrugged. "Maybe you're right. But it's not like I mean to."

"I didn't say you did."

"Whatever. Let's go watch." He turned his head toward the group of kids and saw that Chelsea and Johnny had joined the circle. "Wow, that didn't take long."

"Oh, cool. C'mon, let's go," Samantha said, already rushing to join them.

As Casey got closer, he noticed that a big crowd was watching the group play their game. He began to have second thoughts. *I can't head the ball like them. This is going to be embarrassing.* He watched as Johnny got his chance and headed the ball. Instead of sending it in a high arc like the others, Johnny sent a line drive that hit the kid across from him in the chest. Of course, the boy happened to be one of the biggest and toughest looking in the group. The other kids in the circle went silent. The boy scowled and glared at Johnny.

"I'm sorry. I didn't mean it," Johnny stammered.

I knew this wasn't a good idea, thought Casey as he rushed toward his friend's side while keeping an eye on the big kid who had been hit.

The boy's fierce look slowly turned into a grin as he pointed to his head. "Muy bien. Tienes una cabeza dura."

Casey only understood muy bien, but the group's laughter and the slaps on Johnny's back from those flanking him made it clear that everything was okay. Johnny began to laugh, too.

Casey sighed and stopped outside the circle. He watched as the game resumed, and Chelsea, who was standing right in front of him, headed the ball in a nice arc to the boy across from her. Some of the kids clapped. Then, after the next header, the ball flew back in Chelsea's direction but sailed high over her head. It landed in front of Casey, splashing him in the face.

More laughs emanated from the circle. After rubbing the water from his eyes, Casey saw Chelsea gesturing for him to join the circle.

He tossed the ball to one of the guys and shook his head. "No, I suck at heading soccer balls."

Then, the pretty girl in the bikini who was standing next to Chelsea reached her hand out to him. "Vamos, es divertido," she said with a smile so big, it practically made Casey melt into the pool.

"Okay, but I warned you," he said anxiously as he took her hand and stepped between the two girls.

"Listo?" the boy with the ball asked, looking at Casey. "Aqui, practíca."

"No entiendo," Casey said, uttering the two Spanish words he knew best.

"He's going to toss you one for practice," Chelsea said.

"Okay," he said reluctantly.

Casey focused as the ball came his way in a softly thrown arc. He timed it perfectly and jerked his head forward, hitting the ball low on his forehead, sending it down just in front of him with a big splash. The pretty girl plucked the ball from the water and said, "Mirame."

"Huh?"

She smiled at him, and while holding the ball in her left hand, she pointed at his eyes, then toward the ball with her right hand. "Mira."

She tapped the middle of her forehead and shook her head. "No." Then, she touched her hairline. "Aqui."

Casey watched as she tossed the ball high in the air and waited until the right moment to flick her head forward. She connected with the ball and sent it across the circle, back to the boy who had thrown it to Casey. She looked at Casey again, pointed at him, and said, "Tu turno."

"Listo?" repeated the boy with the ball.

Casey looked at him and raised a finger. "One second." He rubbed his face, steadied himself with his arms stretched out just above the water, and with a look of determination, said, "Listo!"

Casey focused on the ball as it approached. He hit it harder this time, and a little high on his head. The ball flew over the boy's head, directly across from Casey. Nods of approval mixed with a few claps. The girl in the bikini tapped him on the shoulder. "Mejor. Mira." She tapped the top of her head and said, "No." Then, she tapped the center of her forehead, and repeated, "No." Finally, she placed the tip of her finger on her hairline, and said, "Aqui!"

Casey nodded.

"Mira," she said, pointing at a younger boy standing outside the circle in shallower water. He was heading the ball repeatedly, seemingly unaware that anyone was paying attention to him. Casey watched in awe as the ball bounced about ten inches, straight up and down continuously with only small movements of the boy's head. He made it look easy, almost effortless. Casey was impressed by the boy's absolute focus.

A loud shout snapped Casey from his mesmerized stare. He spun his head toward the circle just in time for the soccer ball that was approaching like a missile to hit him squarely in the face. The sickening crack of his nose was drowned out by the louder smack of the ball against his face.

"Ow." He raised his hands, covering his nose and tearing eyes.

Laughs from a few of the kids stopped abruptly as Casey lowered his hands. Everyone was staring at him. He was in pain, but didn't want anyone to think he was a wimp. "I'm alright. Listo."

With all eyes remaining on him, he became anxious. "Why are you all staring?" He reached up with cupped hands and gently felt his nose. It hurt, but the pain was tolerable. His eyes widened as he looked at his palms after removing them from his face. They were covered with blood. Looking down, he quietly gasped at the blood streaming down his chest and stomach into the pool.

"Somebody get him a towel!" Samantha shouted as she splashed her way to his side. "Are you okay?"

"Yeah. It hurts, but not so bad." He looked at everyone staring. "I guess it looks a lot worse than it is."

"I bet you broke it again, dude," Johnny said, leaving a wake in his path as he rushed through the water with a towel in his outstretched hand.

"No. It's not broken," Casey said, reaching up again with both hands and touching his nose. "Ouch. Maybe it is. Is it crooked?"

"I can't tell. There's too much blood." Johnny handed Casey the towel. "Here, wipe it off, and I'll check."

"Look at it later," Samantha said. "Just cover it up, and let's get you out of the pool."

"Yeah," Johnny said. "You're making a pretty big mess."

"Shut up, Johnny," Chelsea said.

"Well, he is."

"He's in pain. Just be nice."

"Oh, come on, it's only a broken nose. It's no big deal."

"Oh yeah?" she said. "Well, how would you feel if it was you?"

Johnny shrugged and rolled his eyes. "You know how many times I've broken this?" He placed his forefinger on the tip of his nose.

"From the look of it, probably a whole lot," Samantha said as she took Casey by the arm and led him toward the steps.

Casey and Chelsea laughed.

"Ow." Casey groaned through the bloody towel. "It hurts to laugh."

Johnny proceeded to touch and rub his own nose. "Is it really that bad?"

"Stop worrying about yourself and help us get Casey out of the water," Samantha said.

They walked by the young boy who was still heading the ball up and down repeatedly.

"Wow, he's good," Chelsea said. "Kind of looks like he's in a trance or something."

The others nodded.

Casey's parents were waiting for them at the top of the stairs.

"Samantha," Reid Clark said. "You didn't have to punch him that hard, did you?"

"What? I didn't…" Samantha said defensively before looking up to see Reid's grin. "Oh."

"How bad is it?" Casey's mom asked.

"I'm pretty sure it looks way worse than it is," Casey said.

"Well, let's get you cleaned up and see if we need to take you to the hospital."

"Hospital? No way!"

"Sure. Who needs a hospital?" Casey's dad said with a chuckle. "You'll look great with a crooked nose."

"Yeah," Chelsea said. "It will look just like Johnny's." She turned, ready to defend herself. "Hey, where is he?"

"Who knows?" Casey said. "Dad, do you really think it'll be crooked if I don't have it set?"

"Let's find you a chair and take a closer look."

"There's one." Samantha pointed a few rows back.

Casey sat and pulled the red-streaked towel from his face. He flinched as he gently wiped away the blood from around his nose.

"Ooh!" Reid grimaced. "Nice job, bud. You look like DeNiro in *Raging Bull*."

Casey gave his father a questioning look.

"You never saw *Raging Bull?*"

As Casey slowly shook his head, Johnny approached. "Whoa! It looks just like McGillivray's."

"Really? It's that bad?" Casey asked, touching his nose again.

"No. Not really," Johnny said with a laugh.

Casey smiled.

"Who is McGillivray?" asked an older man with a long, gray, braided ponytail standing just behind Johnny.

"A UFC fighter. His nose got smashed really badly," Casey said, eyeing the man's tie-dyed, calf-length swimming trunks and matching shirt with peace signs and "Grateful Dead" on them.

"Who is your friend, Johnny?" Reid asked.

"Oh, sorry! This is Doctor…," Johnny scrunched his face as he turned toward the doctor. "Sorry, I forgot your name."

"Julio Esteban," the man said, turning to Casey. "Hmm, may I?" He began reaching toward Casey's nose.

"Hold on a second," Casey's mom said. "Who exactly are you?"

"I apologize, ma'am. You must be his mother."

She nodded.

"I run a clinic in Buenos Aires."

"A clinic?" Shane sounded skeptical. "What kind, if you don't mind my asking."

"Why would I mind? Currently drug addiction. But don't let that scare you. I retired from my family practice about eight years ago in order to offer my services to the needy. If it helps ease your concerns, I have re-set many broken noses in my time."

"How did you know about Casey?" she asked.

"I heard the announcement looking for a doctor and I responded."

"Announcement?"

"Yeah," Johnny said. "I figured there had to be a doctor somewhere in this crowd, so I ran to the concierge and asked them to announce it."

Happy that he wouldn't need to go to the hospital, Casey gave Johnny a thumbs-up.

"I don't want to seem paranoid or ungrateful, but do you have any credentials with you?" Shane asked.

Esteban made a silly face as he pulled the pocket linings out of his swimming trunks. "I can go get them if you wish. My wallet is in our cabana." He pointed to the row of cabanas behind the crowd on the other side of the pool.

Shane chewed her lip while staring at him skeptically.

"Honey," Reid said, pointing at Casey's bloody nose. "Why would anyone but a real doctor offer to touch that?"

Everyone except Shane chuckled, even Casey. "Thanks, Dad!"

"Well?" Reid said, reemphasizing his point.

"Alright," Shane said reluctantly. "I'm sorry, Doctor. I hope you understand."

"Of course I do. He's your son, and I'm sure I don't look much like a doctor in my pool attire."

Shane smiled.

"May I?" the Doctor asked as he approached Casey again.

"Sure," Shane said.

"I'm going to be as gentle as possible, young man, but it may hurt a little."

"Okay," Casey said with a slight nod.

Doctor Esteban delicately slid his thumb and forefinger up and down the sides of Casey's nose. Casey winced.

"Did that hurt?"

"A little."

The doctor nodded and spoke as Casey's mom held her son's hand. "It is definitely broken and needs to be set. I can do it fairly quickly right here, or we can take him to your room for some privacy."

"Your call, Casey," his mom said.

"Let's just get it over with here."

"Good. A brave young man." The Doctor turned to Johnny. "Johnny, would you please go find me two plastic drinking straws and a couple of wooden ice cream bar sticks or spoons."

Johnny nodded, turned, and ran.

Next, Doctor Esteban looked at Chelsea and Samantha. "Could you girls please get some ice, clean towels, and Q-Tips?"

"Sure," Samantha answered.

Then, he looked at Reid. "I guess you're Casey's father?"

"Yes, doctor, I'm Reid Clark," he said, reaching to shake hands.

Esteban smiled. "I may not look it, Mr. Clark, but I'm an avid golfer and big fan of yours."

"Thanks, Doc. I'm sure I'll say the same after you've taken care of that hook." He grinned, pointing at Casey's nose.

"Oh, Dad! That was so bad!" Casey moaned.

"No, Casey," Esteban said with a snorting laugh. "It may have been at your expense, but it was an excellent golf joke." He turned back to Reid. "I have more of a slice than a hook, though. Maybe you'll help me with it later. But at the moment, would you do me a favor?"

"Of course."

"Go ask the bartender for a glass of the highest proof alcohol they have."

"Are you going to get him drunk or use it as a disinfectant?"

"No, it's for me. I always do a shot or two before working on my patients."

"What?" Casey's mom shrieked.

Esteban laughed. "I'm going to use it to disinfect everything. Sorry, I couldn't resist."

Shane rolled her eyes.

"That is unless you would like some, Casey?" Esteban asked. "It might help ease the pain."

Casey looked at his parents questioningly.

"Fine with me," Reid said.

They all looked at Casey's mom, who looked back at each of them and finally shrugged. "I guess if it'll help. But just a little."

"Wow. Cool," Casey said.

"I'll be back in a flash," Reid said.

"Okay, Casey," Esteban said. "I think we should move you to a more comfortable lounge chair." Scanning their surroundings, he saw that they now had a sizable audience. "Tell you what, let's head over to my cabana. I don't think we want to put on a show."

"Good idea," Casey's mom said. "Thank you, Doctor."

"No problem. My wife will appreciate the company anyway." He grinned.

"Oh, no. We can't do that to her."

"Nonsense. I never work without her by my side. She'll not only understand, she'd be annoyed if I did this without her."

"If you say so."

Doctor Esteban nodded.

"Let me help you." Casey's mom reached for his arm.

"I'm okay, Mom. It's only my nose."

"I know, but you got hit hard, you might be dizzy."

"Thanks, but I can do it," he added a little testily.

"Fine." She pulled her hand away. "I only wanted to help. You don't need to be so grumpy."

"Sorry, Mom, but this is really embarrassing. I don't want them to think I need my mother's help." He gestured his head toward the kids in the pool and flinched when he saw the girl in the bikini looking right at him.

"Oh, I understand. Okay, you're on your own. Would you mind if I walk closely behind you? Just in case?"

"Uh, yeah, I guess," he answered, hardly paying attention to his mother.

"Gee, thanks."

As they weaved their way through the prone, glistening bodies toward the cabana, Johnny, then Chelsea, Samantha, and Reid, joined their procession.

Before entering the billowing, white, gauzy entrance to the cabana, Esteban turned, looked at each of them, and said, "Ah, muy bueno. I see you have each accomplished your assignments. Gracias."

The kids placed their gatherings on a chair next to the cabana.

Esteban looked at the glass of clear liquid in Reid's hand. "Vodka or rum?"

"Tequila."

"But I asked for something with a very high alcohol content." Esteban sounded annoyed. Reid held up the glass and nodded. "150 proof."

"Really? I didn't know there was such a tequila."

"Me neither. It's Sierra Silver, the highest proof stuff he had. He said if you need something stronger, he could get a bottle of Everclear 190 from the indoor bar?"

With a chuckle, Esteban said, "No, this will be fine." He turned and pushed aside the hanging cloth entrance. "Just give me a moment to inform my wife."

A moment later, he exited the cabana, followed by an attractive, full-figured, mocha-skinned woman in a bright yellow, one-piece bathing suit. She looked at the group as she tied the sash on her long, sheer, purple robe.

The doctor turned toward her. "Darling, this is Casey Clark, his parents, and his friends." He turned to the group, "And this gorgeous creature is my wife, Camila."

After quick hellos, Esteban said, "Ready, Casey?"

"Yup."

"Please join me in my office along with your parents." He turned, waved the gauze material aside with an exaggerated flair, and entered the cabana.

Camila rolled her eyes and shook her head as she followed her husband. "Estas loco, mi amor!"

Chapter 3

"WAKE UP, SLEEPING beauty!" Chelsea said.

"Beauty?" Johnny questioned. "If that's beauty, I must look like Prince Charming."

Casey raised his eyelids just enough to see his three friends staring at him. He rolled his head slowly to the side and saw the sun setting into the ocean. "Lemme sleep," he mumbled unintelligibly.

"Wow," Johnny said. "How much of that tequila did they give you?"

"Huh?" Rubbing the sleep from his eyes, his hand brushed against his nose. "Ow! What is this?" he slurred, touching his bandaged nose.

"Do you have any idea at all?" Chelsea asked.

"About what?" He grumbled.

"You broke your nose. Doctor Esteban set it and gave you some tequila to ease the pain."

"Tequila?" he groaned quietly. "So that's the horrible taste in my mouth." He touched his bandaged nose again. "How bad is it?"

"Pretty bad," Johnny said.

"Shut up," Samantha said, giving Johnny a shove.

With a lazy, crooked smile, Casey slowly raised his head and looked around. After patting the pockets of his swim shorts, he muttered, "Where's my phone?"

"Don't know, mate," Chelsea said. "You want to call someone?"

"No. I just want to see what I look like."

"Oh. Here you go." Chelsea swiped her phone's screen and handed it to him.

He held it up to his face. "Oh, come on!"

"I've had worse," Johnny said. "So have you, Dude!"

"I don't care about my nose or my black eyes. I'm talking about the stupid Dory bandage. And, what's with the sticks?"

"Dr. Esteban had to get a little creative. He used sticks from ice cream bars as splints, and we got the bandages from a mom near the cabana."

"What are the red things in my nostrils?"

"Q-Tips to control the bleeding," Samantha explained.

Casey started to peel off the bandages and quietly groaned.

"Wait," Samantha said. "Don't take it off."

With one more quiet whimper, the protective covering was off. "I'm not wearing that dumb-looking thing."

"Oh, so you're going to be vain now?" Chelsea said. "Got someone you're trying to impress?"

"What? No, I just don't want to look like a jerk."

"Come on," Chelsea goaded him. "Admit it. I saw the way you looked at that pretty girl in the pool."

"Me too," Samantha agreed.

"No way!"

"Oh sure," Chelsea said. "Well, if it makes you feel any better, she was looking at you too. I saw her turning her head this way, with a concerned look, all afternoon."

"Wait," Johnny said. "Are you guys talking about the girl who showed him how to head the ball?"

Samantha nodded, wide-eyed.

"Wow. How did I miss all that? She's smokin' hot!"

Samantha's strong nudge almost made Johnny fall into the flower garden next to them.

"Will you stop? That's twice now! Cut it out!"

"Stop being a jerk, and I'll stop," she said with a grin.

"A jerk? All I said was…" after a quick moment, he continued, "Wait, she's not as hot as you!"

"I was just kidding," Samantha kissed him on his cheek.

"Aw, how cute," Chelsea said, looking at Samantha's and Johnny's blushing faces.

"We need to tell him," Johnny said to the girls, suddenly very serious.

Samantha and Chelsea nodded.

Johnny and Samantha sat on the edge of the chaise lounge next to Casey's. "Chelsea, sit," Samantha turned to Johnny, "Squeeze over, mate. Make some room."

Once they were all seated, Johnny said, "While you were sleeping, we played more of the header game in the pool with them," he nodded toward the kids in the pool. "Not realizing that Sam and Chelsea understood Spanish, two of the boys talked about yesterday's abduction."

Pushing aside his hazy feeling, Casey leaned closer and asked, "What did they say?"

"They spoke too fast for me to catch everything," Samantha said. "But I think the father of one of the boys is involved with the kidnapping."

"Wow! Really?" Casey said, then winced.

"Hurt's bad, huh?" Samantha asked.

"Yeah. Pretty bad, but who cares. Tell me more."

"I didn't hear much more than that. They were talking quietly."

"We did hear some other stuff," Chelsea said. "Like most of the kid's fathers or uncles are on the Colombian soccer team."

Casey nodded. "Well, that explains why they're so good at that heading game. They're probably awesome on the field too."

"Just cause their dads are good doesn't mean they are too," Johnny said.

"Oh come on," Casey said. "They were probably all given soccer balls the minute they were born. While we were drooling, they were dribbling."

Samantha laughed. "That's good. Gross, but good."

"Kinda stupid if you ask me," Johnny said.

"Yeah, well nobody did," Casey remarked. "Who cares anyway? Let's get back to what you overheard," he said to the girls.

"They didn't say much more than that," Samantha said. "But I watched one of them when he got out of the pool. He walked over and sat next to the man who yelled at you earlier."

"Huh?" Johnny said. "Why did he yell at you?"

"He was talking to a couple of other men as I swam by. He yelled, but I don't know what he said. I think he thought I was listening to their conversation."

"Were you?" Chelsea asked.

Casey nodded slightly.

"Are you always looking for trouble?" Chelsea asked.

Samantha laughed. "This sounds exactly like our conversation, doesn't it?"

Casey gave another nod, this time with a goofy, guilty look.

"Okay, this is beginning to sound interesting," Johnny said. "The boy's father is involved in the kidnapping and he's here at the hotel."

"Wait a second. Slow down," Samantha said. "We don't know anything for sure. We don't even know if that was his father."

"You're right," Casey said. "But we better find out quickly."

"You think we can help find the women and kids?" Johnny asked.

"I don't know, but we gotta try! Right?"

Samantha, Chelsea, and Johnny nodded.

"Good," Casey said. "Let's not tell anybody about this yet. It'll only get our parents worried."

"Hold on a second," Chelsea said. "Last time, in Australia, we worked with the police and Olympic security. Now you're saying you don't want to tell anyone? Don't you think it might get dangerous?"

"Yeah, Casey," Samantha said. "I don't know much about cartels, but from what I've heard, they are really dangerous. That guy El something or other. You know, the guy that escaped from jail then was caught again."

"El Chapo," Johnny said.

"Yeah, him. He's like this really big drug lord. He's killed tons of people. He'd probably shoot us in a second."

"I know, I know," Casey said. "But we can't go to the police yet. First, we have to get some evidence, so they'll believe us. Then, like last time, Johnny and I will tell our dads. They'll help us explain it to the police."

No one said a word.

"Well?" Casey said.

"Well, what?" Johnny asked.

"Are you in or not?"

"You're kidding, right? Of course, I'm in!"

Casey looked at the girls.

"Yeah, me too," Samantha said.

They all looked at Chelsea, who remained silent.

"I don't know," she finally said with a pained look. "I mean, cartels are ruthless. Just the thought of it is freaking me out."

The others nodded and remained quiet, giving her time to think.

"Helping save that gymnast at the Olympics was very cool, but it was scary too. And the man and woman we caught were just assassins. They weren't in cartels."

Samantha and Johnny fought to refrain from laughing. Casey chuckled, then quickly covered his mouth. "Sorry," he said.

Chelsea scrunched her face and giggled. "I guess that did sound pretty dumb. But you know what I meant, right?"

"Of course we do," Johnny said. "Don't feel pressured. You may be right. This could be more dangerous than our work on the Australian Caper."

Samantha burst out laughing. "You named it?"

"Are you going to make fun of everything I say?"

"No, but isn't a caper kind of like a silly type of mystery?"

"Yeah, but isn't everything we do kind of silly?"

"Good point, mate. In fact, it'll work even better here, the Colombian Caper."

"That's great." Johnny's eyes rolled.

"No, I mean it. It sounds cool, doesn't it?"

"Okay, guys," Casey interrupted. "If we're going to do this, we need a plan."

"A plan?" asked Casey's dad, approaching from seemingly out of nowhere. "What are you planning?"

"Nothing, Dad, don't worry."

"Really? It seems to me that when the four of you plan things that you can't talk about, things get very interesting."

"Dad, there's nothing to worry about."

"If you say so."

Casey nodded.

"I just came to see how you're feeling and ask if you all want to come to town with us. We're taking Doctor Esteban and his wife to dinner. We're leaving in about half an hour. You don't have to join us if you'd rather stay here. I heard the burgers and pizza in the hotel pub are great."

Casey looked at the others, "I think I'd rather stay here tonight."

Johnny and the girls nodded.

"No problem, if you change your minds, Joel and I will be in the bar, waiting for your moms."

"Thanks, Dad."

"So, how are you feeling?"

"I was a little groggy when I woke up, but I'm feeling better now."

"A shot of strong tequila will do that. How about the schnoz? And, why is the splint off?"

"Are you kidding? No way I was gonna walk around here with that thing on my nose."

"I kind of liked it. It made you look tough."

"Sure, Dad. Dory, the dumb fish, made me look tough. That's exactly what I was thinking when I took the stupid thing off."

"Well, your nose looks pretty straight to me. How bad is the pain?"

Casey touched it and scowled. "Ow. It only hurts when I touch it."

"Okay, just be careful with it. No horsing around with your pal, there." Reid pointed at Johnny.

"Sam and I will keep them separated, Mr. Clark," Chelsea said.

Samantha nodded with a smile.

"Thanks, girls. Okay, kids, enjoy your evening."

"You too, Mr. Clark," Chelsea said.

Once he had walked away, Johnny said, "Come on, let's go eat. I'm starving."

"Me too," Samantha said.

"Hold on, guys," Casey said. "Before we go, we should give Chelsea a chance to decide."

They all looked at her again.

"I want to help. I really do. I just don't want to get…killed. You know?"

"Of course we do," Casey said. "Obviously, we all feel the same way, but there are four people's lives at stake, and we may be able to help. Tell you what, Chels, work with us and if there is anything we do that scares you, just sit it out. You're good at this stuff. We all are. And we're a team, right?"

Chelsea nodded subtly. "Yeah, I guess. Just please don't get mad at me if I back out of something."

"Mad?" Casey said. "No way! In fact, that goes for all of us. If you need to stay out of something, then just stay out. We'll all understand. Everyone agree?"

"Of course," Samantha said.

They all looked at Johnny. His head was down, and his hands were on his stomach.

"Well?" Samantha said.

Johnny slowly raised his head and looked at them. "You talking to me?" he asked quietly.

"Really?" Casey said. "Have you been listening to anything we've said?"

"No. I was listening to my stomach growl. It needs to be fed!"

The girls laughed.

"You never cease to amaze me," Casey said.

Johnny gave him a silly look and shrugged.

"Okay, let's go feed this animal. Otherwise, he's gonna start getting cranky."

Chapter 4

"OH, SO THERE you are!" Casey exclaimed as he and the girls slid onto the green leather benches of a booth in the rear corner of Kick, the hotel's sports bar and grill.

Completely mesmerized by his phone, Johnny didn't even acknowledge them.

"Earth to Johnny," Chelsea said.

Raising his pointer finger, without a word, Johnny continued staring at his phone.

"Would it have been too difficult to tell us where you were?" Casey asked.

No response.

"Hey, come on!" Casey snapped.

Johnny finally looked up and said, "Hi, where have you guys been?"

"Really?" Samantha said with her head tilted and lips pursed. "We've been looking for you. That's where!"

"I told you I'd be in the restaurant."

"Yeah, but you didn't say which one," Casey said. "There are four of them here. We looked in all the others, upstairs."

"Really? I guess I wasn't paying attention when I got off the elevator. I saw this place and walked in. Why didn't you text me? Oh, wait." Johnny swiped his phone a few times and looked up sheepishly at the group. "Sorry, I was reading about the abduction. I didn't look at your text."

"You mean texts." Casey held up four fingers.

"I said I'm sorry. Come on, forget it. Let's order, and I'll tell you what I found." Ice clinked as Johnny lifted his glass and guzzled the bubbly, pink liquid.

"Good lemonade?" Samantha asked.

"It's Colombian apple soda. The waitress recommended it. It's pretty good."

"Why is it pink?" Samantha said. "I've never seen a pink apple."

"I'll bet you've never seen a pink lemon either," Johnny said.

"Good point."

Two waiters approached and placed a small pizza and a few other plates of food on the table.

"Whoa!" Casey said with a smile.

"I was hungry," Johnny said. "So I ordered some appetizers for everyone."

"The pizza looks great. What's the other stuff?" Chelsea asked.

Johnny pointed from plate to plate. "Bacon-wrapped plantains, grilled chorizo, and yucca balls stuffed with cheese."

"Yuck." Samantha wrinkled her nose.

"No. Yucca!" Johnny said.

"I know, and I said, yuck!"

"Don't eat them then," Johnny said defensively.

"Oh, stop it. You know I was kidding." She elbowed him gently.

"Okay, you two," Casey interrupted as he picked up a slice of pizza. "Can we start putting together a plan instead of horsing around?"

"Hey," Johnny said. "Don't go getting all bossy on us. We want to save those moms and kids as much as you do. But this is our vacation, and we're allowed to have some fun."

"You're right, sorry."

"No problem, boss!"

Casey threw his crumpled napkin, hitting Johnny's nose.

"You better watch it, or I'll hit yours," Johnny said with a sneer.

"You wouldn't," Casey said.

"Course not." Johnny chuckled. He reached over with his fork and stabbed one of the yucca balls.

"Come on, guys," Chelsea said. "Let's stop the silliness and start planning."

"Look who's had a change of heart," Casey said.

"You know I want to help. I just don't want to do anything too dangerous."

"Okay, good. We should start by making a list of what we already know and another of the things we need to find out. Chelsea, will you take notes?"

"Sure," she said, picking up her phone.

"I'll start," Casey said. "We need to find out who the man that yelled at me in the pool is. As well as the guys that were with him."

"When Chelsea and I came down here," Samantha said. "They got on the elevator a couple of floors below us."

"Who did?" Johnny asked.

"The men we're talking about."

"Wait, you rode down with them?" Johnny's eyes went wide.

"I'm pretty sure it was them. I didn't get a very good look at them in the pool, but the guy who yelled at you had a dark, bushy mustache, right?"

"Yeah," Casey said.

"I think it was him."

"What did they talk about in the elevator?"

"They didn't say a word. They were talking as the doors opened, but they stopped as soon as they saw us. We should try to find out what rooms they are staying in," Samantha added.

"Why? Are you going to bug their rooms?" Johnny joked.

"No! Well, maybe. I don't know. It was just a thought."

"And a good one, too," Casey said. "Come on, Johnny, we're not experts. Let's agree not to make fun of each other's suggestions."

"Okay. That works for me. I'm the one who usually gets made fun of, anyway."

"So, it's agreed, we'll all stop. At least during this case," Casey said.

"Wow," Samantha said. "First, we name it the Colombian Caper and now we're calling it a case. This is pretty cool."

"It is, isn't it?" Johnny said.

"Uh-huh," Chelsea agreed. "It'll be even cooler if we save them."

"Yup, let's get back to the list," Casey said.

"Aye, aye, boss!" Johnny said.

"Cut it out. I'm not the boss!"

"Oh sure," Johnny said with another silly look.

"Stop it, you jerk," Casey said.

"I'll stop saying it when you stop telling us what to do."

"Will you both just shut up already?" Chelsea said.

"Fine," Casey said with a roll of his eyes.

Johnny nodded and said, "So, I've got some stuff for the list. While I was waiting for you guys, I found out a few things about Sauro. His family has mob connections."

"What?" Chelsea yelped a little too loudly.

"Shh," all three said.

"Okay," Chelsea whispered. "But doesn't that scare any of you? I mean it's bad enough that we're dealing with cartel stuff. Now we have the mafia involved too. Bloody hell!"

"Take it easy, Chelsea. We don't really know who's involved yet," Casey said. "Even the cartel stuff was only a theory."

"Not anymore," Johnny piped in. He slid his finger across the screen of his phone. "It's confirmed here."

"What are you looking at?" Casey asked.

"There's a bunch of posts about it."

"So, as usual, you believe everything you read on the net?"

"Really? You're already breaking your first rule."

"Huh?"

"You're making fun of me."

"Oh, come on, don't be so sensitive."

"Hey, you're the one who always says, a rule is a rule. And you made this one."

Casey rolled his eyes again. "Fine! I'm sorry!"

"Thank you." Smugness spread across Johnny's face.

"Enough, you two," Samantha said. "Time to grow up."

"Hey." Johnny sneered at her.

"She's right," Casey said. "Let's just get back to work."

Johnny mumbled unintelligibly as he shoved a chunk of sausage into his mouth.

"Can I see your phone?" Casey asked.

Johnny flicked his wrist, sliding his phone over the table as he chewed.

Casey picked it up, skated his finger across the screen, and tapped it. After reading for a moment, he said, "So it says here…"

A loud cheer from behind double glass doors in the back of the dining area cut Casey off. They all turned as two boys from the group in the pool emerged through the doorway. They spoke loudly and laughed as they headed toward a door with Hombre carved into the wood.

"Come on," Casey said. "Let's go look."

"In the bathroom? That's weird," Johnny said with a crinkled face.

Casey's chin slumped. The girls giggled as he groaned, "I was talking about the room they came from."

"Oh, okay. That's much better," Johnny said, following Samantha as she slid off the bench and stood.

They all peered through the open doors. The kids from the pool were watching soccer on a big, wall-mounted TV. Some were playing billiards, others were throwing darts. Large trays of food lined a long table against the far wall. Pitchers of various colored beverages, including the same pink stuff Johnny had been drinking, were perched atop a small bar in the corner.

"Ah, look who's here. Come in, come in," one of the boys said, waving them in.

As they started walking in, Samantha said, "I didn't know we were going in. I need to get my phone and stuff from our booth."

Johnny said, "You should probably tell our waiter that we're back here, so he doesn't think we stiffed him. Ask if he'll charge the stuff I ordered to our room."

Samantha nodded and left.

As they walked by the dart game, Casey noticed that the wall surrounding the board had more holes in it than a window screen. The boy standing at the line threw his dart, then pumped his fist as it joined his previously thrown darts in a tight cluster on the board.

Another boy approached the dartboard, pulled out the darts, and made a couple of marks on a small chalkboard. Shaking his head, he removed another dart from the wall that was pierced through a stack of reddish-brown Pesos. He pulled a paper bill from his pocket, added it to the stack, then stuck the dart back into the wall. *Hmm, looks like a lot of money*, Casey thought.

"Chico," another boy said, waving for them to approach from his seat at the far side of the billiard table.

As Casey, Johnny, and Chelsea passed the pool table, Casey noticed another stack of bills on the corner of the table with a blue billiards-chalk cube resting on top.

As they got closer to the boy who had called them over, Casey saw him gesture to his friends at his table to vacate their seats. The three boys stood and stepped away. With another wave of his arm toward the empty chairs, the boy said, "Sit."

The boy placed his drinking glass on the table and crossed his muscular arms. A pack of cigarettes rolled into the sleeve of his white tee-shirt added to his intimidating look. "No hablas espanol, correcto?"

Casey shook his head and held his thumb and forefinger up with a small gap between them. "Poco," he said.

"You want food?" the boy asked in decent English.

As Casey and Chelsea shook their heads, Johnny said, "Sure."

The boy looked at one of his friends standing nearby, and with a nod in the food's direction, he commanded, "Traerle comida."

The friend turned and walked toward the buffet table.

Interesting, Casey thought. He shifted his eyes toward Chelsea, who raised her brow.

"Como esta tu nariz?' the boy said, looking at Casey. "How is…" He tapped his own nose.

Despite the persistent pain, Casey said, He's "No problemo. Gracias."

The boy nodded, then pointed at the area below his own eyes and added, "Looks bad."

Casey shrugged. "Looks worse than it is."

The boy nodded and asked, "Where are you from?"

Sitting between Johnny and Chelsea, Casey tapped Johnny's shoulder. "Johnny and I are from New York." He turned and patted Chelsea's forearm, "Chelsea and Samantha are from Australia."

"Bueno. Maybe I visit?"

"Sure, that would be great," Johnny said as a plate full of food was placed in front of him. His eyes lit up. "Wow! Gracias!"

The boy with the cigarettes nodded. "So, you all play futbol?"

"Not really," Casey said. "Johnny and I practice martial arts, though."

"Martial arts?" he repeated, shaking his head. "No entiendo."

"Karate and Jujitsu," Casey said.

"Ah, si. Muy bueno! MMA y UFC!" He turned in his chair and loudly said, "Estos chicos luchan MMA y UFC!"

Casey quickly looked around the room, saying, "No, we don't fight MMA or UFC. We practice karate and Jujitsu."

Along with a few claps and cheers, Casey saw looks of doubt on many faces. He turned back to the boy he was talking to, "What's your name?"

"Juan. Y tu?"

"I'm Casey. But, Juan, we don't fight MMA and UFC. We just practice Karate and Jujitsu."

"Practica? No entiendo. I love MMA and UFC. Esos tipos estan locos!"

"Si, they are crazy. I'm not, though," Casey said, tapping his finger on his temple.

"No entiendo," Juan said, raising his palms in question and shaking his head.

"Let me try to explain," Chelsea said.

After a minute of their discussion in Spanish, Casey heard Chelsea say to the boy, "Cinta negra." He saw Juan's eyes widen, and they continued their talk.

Chelsea turned to Casey. "He understands and wants to see you guys fight, or spar, or whatever you do in the ring. They'll clear an area over there." She pointed to the corner of the room.

"What? Now? No way. That's crazy." Casey looked at Juan and shook his head.

Juan shrugged and spoke again in Spanish to Chelsea.

"He said, if he tells the group now that you guys don't fight Mixed Martial Arts, they're not going to think very highly of you."

"This is ridiculous. I never said we fought MMA!"

Pulling the bones of a chicken wing from his mouth, Johnny said, "Let's just do it. We'll spar for a couple of minutes, and it will be over. I don't want to lose respect from this group. They'll be fun to hang out with."

"You're just saying that because they fed you. Your stomach rules your mind," Casey said.

"So, you disagree?" Johnny asked.

"I guess not." Casey sighed as he stood from the table. "Let's just get it over with."

Juan barked an order, and immediately four guys started moving tables and chairs from the corner. *He is definitely the boss*, Casey thought.

"Wipe your hands," Casey said to Johnny. "I don't want chicken grease all over me."

As Johnny picked up a napkin, Casey added, "Remember we're not wearing helmets, no hitting each other's heads. And don't go anywhere near my nose, or I will kick your butt when I'm better."

"Don't worry."

"Yeah, right!" Casey's words dripped with sarcasm. "I can't believe we're doing this."

"We had no choice, did we?"

"No, not really. What a mess."

"Look, I won't go anywhere near your head, but I don't want to go too easy, either. I think we need to impress them."

"I agree," Casey said as they reached the corner.

"Wait!" Samantha yelled as she entered the room and ran to them. "What are you guys doing?"

"It's a long story. Chelsea will tell you."

Samantha looked at Chelsea, who quickly explained.

"No way!" Samantha said, jumping between the boys, who were facing each other near the corner and getting ready. "You can't do this. The doctor said Casey needs to rest. I won't let you fight."

Both Casey and Johnny rolled their eyes. "We're not going to fight, Sam," Johnny said. "We're just going to spar."

"No, you're not!"

"Come on, Sam. Get out of the way," Casey said. "I'll be fine."

Planted like a tree between them, Samantha lifted her phone and typed.

"What are you doing?" Casey asked.

"I'm texting your parents."

"What! No way! Stop!" Casey said, reaching for her phone.

"You stop first, then I will." She stared at Casey.

"Both of you stop," Chelsea said. "I have a solution." She held up her phone, displaying a video of Johnny and Casey sparring. "I'll pass this around. It'll impress them enough for now. That way, they'll wait to see the real thing once your nose is better."

At this point, the entire group was watching them. Most with eyes squinted and faces scrunched. Many heads were tilted in curiosity and skepticism.

Chelsea stepped towards Juan and said, "No puede pelear ahora." She pointed first at Casey, then at her nose. "El medico dijo que debiá descansar." She restarted the video and handed her phone to Juan.

His eyes widened as he watched, and he began nodding. "Hijole!" he exclaimed, with his eyes locked on the screen. After about a minute, he handed the phone to one of his friends, looked at Casey and Johnny, and clapped. "Muy bueno."

As the phone made its way around the room, "Hijole" was heard again, and again.

"What does hijole mean?" Casey asked.

"Wow, I think, " Chelsea said. "I don't know exactly, but I do know they're impressed."

"How did you know about that video?" Johnny asked.

"It's on Casey's Instagram. We've shown it and some of your other videos to like a million of our friends."

"I forgot you even posted them," Johnny said to Casey.

"I wondered why they were getting so many views," Casey said. "I'm glad you thought of it. I was kind of worried about Johnny hitting my nose by mistake."

Chelsea smiled.

Juan turned to the foursome with a very serious look and asked, "Will you please come with me? I need a favor." Without waiting for their answer, he began walking toward the door.

Casey looked briefly at Johnny and the girls, shrugged and began following Juan.

Chelsea ran, got her phone from the last boy who had viewed the video, and quickly caught up with the others.

When they walked out of the room, Juan was already down the hallway and about to walk up the slate staircase to the main floor.

"Hey, Juan," Casey yelled just loudly enough for Juan to hear. "Where are we going?"

Juan turned back, held a finger to his lips, and motioned for them to follow.

***

They passed the hotel gym and spa, then walked outside to the pool area. Casey and the others continually gave each other curious looks as they followed him toward, and finally into, a cabana.

He sat and motioned for them to do the same.

"Thank you," he said.

"Para que?" Chelsea asked.

"For coming with me. I will explain as soon as my sister gets here."

"Your sister?" Casey asked.

"Yes, you met her today, in the pool. I think she likes you."

"Me?" Casey's face reddened.

"Yes, I saw her looking at you all day after you broke your nose."

"Told you," Chelsea said.

Casey was silent, but his crimson cheeks spoke volumes.

"Hey, Juan," Johnny said. "Your English is really good now. Why?"

"When I'm with my friends, I speak Spanish. Most of them don't speak English very well, and I don't want them to feel like I'm hiding something when I speak to you guys."

"Hiding something?" Casey asked.

"I'll explain everything as soon as my sister gets here."

As if on cue, the curtain entrance to the cabana was pushed aside, and the pretty girl from the pool entered. A white floral blouse and white shorts contrasted her light brown complexion. She sat and crossed her legs, revealing white strappy leather sandals that wound up her ankles.

"This is Marianna."

They each introduced themselves as Marianna bent forward and shook their hands. Both she and Casey blushed as their hands came together. "How is your nose?" Her English sounded as crisp as Juan's.

"It's okay, thanks," Casey said.

"Looks like it hurts."

"Not so much. Looks worse than it is."

"Good."

Marianna's seat was directly across from Casey, and he was finding it difficult not to stare.

"I asked you to come here because we read about what you guys did at the Olympics in Australia," Juan said. "You know, saving that gymnast from the assassins."

Johnny, Samantha, and Chelsea nodded. Casey was captivated by Marianna's nails. Her fingernails and toenails were painted red, with white and yellow daisies on them. He had never seen anything like them and had never really cared before, but on Marianna, they were very pretty.

"Well," Juan continued. "I'm sure you heard about the Italian players' wives and children, who were kidnapped?"

Casey snapped from his mesmerized stare. He glanced at Johnny and the girls, who were all nodding.

"This may sound crazy, but Marianna and I think our uncle had something to do with it, and we want you to help us save them."

After a quiet moment, Casey asked, "Why do you think he had something to do with it?"

Juan looked at Marianna, who shrugged. Then, while biting his lower lip, his eyes shifted back to Casey. He seemed to be contemplating what to say.

"If you want our help," Casey said. "You need to be completely honest with us."

"Yes, I know we do, but it's kind of tough."

"Why?"

"Because he's a cartel boss."

"Wow!" Johnny said. "That's so cool."

"Shut up," Samantha said, nudging Johnny.

"It's really not very cool," Marianna said. "He's very dangerous. I get scared whenever he's around."

"Wait," Johnny said. "He's your uncle. He wouldn't hurt you! Would he?"

Marianna and Juan gave each other looks of doubt. "Probably not, but he's done some pretty bad things," Juan said. "Including hurting family members."

The foursome expressed their surprise without a word. It was obvious that Marianna and Juan weren't ready to explain in detail. They had made their point, though! They all needed to be careful when dealing with their uncle.

"So, where does he live?" Casey asked.

"Why?" Juan said.

"I'm just wondering, in case we need to go investigate."

"He's got a mansion up on a hill. It's like a fortress. He's got guards with guns. You don't need to go there, anyway. He's here, in the hotel."

"Oh! Why didn't you say that in the first place?"

Juan shrugged.

"Can you show us a picture of him?"

"You already know what he looks like. You met him."

"Huh?" Casey exclaimed.

"He's the man that yelled at you in the pool."

"Holy cow! Wait, how did you know that?"

"When you have an uncle as scary as he is, you keep an eye on him. At least I do. I never know when he's going to lose it. He's always yelling at me and correcting me. He's a pain in my butt!"

"He is," Marianna agreed.

"Do you think he'd hurt you?" Samantha asked.

"I don't think so," Marianna said. "But his temper is really bad. He's raised his hand to hit me a few times, but he's never done it."

"Do you ever see him with weapons?" Casey asked.

"Sure. He always carries a gun. They all do."

"They?"

"His bodyguards. He pays them a lot. Enough so that they'll take a bullet for him if needed."

"Wow, they sound scary," Casey said.

"No, it's not them. It's just him that I worry about. If one of his guards ever laid a hand on Marianna or me, Uncle Jose would kill him in a second."

"Seriously?"

"Dead serious!"

Johnny laughed. "That's good, Juan! Dead serious."

Everyone's eyes darted toward Johnny, shutting him up instantly.

"So, are you staying here with him?" Casey asked.

"No, we're here with our mom. Uncle Jose never lets her travel alone, ever since…" Juan's voice trailed off, and his head lowered.

"Ever since our father died," continued Marianna. "He was Uncle Jose's business partner. He was killed when Juan and I were small. Uncle Jose has kind of taken care of us and our mom ever since."

"Wow, I'm sorry about your dad," Casey said.

"Thanks."

"Do you guys live with your uncle?"

"No, but close. Our house is on the same property, about half a kilometer away. He wanted us to move into his house when our father died, but my mother never completely trusted him, so she wouldn't do it."

"So, I guess his guards also protect you and your home?"

"No. Our house is not inside his...uh…" she drew a circle in the air, "his walls. We have our own security staff, led by my mom's assistant, Carita. She was in the military before she came to work for our family. She's amazing!"

"Do you have access to your uncle's property?" Casey asked.

"Only when he invites us. We can't just go whenever we want, if that's what you mean."

"What would he do if he caught you there without his permission?"

Juan chuckled and Marianna shook her head. "That's not something we would do," she said. "It would be crazy." Her phone buzzed. After a glance at the screen, she looked at Juan.

"What's wrong?" he asked.

"Mom said Uncle Jose is asking where we are."

"We need to go back in," Juan said.

"Okay," Casey said. "Let's go. We can talk more later."

They all stood. "We should probably go first," Juan said. "Then you guys can follow in a few minutes. Just in case he's watching."

"I think it might be better if we all go in together," Marianna said. "If he sees just you and me coming in, he'll wonder what we're up to. If we are all together, he'll just think we made new friends."

"Okay."

"Does he check everything you guys do?" Casey asked.

"What do you mean?" Juan asked.

"Like, does he check your phones? I mean, if you're worried about him seeing us all together, we can just text each other to plan this thing out."

"No, Juan just gets very paranoid when it comes to Uncle Jose," Marianna said.

Juan shrugged. "Maybe I do, but we both know what he can get like."

Marianna nodded. "But it's not because he doesn't trust us. He just worries about our mom and us."

"Yeah, he's been overprotective of us since our dad died."

Marianna lowered her chin as she nodded. Then, after a few seconds she raised her head, put her arm around Juan's shoulders and said, "Come on, let's all go in together."

"Before we go, we should start a group text," Casey said. "It'll make it easier for us to talk. Marianna and Juan, give me your numbers."

Casey's fingers sped along as they rattled off their numbers. He continued to type, then said, "Okay, done." Buzzes, chirps, and musical notes followed as they each received his text. Then, the sound of gunshots made everyone duck down.

"Oh sorry," Johnny said. "I forgot I downloaded that ringtone this morning. I should probably change it."

"Ya think?" Samantha said, elbowing him.

Johnny's silly expression and shrug made them all laugh.

"Come on, let's go," Casey said.

"I wonder if there's any food left?" Johnny said as they walked.

"You're kidding, right?" Chelsea asked.

"He never jokes about eating." Casey chuckled. "That's why everyone calls him the bottomless pit."

"What can I say? I'm a growing boy."

"How do you stay so skinny?" Samantha said. "I'm jealous."

"Jealous?" Johnny said. "That's crazy! Your body is perfect."

Samantha's nose and eyes crinkled as she smiled with reddening cheeks.

"Aww," Chelsea and Marianna expressed simultaneously.

***

Walking through the hotel hallway, they passed one of the fancier restaurants on the main floor.

Juan groaned. "Damn. I just caught Uncle Jose's eye. He's having dinner with our mom and our cousin, Diego. They're at a table near the door, and Uncle Jose saw me as we passed. He was obviously watching for us. He motioned for us to come in. Give us a minute." Juan gestured for Marianna to join him.

"Should we wait here in case he wants to meet us?" Casey asked.

"No," Juan said. "Go downstairs. We'll be there in a few minutes."

∗∗

Juan's and Marianna's friends were still in the billiard room. As the foursome entered, all eyes were on them.

Casey gave a slight wave and said, "Hi. Juan and Marianna will be here soon. They're upstairs with their uncle." The blank stares he received were a little unnerving.

Chelsea repeated Casey's words in Spanish.

"Bueno," said one of the older boys. He gestured to a table, "Sit." Then gestured toward the billiard table and dartboard. "Play." And finally, he swept his arm toward the buffet. "Eat."

"Gracias," Chelsea said with a big smile.

The boy smiled back at her.

Samantha whispered into Chelsea's ear. "He's cute."

"I noticed," Chelsea said coyly.

Casey turned toward the girls. "Billiards anyone? Wait, where's Johnny?"

Samantha pointed her chin toward the buffet table. Johnny was already filling a plate.

"He doesn't waste any time, does he?" Casey said with a laugh. "Let's sit until he finishes. Then we'll go shoot some pool."

"Sounds good to me," Samantha said.

As they took seats at a table, Juan and Marianna entered the room with the young boy who had been continuously heading the soccer ball in the pool.

Juan grabbed two chairs and slid them over.

Gesturing toward the younger boy, Marianna said, "This is our cousin Diego. Diego, these are our new friends, Casey, Samantha, and Chelsea."

"Hi Diego," they all said.

Diego was looking at the other side of the room.

"Diego, say hello," Marianna said. When he didn't respond, she lowered her face to his and quietly spoke to him. Marianna looked in the direction Diego was staring. One of the older boys at the dartboard was waving Diego over. "You want to go to Mateo?"

Diego nodded without looking at her.

"Okay, go."

As Diego left, Marianna took a seat and said, "Sorry. He's not being rude. He's autistic."

Chelsea, Samantha, and Casey gave understanding nods.

"He's really sweet, and very smart. But sometimes, he's difficult to deal with. He's Uncle Jose's son."

Johnny had approached, placed his overfilled plate on the table, and sat.

"That nickname, bottomless pit, really does suit you," Samantha teased.

Already gnawing on a chicken wing, Johnny gave her a slight shrug.

"So, what did your uncle have to say?" Casey asked.

"He asked where…" Marianna stopped talking as all their phones sounded off, or buzzed with an incoming text.

Juan: *Don't talk about Uncle J or what we r planning. You never know who is listening. Text only!*

Casey: *Good point.*

Marianna: *Uncle J asked about you all. We didn't tell him much. Didn't want him to Google you & see how you solved the case in Australia. Don't want him to get suspicious.*

Casey: *Good thinking. OK, we need a plan. Have any of you thought about where we should start?*

"I think…" Johnny stopped speaking as everyone abruptly turned and glared at him.

"What?"

Samantha aggressively raised her phone.

"I can't text well while I'm eating," he said, holding up a greasy chicken bone.

Casey: *Who are you kidding? You text faster with one hand than most do with two. And don't talk with your mouth full. It's gross.*

Johnny bit the rest of the chicken off the bone.

Casey: *Do you guys think ur uncle has them in his house?*

Marianna: *No way!*

Juan: *She's probably right, but we need to check anyway. They could be down in his cellar.*

Marianna: *That's crazy. How do we get in?*

Juan: *The tunnels!*

Marianna let out a quiet yelp. Everyone flinched and Johnny dropped his half-eaten sausage, wiped his hands quickly, and picked up his phone.

Marianna: *Too dangerous!*

Johnny: *What tunnels?*

Juan: *They're everywhere underneath our houses. We used to play in them when we were kids.*

Marianna: *Not anymore. They're in case uncle j has to escape. Lots of locked steel doors. No way we can get in!*

Juan: *Diego can let us in*

Marianna stomped on the floor, causing everyone to flinch again. She glared at Juan as she typed.

Marianna: *NO! Do not get Diego involved.*

Juan: *You want to let 2 women & kids die?*

Marianna shook her head while looking down in defeat. She sighed as she typed.

Marianna: *Fine. But I will be the one to talk to him. Not u*

Juan: *Agreed*

Marianna closed her eyes for a moment and slowly shook her head. Her chest heaved, and she sighed again. Then she typed.

Marianna: *I really don't like this. Diego shouldn't be involved.*

Juan: *Do you have a better idea?*

Marianna: *How about Manny?*

Juan: *No!*

Marianna: *He'd be more reliable than Diego*

Juan: *Can't trust him*

Johnny: *Who is Manny?*

Juan: *One of Uncle Js security guards*

Marianna: *Nice guy. He always looks the other way when I take Diego to our house without permission.*

Juan: *That's because he has a crush on you*

Marianna snapped her head toward Juan, wide-eyed and mouth agape. Her thumbs danced quickly on her phone's screen.

Marianna: *No way!*

Juan looked at her. His head tilted and nodding, his lips pursed.

Marianna: *Eww!*

Casey, Chelsea, and Samantha laughed. Juan typed.

Juan: *I thought you knew*

Marianna's face was etched in horror as she shook her head. She stuck her finger into her open mouth and pretended to gag.

Juan: *So will you allow Diego to help us?*

Marianna shrugged and nodded resignedly.

Casey: *When can we do it?*

Juan: *Tomorrow morning when uncle j goes for his run*

Casey: *I thought your uncle was staying here?*

Marianna: *No. He has a suite here for entertaining during the World Cup, but he prefers to sleep at home.*

Casey: *Okay. But tomorrow morning is pretty quick. We should make a plan before doing this.*

Juan: *Isn't that what we're doing now?*

Marianna: *That doesn't give me much time to prepare Diego*

Juan: *Diego is smart. He'll be fine. You just need to talk to him.*

Marianna: *Well, we better do it now. Uncle J will probably take him home soon.*

Juan: *Casey can we go up to your room?*

Casey: *We should probably use Chelsea's and Samantha's room. Ours is right next to our parent's suite.*

Chelsea: *But our room is next to yours, on the other side.*

Casey: *That's still better than ours*

Samantha: *Hope you don't mind a mess*

Casey: *Can't be any worse than my roommate's mess!*

Johnny rolled his eyes, then crammed more food in his mouth.

Juan: *Let's go up in pairs. Less noticeable that way. Chelsea & Samantha 1st. Casey & Johnny 2nd. Then me Marianna & Diego. What's your room number?*

Chelsea: *809*

Marianna: *Will I be able to get some privacy? I need to talk to Diego without any distractions.*

Johnny: *Yeah, there's a door between our rooms. You can use one while we're in the other.*

Casey: *I didn't even notice the door. I'll bet you already opened it, didn't you?*

Johnny: *No. It's locked on both sides.*

Chelsea: *So that means you tried. You didn't even know that it was us on the other side. What if it was someone else and they were naked? Eww!*

Johnny's goofy grin got a chuckle from everyone except Chelsea.

Juan: *Chelsea & Samantha go up now*

***

Fifteen minutes later, they were all in Chelsea's and Samantha's room.

"Let's go into our room and leave Marianna here with Diego," Casey said as he unlocked the adjoining door. "Johnny, come with me. We'll unlock it from our side."

A few minutes later, Casey opened the door for Samantha, Chelsea, and Juan. Their jaws dropped when they saw Johnny on the hotel phone with a menu in his hand.

"What?" Johnny said. "I didn't have dessert. Is it a crime to order some chocolate cake?"

"Forget bottomless pit, you're like a human rubbish bin," Chelsea said.

"Yeah, whatever. Does anyone want anything?"

"Cervesa," Juan said.

"Ooh, me too," Chelsea said with a sly smile.

"That's beer, right?" Johnny asked.

Juan nodded.

"Unh-uh," Johnny said. "No beer. Our parents are right next door, and besides, beer tastes terrible! You want Sprite or Coke?"

"Never mind." It was Juan's turn to roll his eyes.

"I'll take a Sprite," Samantha said.

"Me too," Casey added. "And order cheeseburgers and fries for all of us. You were the only one who ate downstairs."

As Johnny was ordering, Juan's phone chirped. He looked at it and sighed. "Uncle Jose is looking for Diego. We need to bring him downstairs now."

***

Minutes earlier in the adjacent room.

As soon as the door closed and the room was quiet, Marianna sat on the edge of the bed and gently said, "Diego, I need you to help me with something very important. Okay?"

Diego had picked up a pencil and was tapping it in a rhythmic beat on the room's desk.

"Are you listening to me, Diego?" Marianna asked quietly.

Diego gave a slight nod.

"Would you like to help us save the lives of two little babies and their moms?"

His nod was a bit more pronounced.

"Good. Tomorrow morning, when your dad leaves for his run, I'd like you to go down to the tunnels and unlock the door to our side of the tunnel. That way we can come visit your side."

Diego frowned.

"You can show our new friends your murals."

Diego's frown curled into a slight smile and his drum beat quickened.

"You'd like that, right?"

He turned his head slightly toward her and gave a small single nod.

"Thank you, Diego. I knew I could count on you. It will feel good when we save those kids and women, right?"

"Save kids. Feel good."

"Great. Your dad usually leaves at 9:30, right?"

Diego nodded.

"Then you can open the door for us at 10 o'clock, okay?"

"10 o'clock, 10 o'clock, 10 o'clock."

"Very good," Marianna said. "I love you, Diego. Would you please come here for a head bump?"

Diego approached until he was standing in front of Marianna. He tilted his head forward.

Marianna leaned her head till their foreheads lightly touched.

"I love you, D," she said.

"I love you, M."

Her phone buzzed. She read the text and said, "Come with me, we need to go get Juan."

Diego followed her as she opened the door to the adjoining room and walked in.

"You saw his text, right?" she asked Juan.

"Yeah, we gotta go."

"How was your talk?" Casey asked, looking at Marianna.

"Good. Diego will open the door in the basement for us tomorrow morning at 10 o'clock. Right Diego?"

Diego looked around the room but avoided any eye contact until he got to Juan.

"It's okay, little buddy," Juan said, smiling at the boy. "They are our friends. You can talk."

Diego turned and looked out the window without a word.

"Maybe tomorrow morning is too quick," Casey said. "Maybe we should give him another day. That way, we can also plan a little better."

"Diego's fine. If he told Marianna he'll open the door, he will."

Marianna nodded. Diego's finger was now on the window, tracing the movement of a bug crawling outside on the glass.

Watching Diego through squinted eyes, Casey chewed his lip with his head askew.

"Casey," Juan continued. "I understand why you're worried, but I'm telling you he can handle this. He is totally reliable whenever he is given a task. And besides, four lives may be at stake unless we move quickly."

Casey nodded slowly, swallowing hard.

"I'll tell you what. Marianna will take Diego downstairs and go home with our mom and uncle. I'll stay here tonight so we can make a plan."

"That sounds better," Casey agreed.

"Good. I'll get Antonio to pick us up in the morning," Juan said, looking at Marianna.

She nodded.

"Who is Antonio?" Samantha asked.

"Another one of our cousins, you saw him downstairs," Marianna said.

"How's he going to feel about this?" Casey asked.

"We won't tell him much," Juan said. "I give him a lot of my stuff, so he'll be willing to do whatever I ask."

"Stuff?" Johnny's forehead wrinkled in skepticism.

"Why the look? Wait, you think I meant drugs? Come on, just cause my uncle is in that business doesn't mean I am. I don't want anything to do with that junk."

Johnny shrugged. "Sorry."

"It's alright. I guess I understand how you could think that. What I meant was that I give Antonio all my old sports equipment and clothes, and stuff like that. His family doesn't have much money, so he appreciates whatever I give him."

"How will he feel about what we're doing?" Chelsea asked.

"He's as sick of Uncle Jose as we are. The business makes life difficult for the whole family. Always being worried and having to look over your shoulder is hard. We all live in fear that one of us will get kidnapped or killed."

"I know that feeling," Casey said. "I hadn't been born yet when my father received death threats from some psycho while dad was playing golf in the Masters Tournament, but ever since then, my family has lived with the same fear. You get kind of used to it, but it really sucks."

Juan and Marianna nodded.

"I should go now," Marianna said. "Before Uncle Jose gets impatient. Come Diego, let's go." She held out her hand. Diego remained at the window, following the bug round and round with his finger. Marianna walked over and gently put her hand on his shoulder from behind. He flinched hard at her touch, but she kept her hand where it was. "It's just me," she said soothingly. "We need to go. Your dad wants to take us home now."

Suddenly the bug flew from the window, and Diego froze in place, staring out.

"It's okay. Let's go find another bug," she whispered in his ear.

Diego turned, took her hand, and without looking at anyone, silently followed her.

Marianna waved with her other hand as she walked toward the door. "Buenas noches. See you in the morning."

Chapter 5

"HERE HE COMES," Juan said as an old pickup truck made its way up the hotel driveway, expelling an oily trail of smoke into the misty morning air. The vehicle's faded yellow paint was losing its battle to reddish-brown hues of rust.

"Nice ride," Johnny said.

"Shut up and jump in," Juan said as he walked around the cab to the passenger door.

Casey and Chelsea were already climbing into the truck's straw-covered, metal bed, using the rear bumper as a step. Johnny helped Samantha, then followed her, climbing up the passenger side, rear wheel well, and over the sidewall.

As they were all settling in, Juan turned from the passenger seat and said through the open rear window of the cab, "This is my cousin Antonio. He doesn't speak much English."

Antonio turned his head slightly, and raised his hand, greeting them with a peace sign. His forefinger had a black ring on it. Black sideburns were visible below a tattered, straw cowboy hat, and a circular tattoo with the words, Federacion de Colombiana de Futbol in an arc above a red soccer ball, covered the side of his dark brown, muscular bicep.

"Hi Antonio," Chelsea said, as she, Samantha, and Casey waved.

"Buenos dias, Antonio" Johnny yelled, returning Antonio's greeting with a sideways peace sign.

"Who do we have here?" Chelsea cooed as a tiny, black-spotted, pink-nosed piglet awoke from its nap and eyed its new visitors cautiously before standing. It waddled to Chelsea, climbed into her lap, and lay back down, snuggling inside her crossed legs, resting its jowls on her thigh. As Chelsea rubbed its head, it let out a tiny, satisfied snort and closed its eyes. Chelsea gently turned the dirty, pink bandana tied loosely around the pig's neck until she found a small leather tag.

"Hi, Isabella!" she said, reading the tag. "You are the most adorable thing I've ever seen."

"Isabella, that's sweet," Johnny said, lying sprawled out on as much hay as he could pile in the center of the truck bed.

"Oh, shut up, Johnny!" Chelsea said, just loud enough to be heard over one of the truck engine's occasional misfires. Isabella squealed as if in agreement.

"Shut up? Why?" Johnny asked with a baffled look.

"'Cause, you're making fun of her name."

"No, I wasn't. Isabella is a sweet name for a pig!"

Aside from the sporadic backfires, the ride wasn't so bad once they had gained enough speed for the fumes to dissipate behind the vehicle. Bits of hay flew around, getting tangled in everyone's hair, but at least it cushioned the metal bed. The ride became rough when they turned off the paved road onto an uneven dirt path. Isabella was getting tossed all over the place until Chelsea clamped her in a protective bear hug. After a few very uncomfortable minutes of being thrown around and lashed at by low-hanging, curved Mahogany tree branches, the truck stopped.

Juan got out, moved some logs from the side of the road, and waited as his cousin drove onto the barely visible path the logs had been blocking. The truck stopped again, and they waited for Juan to replace the logs and return.

"How is everyone holding up?" he asked.

"We're okay," Casey said, pulling hay from his hair.

Isabella squealed, then squirmed from Chelsea's lap and walked to Juan.

"Hi, Izzy!"

She snorted and licked Juan's fingers as he picked her up.

"Yes, you can ride inside with me." Juan looked from Izzy to the others in the truck bed. "Sorry for the bumpy ride. We're almost there."

After a few more deep potholes, the dirt road transitioned to smooth paving stones. Orchids and other beautiful flowering plants lined the road on both sides. Someone worked very hard to maintain a natural yet magnificent landscape. They drove past a turnoff that led to wrought iron gates that resembled interwoven branches. Even the large stone pillars at the sides of the gates blended nicely into the setting. An entanglement of flowering vines obscured the fence that surrounded the property. As the truck slowly continued, Casey noticed razor wire and sharp, vertical steel spikes poking through the vines at the top of the fence.

A few moments later, the vehicle slowed and turned off the road toward another set of similar pillars and gates. Antonio stopped adjacent to a metal box attached to a tree that hugged the driveway.

Casey craned his neck to watch as Antonio reached into the box, punched a code on a keypad, then pressed his hand flat on a glass surface. The wrought iron gates opened from the center, arcing slowly away from the truck.

"Wow, a handprint reader," Casey said.

"Cool, where?" Johnny sprang to his knees.

Casey pointed to the box as they drove by. The truck moved through the gates and stopped, leaving just enough room for them to swing closed. Not until they passed the large pillars did Casey notice the moat-like waterway that bordered the property. Juan slid open the cab's rear window.

"Watch this," he said as he tossed something down into the water. Within seconds the water frothed and turned red. He tossed another. The same bubbling and splashing occurred. This time, big, black beady eyes and a long spiny back broke the surface. Then, a long tail raised from the water and smacked down with a splash.

"Whoa!" Chelsea shouted.

Samantha and Johnny shrieked.

"I just wanted you all to see that, so you'll know to be careful," Juan said.

"Crocs or gators?" Samantha asked.

"Crocs and piranhas," he answered. "And they're always hungry."

The kids' eyes displayed intense shock and fear.

After a moment, Casey began to laugh.

"What's so funny?" Chelsea asked.

"Nothing," he said, shaking his head. Then he chuckled again.

"Come on, what is it?" Samantha said.

Casey just shook his head again with a silly grin.

"Will you just tell us already?" Johnny pleaded.

"Unh-uh."

"Wait, you're laughing at Johnny's squeal, aren't you?" Samantha said, smiling.

Casey smiled and nodded. "Sorry, dude. It was funny."

Johnny shook his head. "Oh, man. I was hoping none of you noticed. It was pretty bad, wasn't it?"

"No, not bad," Casey said. "Just funny. Sounded a little like Izzy!" They all laughed.

"Well, they are scary, aren't they?" Johnny said.

"You bet they are, mate!" Samantha agreed. "I wouldn't want to fall in."

"Yuck." Casey's nose wrinkled.

As the truck parked near the garage of the large, beautiful, log home, Marianna walked out to meet them.

"Good morning," she said very quietly.

"Hi," Casey said a little too loudly.

Marianna raised her finger to her lips. "Our mother is still sleeping. Let's try to keep it that way. The fewer questions we have to answer, the better.

Casey mouthed, "Sorry."

"We can talk," Juan said, walking around the rear of the truck. "Just be very quiet."

Everyone climbed out of the truck.

"Ready?" Marianna asked.

They all nodded.

Without a word, they followed Marianna and Juan through the multi-bay garage, where they passed two shiny, topless Jeeps. One was powder blue, and the other was beige, green, and brown in a camouflage pattern. The knobby offroad tires of a motorcycle and an ATV in the rear corner were caked with dried mud. A shiny white convertible Mercedes was parked near the furthest of the three overhead doors.

"Those are awesome," Samantha whispered, nodding towards the Jeeps. "Are they yours?"

Marianna nodded.

"Wow, that's so cool. I can't wait to drive," Johnny said quietly.

"Come on." Marianna glanced at her phone and then waved them on. "We have less than five minutes till Diego opens the door. If we're not there, he'll freak out."

All talk stopped as they hurried behind her into the house and down a staircase.

"Let's take the elevator," Juan said. "It's quicker."

"Too noisy. I don't want mom or the others to hear us."

"The others?" Casey asked.

"Mateo, Alejandro, and Isabella," she responded. "The morning shift of our security team."

"Isabella? Like the pig?" Chelsea asked.

"Yeah. Antonio named Izzy after her," Juan said. "She's totally hot. He's had a crush on her forever."

"Really," Johnny said. "When do we get to meet her?"

Samantha backhanded Johnny lightly on the side of his head.

"Hey! Stop!" he said loudly.

"Shh," everyone admonished.

Johnny put his hand over his mouth and whispered, "Sorry."

"Where is Izzy, anyway," Chelsea asked, looking at Antonio.

"No hablo ingles," Antonio said.

Chelsea nodded.

"He put Izzy in the pen with El Pibe," Juan said.

"El Pibe?" Chelsea asked.

"Yes, he's Marianna's pig. They're brother and sister."

"Who is he named after?"

"Carlos Valderrama," Juan said. "Colombia's best soccer player, ever. Google him. You'll laugh."

"You better not laugh," Marianna warned.

"Wow look, he's got a huge blond afro." Johnny held his phone up for the others to see. "What a mop."

"Don't you dare make fun of El Pibe." Marianna gave Johnny a nasty look.

"Okay, okay. I'm sorry." Johnny raised his hands in surrender.

"Izzy and El Pibe. They must be so adorable together," Samantha said.

"They are, and it's even more fun to watch when their sister, Shakira, is with them," Juan added. "She's Diego's."

"Come, this way," Marianna said, turning right at the bottom of the fourth flight of stairs.

"How far down are we?" Casey asked.

"About forty feet," Marianna said. "We have another few flights to go. The tunnels are a little over seventy feet down."

"Wow," Chelsea said. "This is so cool."

"We need to hurry," Juan said as he took the lead and stepped up the pace. They all bounded down after him.

Marianna pulled hard on the wrought-iron handle of an oversized metal door. Juan moved quickly through the opening with the others following close behind. When Marianna pulled the door shut behind them, Juan said, "Marianna, you better run ahead to make sure Diego is nice and calm when we get there."

She nodded and took off, sprinting into the tunnel. Juan started to jog, and they all followed, keeping pace as he increased his speed. Light bulbs in small ceramic sockets protruded from the arched concrete ceiling every so often, creating just enough light so that no one tripped.

A few minutes later, between gasps, Samantha asked, "How much further?"

"Not much," Juan answered, barely out of breath.

"Thank God," Chelsea panted. "I hate soccer players. You guys can run forever."

Casey laughed. He and Johnny were holding up okay, too.

"Wait, so you guys aren't winded either? Sam and I are the only ones out of shape here?" Chelsea said between labored breaths.

"We run at home as part of our karate training," Johnny said effortlessly.

"I thought you hated running?" Samantha asked.

"I do, but if I don't train harder than him," he gestured toward Casey. "He'll kick my butt in the ring."

"Yeah. Well, I hate you both," Chelsea wheezed.

Samantha's laugh came out with a snort, making everyone laugh harder.

The laughter ceased as they followed Juan around a corner and saw Marianna and Diego ahead.

When they reached her, Marianna quietly said, "It's about time. We need to hurry."

"How much did you tell Diego?" Juan asked.

"Just that we're looking for two kids and their moms. I figured he's down here so often he probably knows the tunnels better than we remember them. Maybe he can help us find them."

Juan nodded. "Lead the way."

Marianna took Diego's hand, and led him through the doorway he had just unlocked for them.

The tunnel on the other side of the door was a little less raw looking than the one they had just run through. The lightbulbs were encased in glass lanterns, the concrete floor and walls were painted, and there were big, colorful, murals of musicians on the walls.

As they passed a mural of Jimi Hendrix, Casey reached out to touch the creases and folds in the painted headband. "It's amazing. They look so real," he said quietly. Looking below the guitar, Casey noticed a bold, slightly crooked, D.

Passing the next mural of Carlos Santana, Casey eyed the same D. Then, as they passed a much larger mural of Shakira, the D was bigger and bolder, sending a subtle message that the artist was more proud of this piece of work.

Noticing that Diego had turned his head toward the mural and moved closer to it as he passed by, Casey asked, "Diego, did you paint these?"

Diego did not answer.

"Yes, he did. He's talented, isn't he?" Marianna said proudly.

"Wow," Samantha said. "They're beautiful and so lifelike."

"Bravo Diego!" Casey said.

"So, you're an awesome artist, and you're amazing with a soccer ball. That's very cool, Diego," Johnny said.

"Not bad for a nine-year-old, right? And, you should hear him play his drums," Juan added. "He's incredible."

"Really? That's ace, mate," Chelsea said.

Marianna reached for Diego's hand. "Say thank you, Diego."

"Thank you, thank you, thank you, thank you," Diego repeated quietly.

"Hey Chelsea," Juan said. "Did you just say, 'ace mate'?"

"Yeah. It's like saying, 'that's excellent, my friend.'"

"That's ace!" he said, winking at her.

"What's that?" Johnny asked as they passed a large, dimly lit room filled with flasks, bottles, and long, interwoven, coiled tubes.

"A distillery. Uncle Jose is proud of his Arguadiente," Marianna said.

"His what?" Samantha asked.

"It's Colombian liquor. It's really bad," Juan answered.

"So, why does he make it?" Johnny asked.

"It's Colombia's national drink. He gives it away as gifts along with his cigars and wine."

As he finished saying it, they walked by another room with long tables and lots of chairs. In front of each chair, there was a grooved wooden plank and a pile of large, wrinkled, brown leaves. More leaves hung above the tables on wires that stretched from wall to wall.

"Cigar making?" Casey asked.

Juan nodded.

"Casey and I saw a man rolling cigars when we were in a cigar store with our dads," Johnny said.

The next room they passed was huge. Wooden barrels were stacked, lining an entire wall, and five tremendous metal tanks stood side by side along another wall.

"Wine?" Chelsea asked.

"Yup. Some of it's pretty good."

"So, your uncle employs a lot of people here, huh?" Casey asked.

"Yeah, he busses them in from the two neighboring villages. Even more villagers work out on the farms where he grows the grapes, sugar cane, and tobacco for making all this stuff."

"I guess he's well-liked around here?" Casey asked.

"More feared than liked, I think. He's a good boss until you do something wrong. Then…well, he's not so nice."

"Where are all the workers now?" Casey continued.

"They work in the fields in the morning, while it's not too hot. Then, a bunch of them come here after lunch when the sun is blazing."

They passed a few closed doors and an elevator entrance. On the wall, across from the elevator, was an enormous mural of Diego's father's head. His sun-drenched face looked very serious, and his faded fedora had an emblem on the dark band that read, Jefe.

"Our uncle likes to remind everyone who exits the elevator that he's the boss, and that he's always watching," Marianna said.

They had reached the end of the tunnel.

"What about the closed doors we just passed?" Casey asked.

"They're bathrooms and locker rooms for the workers," Juan said.

"So, that's it? We're done?" Samantha asked.

"No," Marianna said as she gestured her chin toward Diego, who was moving a brick in the wall at the end of the tunnel. A hidden doorway of bricks slowly moved to the side.

"Wow. How much more?" Johnny asked.

"A lot," Juan said quietly. "There are four more levels. We'll split into groups of two. Johnny and Samantha, you take the floor below us. Casey and Marianna, you take the next one along with Diego. And, I'll take the third floor with Chelsea and Antonio. Then, if we don't find anything, we'll all meet on the bottom level and search that together. He glimpsed at his phone. We need to move fast. Text if you find anything, or, when you reach the end of your tunnel if you don't find anything. Everyone ready?"

"Wait," Johnny said, looking at his phone. "Can we text down here?"

"Yeah, there's WIFI everywhere," Juan said.

"Let's go. We don't have a lot of time," Marianna said.

Johnny peeked through the opening. "Wow, it's dark in here." He turned on his phone's flashlight.

"There are lights," Marianna said. "It's just not as bright as it is out here. Turn off your flashlight and walk slowly until your eyes adjust."

"Okay," Johnny said, stepping through with the others following.

At the bottom of the first flight, Johnny opened the metal door. "I'm not a wimp, but this is creepy."

"Don't worry, this level is mostly wine storage," Juan said. "Just open each door and confirm that they're not in there. When you reach the end, come back out, and head to the bottom floor. We'll all meet there."

Samantha's eyes were wide as she grabbed Johnny's sweaty hand, and they walked through the doorway. The door clanged shut behind them, making them both jump.

Marianna quickly led the way down to the next landing and opened the heavy door. She held her hand out, and Casey's heart fluttered as he reached for it, but Diego snatched it first. She turned her head and smiled at Casey.

"I'll be faster next time," he said quietly, with an ear-to-ear grin.

She winked and headed through the open door. Metal doors lined both sides of the tunnel. The first room they looked in had a sickeningly sweet odor. Crates of long, thick, green stalks were stacked in rows.

"That's sugarcane for the aguardiente," Marianna said as she closed the door. "It needs to be used soon after it's harvested, or it goes bad. The smell gets very strong."

"Yeah, I noticed," Casey said.

"No, this is nothing. The cane was probably just cut yesterday, and they'll use it today. When it goes bad, it gets really stinky."

"Stinky, stinky, stinky, stinky," Diego repeated.

"Yes, Diego, that's right. P.U." She waved her hand in front of her nose.

Diego looked at her, scrunched his nose, and waved his hand too.

Casey smiled and thought, *She is so good with him. I wonder if he gets help in school like the autistic kids back home.*

They continued to the next door, and Marianna snapped to attention as they neared it. "Shh, did you hear that?" she whispered.

"Hear what?" Casey asked.

"A thumping or something behind the door. I'm not sure, but I thought I heard movement."

"Maybe it's them. Open it!"

"You open it," she whispered, with her eyes wide.

Casey reached for the knob. The locked handle slid through his sweaty palm as he pulled. "It's locked. Where are the keys?"

"I don't know," she said.

"Keys, keys, keys," Diego said, digging into his pocket. He pulled out a small keyring with two keys on it, and handed it to Marianna.

"You are awesome, Diego," Casey said.

"Awesome, awesome, awesome."

Marianna handed the keys to Casey. He tried the first one—no good. The click of the lock as he turned the second key made him flinch. His nerves were tight, and his breath held as he slowly opened the door and peered through the opening. A loud, fierce growl came at him. He slammed the door shut while jumping backwards away from it, crashing into Marianna. They both fell hard on the concrete floor.

Diego covered his ears and began pacing and mumbling.

"Sorry," Casey said, rubbing the back of his head.

"It scared me too. Are you okay?"

"Yeah, I'm fine. I just hit my head on the floor. Are you alright?"

She nodded. "Uh-huh."

"What's in there? A tiger?"

"No. They're Jaguars. My uncle is obsessed with them. The animals and the cars. He's got like five of them."

"Five live Jaguars?"

"No, five cars. There are only three animals."

"Only three, huh?" Casey said with a snicker. "Why does he keep them down here? I mean if he's so obsessed with them, I'd think he'd give them a more natural outdoor environment. It can't be very good for them down here."

"I didn't even know he kept them down here. I've only seen them in their enclosure out back or their room in his house. They usually get treated very well."

"That's good. I guess, as long as they don't eat me, he can do whatever he wants with them."

"I'm sure he'll be relieved to hear that," she answered. They looked at each other and smirked.

"Will he be okay?" Casey gestured toward Diego, who was still mumbling and pacing.

"Yes, it'll just take a minute or two." She stood and went to Diego's side to comfort him. Without touching him she soothingly said, "It's okay, D. The Jaguars are alright. I'm okay, and you're okay. Everything is perfect. Let's take a few deep breaths together."

"Deep breaths. Deep breaths. Deep breaths."

"Yes, D. In through the nose," Marianna said quietly.

"And out through the mouth," Diego said.

By their fourth deep breath, Diego had stopped pacing.

After giving him another thirty seconds, Marianna said, "Are you feeling okay, D?"

He nodded once.

"Good. Can we continue?"

Another nod.

Marianna led the way to the next door. Casey saw that she wasn't reaching for the knob, so he moved closer and put his ear to the door. Hearing nothing, he slowly turned the handle and pulled just enough to peek in. Rows of freezers lined the walls of the room. Casey opened the door wider so Marianna could see.

She nodded, and he closed the door. The final two rooms were filled with shelves of canned and dry foods.

"So, is your uncle worried about the apocalypse?"

"No. He worries about his rivals. He has to be ready to run at a moment's notice. In his business, you never know who might come after you. It can be scary."

"Aww, poor Jose," Casey said sarcastically.

"Don't joke about it," she reprimanded. "We need to go."

"Oh, come on, don't get mad."

"I'm not. Let's just go." She took Diego's hand, turned, and began walking back.

Casey followed. "You're cute when you're mad."

"Oh, shut up!"

Casey laughed and quickened his pace to keep up.

Their phones chirped.

Juan: *Marianna, where are you? We're all waiting on the bottom floor.*

She typed.

Marianna: *We'll be there in a minute. I guess no one found them?*

Juan: *No. Hurry up. We're running out of time. We're going in.*

Marianna, Diego, and Casey ran down the stairs. The heavy door was open at the bottom level, and they ran into the tunnel to catch up.

"Nothing down here either?" Marianna asked as they reached them.

"No, but we haven't opened this one yet," Juan said as he tried turning the doorknob in front of him. "Damn, it's locked."

"Here. Try these," Casey said, holding the keys out to Juan.

"Where did you get these?"

"Diego had them," Casey said.

"Good job, Diego," Juan said, unlocking the door. The hinge squeaked as he pushed the door. Four mattresses with rumpled sheets were on the floor. They walked in for a closer inspection.

"Look at this," Chelsea said, picking up an old, dirty troll-doll with matted pink hair that had been sticking out from under a sheet.

"I guess they were here," Juan said solemnly. "They must have moved them."

"Or maybe…" Johnny's voice trailed off.

"Maybe what? Killed them? Unh-uh!" Juan said. "If Uncle Jose took them, he did it for a reason. He wouldn't kill innocent women and children. No way!"

"I agree," Marianna said. "But Pedro might."

Juan's nod was barely perceptible.

"Pedro?" Casey asked.

"Our uncle's lugarteniente. He's like his advisor," Marianna said. "He helps run the cartel. Uncle Jose keeps him away from us. He does everything he can to keep us and his business separated."

"Pedro is mean," Juan said. "I'm not sure whether Uncle Jose respects him or if he's a little scared of him. He handles most of the cartel's dirty work."

"Ha. Uncle Jose isn't scared of anyone. What could possibly make you think that?" Marianna asked.

"Because I listen closely whenever Uncle Jose is on the phone. He speaks with Pedro differently than he does with everyone else. You know, like he did with Dad."

"But your dad was his brother, right?" Casey asked.

Juan nodded. "And business partner."

"Oh," Casey said.

"So that means we need to search Pedro's properties too," Johnny said.

"Maybe," Juan said, glancing at his phone. "Wow, I didn't realize how long we've been here. Uncle Jose will be back soon. We need to go right now!"

Juan turned and ran with everyone following. They were completely out of breath when they reached the spot where Diego had met them.

"We should just take him with us," Marianna said.

"No," Juan said. "He needs to put the keys back where he got them. He'll be fine."

Marianna bent down, face to face with Diego. "Are you scared?"

Diego looked toward the floor and shook his head.

"Okay. Go put the keys back where you found them and then come to our house. If your dad asks where you're going, tell him I asked you to come play with Izzy and me. Okay?"

"Izzy!" Diego's face lit up. "Shakira loves Izzy."

"Bring Shakira with you."

Diego jumped up and down with his mouth open and eyes wide. "Izzy, Izzy, Izzy, Izzy."

Marianna smiled and opened her arms, ready to hug him when he was ready. The others all had concerned looks.

"Mar, we have to hurry!" Juan said.

She held up her index finger. "We have to give him a minute."

"I know, but…"

She glared at Juan and stiffened her upheld finger.

Juan closed his eyes, breathed in deeply, and quietly, through clenched teeth, said, "We don't have time for this."

Marianna shot him another fierce stare.

Juan raised his hands in surrender.

Diego finally calmed down but avoided Marianna's hug. As Juan opened the door, Diego turned and, without a word, walked away.

"I hope he's alright," Samantha said.

"He's fine," Marianna assured her.

"Let's go," Juan said.

Chapter 6

MARIANNA STEPPED THROUGH the doorway into her mother's kitchen and immediately recoiled. Unprepared for the quick stop, Casey bumped into her, then Chelsea into Casey, and the domino effect continued through the rest of the procession. At the end of the line Johnny walked into Samantha and began to laugh before looking up to see the cause of the pile-up. His laugh ended abruptly with a gasp. Uncle Jose was standing at the counter, with his back towards them, pouring himself a cup of coffee. His sweat-soaked tee-shirt and running shorts clung to his stocky body. Marianna scanned the surrounding area. Uncle Jose's bodyguards were outside the kitchen door, smoking cigarettes.

Jose looked over his shoulder. "Ah, there you are." His eyes roamed from one kid to the next, and his face wrinkled in question. "Where's Diego? He wasn't home when I finished my run, so I figured he was with you."

"He was," Marianna said. "But I took him home. We must have just missed you."

"So, you're saying you just walked him home now, and then you came right back?" His voice reeked of skepticism.

"Yes."

"Then tell me, my dear. Why didn't we cross paths?"

"We took the tunnel. Diego wanted to show me his latest mural."

"Ah yes, my little artist. What did you think?" he said, grinning and raising his hand to his chin. "Very, realistic, no?"

"Yes, Uncle Jose. He captured you quite well."

He nodded happily. "And the positioning is excellent. Don't you agree? I don't want my workers to forget who pays them."

"Yes, it's some reminder," Marianna's and Juan's mother said as she walked in. She looked like an older version of Marianna. Her feet were bare, and she wore a thigh-length, pink silk robe over matching sleepwear. "I've heard that many of the employees salute you as they walk by."

Jose nodded and smiled. "Excellent!"

"I didn't mean that type of salute," she said with a smirk.

The kids held back their laughter.

"Where did you hear that, Luna?" Jose seethed.

"Just around." She turned toward the kids. "Sorry for my attire. I didn't realize we had guests."

"It's okay, Mom," Marianna said. "These are our friends, Casey, Johnny, Chelsea, and Samantha."

"Nice to meet you. I'll bet you'd all like some bacon and eggs." She opened the double doors of the refrigerator and took out a dozen eggs.

"You really don't have to do this, Mom," Juan said.

"What have I told you about guests in our house?"

"That they should never leave hungry or thirsty," he said with a roll of his eyes.

She nodded.

"But we're not. We're fine," Juan said.

"Yeah? Take a look at him," she said, pointing her chin at Johnny. "If that's not the look of a hungry boy, I don't know what is. Am I right?"

Johnny shrugged, smiled, and nodded. "Bacon and eggs sound pretty good to me."

"You see," she said, before sticking her tongue out at Juan. "Now make yourself useful. Grind some coffee beans, and put on a fresh pot. It looks like your uncle just finished what was left. Marianna, please grab the bacon and a couple of frying pans."

Within minutes the sumptuous aromas of frying bacon and fresh ground coffee beans filled the tremendous kitchen.

Luna looked at the other kids and pointed. "Plates are up in that cabinet, and silverware is in the drawer below. Please set the table out on the patio. How many are we?" she looked around the room, mouthing numbers silently. "Nine, plus Esteban, Felipe, Pedro, and Diego. Better set the table for thirteen. Will someone please get me another dozen eggs and start making toast?"

Casey gave Juan a questioning look at the mention of Pedro's name. Juan subtly shook his head.

"I don't dine with my guards," Jose grumbled.

"At my house, you will." Luna gave her brother-in-law a stern look. "Everyone eats together here."

He sneered at her as the kitchen buzzed with activity.

Setting the table outside, Johnny said to Casey, "I didn't think we'd be here this long."

"I know. We better text the 'rents. They know we don't sleep this late, at least not me."

Johnny nodded as his thumbs raced across his phone's keypad. "Done."

"Hey, you," growled Jose as he walked out the kitchen door while glaring at Johnny. "No taking pictures here."

"Uh, I wasn't, sir. I promise."

"And you," he said to Casey. "You're the boy from the pool yesterday. I never forget a face." He pointed his finger at Casey. "You should mind your own business. Listening to other people's conversations can get you in trouble."

Casey took a deep breath to keep himself from trembling. "I'm sorry, sir. You are right. I was listening, but I didn't understand a word.

I was just trying to figure out how many languages were being spoken throughout the pool."

"Why?"

"I was just curious."

Jose nodded. With squinting eyes and his head atilt, he asked, "How many?"

"I counted four in the pool. Then another five on the surrounding patio."

"Hm. So, what were they? Besides Spanish, Italian, and English?"

"Some Asian, some French, I think a few were Russian, a couple were Arabic, and one was Scandinavian. The whole world loves soccer. Uh, I mean futbol."

"That's right. It's so popular it's got two names." Jose roared with laughter.

Casey and Johnny looked at each other and laughed too. More at Jose than at his terrible joke.

"That was a good one. So popular it has two names." He continued to laugh. "Very funny, right?" His eyes went from the boys to his guards.

Still chuckling, Casey and Johnny nodded. Casey looked at the guards, who were also, obviously, forcing laughter.

"What's so funny?" Luna asked, carrying out a big, colorful, ceramic platter of food.

"Futbol," Jose said. "It's so popular it has two names." He laughed again.

Luna placed the platter on the table while giving her brother-in-law a deadpan look.

Jose spread his arms, and his eyes opened wide with shock. "Futbol and soccer!"

Casey had to choke back from laughing as Luna rolled her eyes.

"What? It's funny," Jose said defensively.

She sighed and shook her head, looking toward Casey and Johnny. "Don't mind him, he's un poco loco."

"Poco loco, poco loco, poco loco," repeated Diego as he walked around the corner with Shakira trailing on a leash. Casey and Johnny laughed at her intermittent snorts and squeals. She was way more amusing than Jose's terrible joke.

"Ah, there's my little artist," Jose said. "I've been looking for you. Do you want to go to the plantation with me?"

Diego nodded.

"Come on everyone. Time to eat," Luna yelled

Everyone sat quickly and dug in. Jose grumbled something as he took the last available chair between two of his guards. They quickly moved their chairs, giving him more room. With a sour look, he sipped his coffee and slowly ate a strip of bacon. As soon as Diego finished eating, Jose rose from the table and said, "Come, Diego, it's time to go." He shot a serious look at his guards, who each immediately put down their forks and stood.

***

Alone outside, as they cleared the table, Casey said quietly to Juan, "When I heard your uncle say the name Pedro, I thought—"

"Yeah, I know. Don't worry, he was talking about one of his guards. Pedro is a very common name. Same as Jose and Juan. Two of my friends are named Juan. It gets ridiculous when we're all together, especially on the futbol field."

"I guess I'm lucky my name is kind of unique."

Juan nodded.

When they walked inside, Luna was asking Chelsea and Samantha where they were from.

"Australia," Samantha answered.

Instead of responding, Luna went quiet for a moment, then wiped a tear from her eye and said, "My husband had planned a trip to Australia for all four of us. But he was killed a few weeks before we were scheduled to go."

"I never knew that," Marianna said.

"Me neither," Juan added.

"I had a lot on my mind then, and I couldn't bring myself to tell you. We probably should have gone anyway, but I just didn't have the strength."

Marianna nodded.

Juan looked at his mother for a moment, then said. "Mom, I'm sorry, but I need to switch the subject and ask you a question."

"Go ahead."

"These guys," he gestured his arm towards Casey, Johnny, Chelsea, and Samantha. "Didn't come here for breakfast.

The kids all snapped to attention.

"No, Juan, don't," Marianna pleaded.

"We think Uncle Jose may have taken the women and kids that have been on the news. You know, the Italian players' families who were kidnapped."

"Of course, I know, but why do you suspect your uncle?"

"The news said it might be a cartel versus mafia thing, and who else around here would do something like this? And because he yelled at Casey yesterday in the pool when he thought he was listening to his conversation."

"Jose yells at everyone. You know that," she said. "And there are many cartel bosses in Colombia. Besides, Jose wouldn't kidnap innocent women and children."

"Really, Mom? Who are you kidding?" Marianna said. "He hates the mafia. This is exactly something he might do, and, if not him, Pedro certainly would."

Luna sneered. "You're right, Pedro would. That man makes me sick. Your uncle knows that if I ever saw him around here, I would probably kill him." Luna's tone was venomous.

"Whoa. Mom," Marianna said, studying her mother's face. "You're serious, aren't you?"

Luna took a deep breath and slowly expelled it. "We'll talk about it later."

"Sorry," Marianna said.

"Forget it, let's just move on. Tell me what else you know."

Concern and curiosity showed on Juan's face as he looked at his mother and said, "We already searched the tunnels, and in the last room on the bottom floor, we found four empty beds that looked like they were recently slept in. I think he was keeping them there."

Shaking her head, Luna said, "You know what your uncle would do if he knew you were snooping around down there?"

"Well, he wouldn't kill us, if that's what you're thinking. But that's probably what's going to happen to those women and kids unless we find them."

"I can't believe we're even discussing this. I'm not going to let you do it. You're just kids and it's way too dangerous. Whether Jose kidnapped them or not, if he finds out that you even suspected him enough to search his properties, he will totally lose it."

"Mom," Juan said aggressively, causing Marianna to put up her hand to stop him. His eyes widened, then he took a deep breath and settled down.

"Mom, we can't just sit around and do nothing," Marianna said in a soothing voice. "We know his properties better than anyone else. We are the best chance those women and children have."

"I agree, but this is way too dangerous for you kids."

"So, we should just leave it to the police, right?" Chelsea added.

"No," Luna said. "Jose owns them."

"What do you mean?" Casey asked.

"Most of the police here are happy to accept his money," Juan said. "And Uncle Jose is very generous with them. If we go to them, he'll be informed immediately."

"That's exactly why we need to help, Mom," Marianna said.

Luna raised her palm toward Marianna. "Stop pushing me. I said no and I meant it. It's too dangerous. Just give me a moment to think. I've got to know someone who can help."

"We do," Casey said.

"You do what?" Luna asked sharply.

"We have some people who can help," Casey said sheepishly.

"Who?"

"My father's security and investigation team."

"Your father is an investigator?"

"No, he's a professional golfer."

"Oh, really? How is that going to help us?"

"I guess that does sound kind of weird."

"A little. Why don't you explain?" Luna said.

"Years ago, he received a death threat while playing in the Masters Tournament."

Luna's eyes bulged. "Your father played in the Masters?"

Casey nodded, "Yes. In fact, he won it that year."

"Hold on, are you telling me that your dad is Reid Clark?"

Another nod. "So, I guess you know who he is?"

"Of course, I do. Who doesn't? I can't believe you're his son. That's amazing!"

"Do you golf?"

"She's a great golfer," Marianna said. "She and my dad used to win their club championship every year."

"We can talk about that later," Luna said. "Tell me more about this investigation team."

"Well, when Dad got the threats, he hired a team. Johnny's dad, Joel, is one of the bosses. Johnny and I grew up together at AllSport, a camp where my dad's foundation trains talented, but very underprivileged young adults to become pro athletes. Most of the recruits are from inner cities."

"I've read about AllSport. It sounds like an amazing place."

Casey nodded. "It is, but it's also dangerous sometimes. Lots of the athletes who train there were members of street gangs before they were recruited. There are always fights on campus. There was even a murder a few years ago."

"Really?" Luna said.

"Yeah, my dad's best friend was killed. He was AllSport's CFO. His body was found by Secret Service agents while my dad was giving the President and First Lady a campus tour."

Luna raised her eyebrows. "Sounds similar to things that happen around here. So, just like Juan and Marianna, you boys are somewhat used to this kind of stuff. How about you two?" she asked, looking at Chelsea and Samantha.

"We met Casey and Johnny a few years ago when the Olympics were in Australia," Samantha said. "We helped them stop assassins from killing a gymnast."

"Oh yes, I remember that, too. So, you've all had experience with things like this."

The foursome smiled and nodded.

Then, everyone fell silent as Luna's eyes moved skeptically from one kid to the next, ending on Marianna. "So tell me, how did you get into Jose's side of the tunnels, anyway?"

"Diego let us in," Marianna said with trepidation.

"What? How dare you involve that boy! Life is difficult enough for him without having to deal with the wrath of his father. That is unacceptable!"

With his elbows on the counter, Juan buried his face in his hands, then looked up at his mother. "What choice did we have? We couldn't have gotten in without him."

"Well, maybe you're looking at your choice. I'm tired of your uncle's constant bullying. If he's responsible for four innocent lives, then I want to help."

"Wait, is everybody cool with my mom helping out?" Marianna asked.

"A little late to ask us now," Johnny said with a laugh.

"I guess it is," Juan said. "Sorry, but I figured she knows more about my uncle than anyone, and I knew, once she heard what we're doing, she'd want to help."

Luna gave her son a slight nod and said, "If we're smart about this, we won't need to take any dangerous chances. It seems to me that your biggest problem will be searching Jose's properties without knowing if, or when, he might show up."

Casey and Juan nodded.

"So, my job will be to watch him and inform you. I'll stick by his side for the next day or two and text you whenever we go anywhere."

"That'll help a lot," Casey said.

"Won't he get suspicious, Mom?" Marianna asked. "I mean he knows you're not his biggest fan. You break his chops all the time."

Luna shrugged. "He makes it so easy, it's impossible to resist. I kind of assumed that role from your father. You may not remember, but he was relentless when it came to teasing Jose."

"I remember," Marianna said, smiling. "He would wink at us every time he did it."

"Yup," Juan said with a chuckle. "I remember too."

Luna looked at the ceiling for a moment, obviously deep in thought. When she lowered her head, her eyes were moist. "Don't worry. I'll be the best tracking informant ever."

"Tracking informant? Is there such a thing?" Juan asked.

"There is now!" Luna said with a smirk.

Casey smiled. "Okay, where do we look next?"

"Good question," Marianna said. "The plantation house, the beach house, the hunting camp, the island cottage, or the guest house. They all have hidden rooms or separate buildings that would be good hiding spots."

"Wow, that's a lot of possibilities," Chelsea said.

"Yup," Juan agreed. "And, if we want to save them, we need to move fast."

Skepticism appeared on Luna's face. She looked at Casey and said, "How is it that you always seem to be in the wrong place at the wrong time?"

Casey grinned.

"What do you mean?" Johnny asked.

"I don't know of any other kids who have done anything like this. And you guys are now on your second..."

"Case," the four kids blurted simultaneously.

Luna flinched. "Alright. Case."

"I named it the Colombian Caper," Samantha said proudly.

Juan chuckled.

"That's so cool," Marianna said. "This is fun."

"No, Marianna," Luna demanded. "It's not fun. It's dangerous. Don't get me wrong, I'm glad to be helping. But we need to take this very seriously, or someone might get hurt. I'm glad you four have some experience, but my kids don't. Although they've seen more horrible stuff than most kids, they've never been involved with anything like this. If you...I mean, we, are going to be involved, there will be no more laughing or fooling around. I don't want anyone here getting hurt."

Everyone stared at her silently until Juan burst into laughter.

Luna glared at him.

"Mom, take it easy. We're kids, remember. Of course, we know it's dangerous, But we can't just stop laughing. If you want to work on this with us, you need to lighten up."

Luna looked at her son sternly.

"Mrs...um...sorry, I don't even know your last name," Casey said.

"It's Camarillo, but please call me Luna, all of you."

"Okay, Mrs...uh, I mean Luna," Casey said. "Juan is right. We know how dangerous this stuff can be, but joking and laughing helps keep us calm when things get scary."

Luna shrugged. "Alright, obviously it's not your first rodeo. I'll back off."

"Another rule, Mom," Marianna said. "No more bad clichés."

Luna closed her eyes, smiled, and nodded once more.

Casey said, "Alright. We need to make a plan and get started. Sitting here isn't going to save anyone."

"We should go search one of the other locations right now while we know your uncle is at the plantation," Johnny said.

"Yeah," Juan agreed. "Let's go to the beach house. It's the closest. We can take the Jeeps."

"No, not the jeeps," Luna said. "They'll bring too much attention. Besides, I'm the only one here who can drive."

"No, you're—" Juan started.

"Legally," Luna cut him off. "You know, like with a driver's license."

Juan rolled his eyes but remained silent.

"We'll take the Suburban," Luna said.

"No way," Juan said. "That old rust bucket leaves a trail of smoke everywhere we go."

"So do most of the other vehicles around this area. That's what makes it perfect. It draws no attention, and besides, it's the only thing we'll all fit in."

"Where are we going?" Johnny asked as they followed Luna across the patio and past the pool.

"The Suburban is back that way." Marianna pointed towards the trees. They walked to the edge of the manicured lawn and followed a path into the woods. A couple of minutes later, a big red barn came into view.

"This was my father's studio," Marianna said. "He was a really good painter and sculptor. He made most of the artwork you saw in the house and around the property."

"Wow," Casey exclaimed. "Did he make that big metal horse near the pool?"

Marianna smiled. "Yes. That is my favorite. He made it when I was born. He named it Mare, which besides being what he usually called me, also means female horse in English."

"That's so cool!" Chelsea said.

"Juan, tell them about yours," Luna said.

"You tell them if you want to." Juan sounded annoyed.

"I thought you were proud of that piece?" Luna asked

"Really? Proud of an abstract sculpture called *Juan of a kind*? That's just stupid."

"Don't say that. Your dad loved that sculpture, and he loved you."

"Yeah, whatever. Let's go."

"Juan, don't," Marianna said.

"Leave me alone. Let's just get out of here and get this thing done."

All conversation ceased as Juan grabbed the barn door handles, leaned back, and heaved them open. The silence continued as they all piled into the big SUV, and Luna subtly crossed herself before turning the key. The engine coughed to life, and smoke billowed from the tailpipe as she drove out of the barn.

Chapter 7

MINUTES INTO THE steep drive down the winding mountain road, the skies darkened, and suddenly a deluge of marble-sized raindrops began pounding on the windshield and roof of the old vehicle. The interior ceiling liner had long since been torn off, leaving the metal roof exposed. The rat-a-tat-tat of the pelting raindrops sounded like they were under attack.

Fists white from clinging tightly to the oversized steering wheel, Luna's eyes were locked on the road just in front of the vehicle. She was accustomed to driving in torrential rainstorms, but this was extreme.

Thirty-four minutes later, they turned off the road onto a long gravel driveway. The storm's intensity had increased as they parked in front of another sprawling, one-level home. They waited in the SUV as bolt after bolt of lightning punched through the atmosphere, illuminating the dark, gloomy sky with powerfully bright flashes.

Casey's nervous excitement from working on the investigation was elevated by each crack of thunder. He looked around the vehicle to see how the others were responding to the storm. Everyone except Juan appeared as anxious as Casey felt. As he was wondering, *How is Juan staying so calm?*, a bright flash followed immediately by an extremely loud crash of thunder caused everyone to flinch, including Juan. *That's more like it,* thought Casey.

"Let's give it another minute or two," Luna said. "Most storms here don't last very long."

"So, we get a little wet. Who cares?" Juan said, opening his door. "We've got a job to do. Let's do it. Waiting could cost lives!" He jumped out and ran toward the back of the house, with Marianna, Chelsea, and Casey at his heels.

"I don't know why they went back there," Luna said to Johnny and Samantha. "Follow me, and you won't get quite as wet."

She stepped from the truck and dashed for cover under the portico at the front entrance. She unlocked the door and held it open as Johnny and Samantha ran up the steps.

Once inside, they walked toward the rear of the house, where the hallway opened into a huge living room with floor-to-ceiling windows lining the back wall. The ocean was less than thirty yards away. Even in the storm, the view was spectacular.

"Woah," Samantha exclaimed.

"Woah, is right!" Johnny agreed.

"Wait, is that a grommet out there?" Samantha asked, pointing at a wave.

"A what?" Johnny asked.

"Oh, sorry, mate. A kid surfing."

"Oh, yeah. Looks like it is. That's insane, with all the lightning. Right?"

"Wouldn't catch me out there right now," she said. "The waves aren't much either."

A loud thud made them both turn. "Luna, are you… Where did she go?" Johnny asked.

As they started toward the noise, someone began banging on the sliding glass doors behind them. They turned and saw Casey at the door.

Johnny ran and tried to open it. He flipped all three latches on the locks and pulled the handle. It wouldn't budge. He flipped the latches back to their original positions and pulled again without success.

Samantha reached down and pushed a button on the bolt lock in the door's track.

Johnny pulled again. The door still didn't move.

Casey banged again and yelled, "Come on! Open it already!"

"Chill, dude!" Johnny shouted. "We're trying."

He flipped the three locks one more time and yanked the handle with everything he had. This time the door opened easily and slid way too fast. It smashed hard against the frame at the end of its track, and glass shattered to the floor in thousands of tiny pieces.

"Whoa!" Johnny groaned as Chelsea, Marianna, and Antonio ran in behind Casey. They were all completely drenched and making a mess of the white leather, chrome, and glass-adorned room.

Luna and Juan entered the room from a hallway, and Luna sighed as she surveyed the chaos. The loud thud Johnny and Samantha had heard earlier had been Juan knocking books off a night stand to the floor as he climbed into the house through a bedroom window. His soaked clothes were now leaving a wet trail along the marble floor.

"How did that happen?" Luna asked, pointing at the pile of glass.

"I'm sorry," Johnny said. "I kept turning locks and pulling the door. When I finally got it unlocked, I guess I pulled too hard."

"Just a bit," Chelsea said with a giggle.

"Don't worry about it," Juan said. "If we find the women and kids, it won't matter, and if we don't, I'll just tell Uncle Jose that I did it. "I've done worse, and he's forgiven me."

Luna and Marianna nodded.

Casey looked around the room. Between the shattered glass, mud, and copious amounts of water, the once pristine room was a disaster. "You've really done worse than this?" he asked.

"Yeah, I totaled one of his old classic Jaguars last year. It was worth over six mill."

Johnny's eyes bulged. "Six million dollars?"

"No, pesos. About four hundred thousand dollars."

"Wow," Casey said. "If he forgave you for that, this should be no problem."

"It won't be quite that simple, but he'll get over it," Juan said. "We don't have time to worry about it now, anyway. We need to search this place."

Marianna nodded and said, "Mom, you and Antonio search the bedrooms. Juan, you take the basement. Johnny and Samantha, go check the garage. Casey and I will look in the attic."

"I'll check the guest cottage after I look in the basement," Juan added.

The group stood where they were, just nodding in silence for a moment.

"Come on. We need to hurry!" Marianna said.

Everyone started off simultaneously in different directions, bumping into each other. It was somewhat comical until Luna slipped on the wet trail Juan had left on the marble floor. She fell hard with a loud grunt.

"Mom, are you okay?" Marianna asked as she turned back to help.

"Yeah, I'm okay," she said as she slowly stood, holding her elbow. "Don't make a fuss. I'm fine. Really. I landed mostly on my butt."

"Are you sure? How about your arm?"

"I'll live. Just go! We need to get this done quickly."

Marianna nodded, stepped gingerly over the wet area, and ran to catch up with Casey.

Fifteen minutes later, after searching the premises and coming up empty, they all gathered at the front door.

"We need to go back to the hotel," Casey said. "My parents keep texting me, and they're running out of patience."

"Mine too," Johnny said.

"What are we going to do about this mess?" Marianna asked.

"I spoke with Carita," Luna said. "She is bringing a cleaning crew and has a glass company already on the way. Jose will never even know it happened."

"Phew," Johnny said. "Thank you. And again, I'm so sorry."

"No apology needed," Luna said. "It was just one of those things. Now, let's go."

The rain had mostly stopped. As they all jumped into the Suburban, Casey said, "Carita sounds like she's a big help."

"She's like our superhero," Marianna said. "She was my dad's assistant. When he died, Mom asked her to stay. She's like part of the family. She manages our house and just about everything else in my mom's life. Including us." She gestured toward Juan.

He looked back from the front passenger seat and gave a quick nod.

"There she is," Marianna said, looking out the window as they turned from the driveway onto the road.

A white Hummer H2 was waiting to turn into the driveway with a van behind it. Luna opened her window and waved as she drove by.

"Wow, a Hummer. I love those," Samantha said.

"You must pay her pretty well. Do you have any job openings?" Chelsea said with a grin.

Juan turned on the truck's radio. A Spanish news station was broadcasting. "Oh good," Juan said with a laugh. "It's going to stop raining soon."

"What?" Johnny asked. "It stopped like ten minutes ago."

"Duh!" Juan's eyes spun as his head bobbled. "I know, you idiot. The weather guy just said that. I was making fun of him. They're always wrong."

"Hey," Luna said. "No bullying!"

"Bullying? Mom, that was completely harmless. Johnny knows I didn't mean it. Right?" Juan turned and looked at Johnny.

Johnny shrugged. "Yeah, he's right. I kind of set myself up for that. I do it a lot."

Casey chuckled.

"Well, I won't stand for that nonsense. While I'm working with you, there better be none of it. Got it?" Luna's tone and the look she gave Juan was all business.

"Okay, okay, no mas!" Juan's hands were up in mock surrender. His tone was comedic, but the angst evident in his squinted eyes conveyed that he knew when not to mess with his mother.

"How much time till we're at the hotel?" Casey asked.

"Around twenty-five minutes," Luna said.

Casey sent a text.

"Uh-oh," he said as he read the response.

"What?" Johnny asked.

"They want you, me, and the girls to come to their suite for lunch as soon as we get there. They have someone who wants to meet us."

***

They entered the hotel lobby.

"You guys go ahead up," Luna said to Casey. "We'll eat lunch down here and wait for you."

"No. Come with us," Casey said.

"Are you sure?"

"Yup. Let's go."

They squeezed into the elevator along with a man and woman.

The woman dabbed her eyes with a tissue while the man tried to console her.

"Sono sicuro che stanno bene," he said.

"Spero che non siano morti," the woman said as she began to cry.

The man hugged her just as the elevator stopped on the sixth floor. "Ci scusi per favore," he said, helping the woman out.

The doors closed. "I wonder what that was about?" Johnny said.

"She is scared that the women and children are dead," Luna said.

"There are going to be people talking about it everywhere," Casey said. "So, we all need to watch what we say. If someone overhears us, they could go to the police, and we know what that will lead to."

"You're right," Juan said. "When in doubt, text it."

"Don't talk, type!" Johnny blurted out with a grin. "Our new motto!"

Casey gave him a look, his head shaking. "Really?"

"No, huh?" Johnny asked.

"Nope."

The elevator door opened, and they all followed Casey down the hallway.

"You guys wait in here for two minutes while we let them know you're with us," Casey said, opening the door to his and Johnny's room.

"You're sure you want us to come in?" Luna asked. "Your parents may not be happy about it."

"They'll be fine. I just want to let them know first. Besides, we'll need you to help explain."

"If you say so."

Casey nodded. "We'll be right back." He, Johnny, Samantha, and Chelsea went to his parents' door and knocked.

The door opened, and Johnny's mom, Cindy said, "Come in, lunch just arrived a little while ago, and we have a surprise for you."

They walked through the entranceway into the suite's oversized living room, where a small group was sitting, waiting for them. The four kids stopped dead in their tracks. Samantha shrieked as they saw Arnaldo Perez, Argentina's star soccer player, sitting on the couch. He was one of the best players in the world, and he was a hunk. A dark blue t-shirt hugged each ridge of his six pack abs. His large, well defined thighs pushed against his dress slacks. High cheekbones were like shelves, holding up his glittering, hazel eyes. His slightly crooked smile revealed bright white, nearly perfect teeth. It was as if the cliché, tall, dark, and handsome was coined just for him. Women around the globe melted when he was near.

Arnaldo approached them and shook the boy's hands.

"So, what does the other guy look like?" Arnaldo asked Casey.

"Huh?" Casey said.

"Nice shiners." Arnaldo pointed two fingers toward Casey's eyes.

"Oh, I forgot all about that. No, I got hit by a soccer ball."

"Ah yes, I've been hit more than a few times."

Casey smiled.

"Don't worry, it makes you look tough. The chicks will dig it."

"It's already working for him, Arnaldo," Johnny chimed in.

"Shut up," Casey said.

Arnaldo laughed, then turned to Chelsea. Her face lit up as he gave her a quick hug.

Samantha was trembling when he approached her. She threw her arms around his muscular frame and wouldn't let go.

Chelsea leaned over and whispered in her ear, "Okay, mate, that's enough."

Samantha gave one final squeeze and slowly removed her arms. Her dreamy look as she mumbled, "Sorry, guess I got a little carried away," made everyone laugh, including Sandra, Arnaldo's gorgeous girlfriend, who was still sitting on the couch holding their child, Justin.

Casey gave Johnny an uneasy look, wondering how he was going to tell his parents about the others and that they needed to speak in private.

"How about lunch?" Casey's mom said with a sweep of her arm toward a buffet table covered with sumptuous dishes.

"Thanks for the offer," Arnaldo said. "But, I have to get to practice. They're issuing heavy fines this week for every minute we're late."

"Arnaldo, could you please wait one minute? I have some friends who'd never forgive me if they found out you were here and didn't get to meet you." Casey ran out the door without waiting for an answer.

A minute or so later, Juan, Luna, Marianna, and Antonio were fawning over one of their heroes. Arnaldo's eyes bulged, and he coughed when Juan slapped his back a little too aggressively, ending their brief bro-hug. Marianna giggled, and Luna almost passed out when they each received a hug.

After posing for pictures with everyone, Arnaldo shook Reid Clark's hand. "It was great to meet you, Reid. Maybe we can get dinner one night after the game. Or better yet, you should all come to the team's celebration after we win."

"Que Chimba!" Juan said with a huge smile.

"What he said," agreed Johnny, bumping knuckles with Juan.

"Adios," Arnaldo said, ducking through the doorway with his little boy on his shoulders.

"Mom, Dad," Casey said. "This is Marianna, Juan, their mother, Luna, and their cousin Antonio."

After quick hellos, Casey added, looking toward his and Johnny's parents, "Let's all get some food, and then we need to speak with you."

"What about?" Casey's mother asked warily.

"We kind of need your help," Johnny said as he piled food on a plate.

"With?" Johnny's mom's tone was even more apprehensive than Shane's.

Johnny looked at Casey and said, "Go ahead, bud."

Casey sat and said, "You know the Italian players' wives and kids who were taken?"

"Oh no. Don't tell us that you guys got yourselves involved. Not again," Shane said.

"We didn't mean to," Casey said. "It just kind of happened."

"Why am I not surprised," Reid said. "Like Yogi Berra said, 'it's like déjà vu, all over again.'"

"Can I please explain without you getting mad?"

"Let's hear it," Reid said.

"We met Marianna and Juan in the pool yesterday, and we talked about the abduction. They told us that their Uncle Jose, Luna's brother-in-law, is a local cartel boss."

"Oh, terrific," Joel said. "Sorry, Luna. I mean no disrespect."

"I completely understand," Luna said. "I can only imagine what this sounds like to you all."

"Well, we're pretty sure he has them," Casey said.

"I suppose you overheard someone saying something again," Shane said.

"Kind of."

"What's that supposed to mean?" Reid asked. "Either you heard something, or you didn't."

"I was trying to see how many languages were being spoken while I was in the pool. Their uncle yelled at me for listening to his conversation. He didn't know that I couldn't understand what they were saying."

"So, it may not have had anything to do with the kidnapping," Reid said.

"Yeah, but when I mentioned it to Juan and Marianna, they agreed that he might be involved, so we kind of started searching for them already."

Shane and Cindy both groaned.

"And?" Joel asked.

"We found a room in the tunnels below his house that had four unmade, recently slept-in beds."

"So what," Joel said. "Anyone could have been sleeping there."

"No, the tunnels are no place to sleep. They're only for storage, or…" Luna let her voice trail off.

"Or?" Reid asked. "Please continue, Luna."

"Uh." She hesitated, took a deep breath, and said, "Hiding in, or escaping through."

"Cartel stuff?" Reid asked.

Luna nodded.

"And this was under one of the pillows." Chelsea pulled the troll doll from her pocket and dangled it by its pink hair.

"Hmm, so a kid probably was there," Joel said. "But those dolls aren't that uncommon. It could have been any kid. Nevertheless, we should call the police."

"He owns them," Luna said bluntly.

"What?" Shane asked.

"Most of the local police are on Jose's payroll."

"Well, that complicates things," Reid said, turning to Joel. "We should call Jay. He's got to know someone down here who can help."

Joel nodded, pulling his phone from his pocket.

"Wait, Uncle Joel," Casey said. "Let us tell you everything we know first."

Joel lowered his phone. "Go ahead. I'm listening."

"Juan," Casey said. "Help me explain."

Juan's eyes bulged. "You tell them," he said nervously.

"Don't be scared," Casey said. "You haven't done anything wrong. They just want to help us."

"He's right, Juan," Reid reassured. "You have absolutely nothing to worry about."

"He's scared of what it will be like after you all leave. Jose may be their uncle and my brother-in-law, but if we turn him in…" Luna shook her head.

"Won't they put him in jail?" Shane asked.

"No judge in this area will convict him. They're either on his payroll too, or they're afraid he'll have them killed."

"Sounds like a sweet guy," Joel said.

"Worse than you can imagine. My husband is dead because of him. They ran the cartel together."

Juan and Marianna both snapped to attention. Their eyes went wide as the bottle cap Johnny had just removed from his drink.

"I'm sorry, kids. I always just figured you were better off not knowing the truth. Uncle Jose set your dad up to save his own hide.

They were ambushed on the road. Jose walked away without a scratch. Your father was not so lucky. Jose began working with Pedro after that."

"That's why you acted like you did before. You think Pedro killed Dad." Juan's lips quivered as he stared at his mother.

Marianna's eyes narrowed as her face slowly twisted into a look of pure hatred. "He's going to pay for that," she seethed. "I don't care what happens to us afterward."

Luna walked to them and pulled them both into a hug. "I know how you both feel. I've been torn by the same feeling ever since it happened."

"Why do you put up with him?" Marianna asked.

"Because I have no proof, and because I love you two and Diego. If I did anything about it or even tried, I'd end up dead. It's bad enough that you have to grow up without a father. I don't want you to be motherless too."

"But you go to dinner with him all the time," Marianna said.

"You're right, and I hate it. But you know what he's like when he doesn't get his way. He's hinted many times that if I don't join him, he'll take it out on you two and Diego."

"He wouldn't!" Marianna said through clenched teeth.

"Of course, he would," Juan said. "We have to put an end to it, now."

"If we're going to do this, neither of you can let on that you know anything about your father. It would make him suspicious, and when he gets suspicious, he also gets nasty."

"Who is Diego?" Shane asked.

"Jose's son," Luna said. "He's autistic."

"Oh, I'm sorry. That has to be difficult."

"Actually, he's a great kid. But Jose doesn't take the time to work with him. Diego loves Marianna, and she is excellent with him."

"What about his mother?" Shane asked.

"She and Jose were not good together. They fought all the time, and she had a hard time dealing with Diego. A few years ago, she just disappeared."

"What do you mean, disappeared?" Reid asked.

"Exactly that!" Luna said. "One day she was here, and the next day she was gone."

"Just like that? You never asked where she went?"

"Of course, I asked, but I never got a real answer. Jose just shrugged and told me to mind my own business. That's his answer to most of my questions."

"Do you think she's dead?" Joel asked.

"While I wouldn't put it past him, I don't think so. I think he just sent her away. She's probably back with her family in Peru. At least, I hope so."

"Aren't you curious?" Reid asked.

"Of course I am, but I've always been afraid of him. When he told me not to meddle, I decided things were already tough enough for me and the kids. Living with him is difficult enough when he's happy."

"I didn't realize you live with him," Reid said.

"We don't live together, but our house is next to his. My husband and he built the estate together. The houses are attached by the tunnels that the kids mentioned."

"I guess that makes it hard to avoid him?" Reid asked.

"Yes. He comes over almost every day, whenever he feels like it. I haven't had the courage to tell him I don't want him in my house."

"That's terrible," Joel said.

Luna nodded. "So, now you understand why I'm helping the kids with this. I've had enough."

"Okay, let's do it then," Reid said, turning toward the kids. "I'm sure you guys have a plan already, right?"

"Well, we already searched through the tunnels and his beach house," Casey said. "He's got a bunch of other homes too. Juan, why don't you explain."

"There's a mansion at his plantation. There's a big barn and another house there too. Then, there's the island house. We need to check them all."

"He also owns houses that he rents to his workers and his security staff," Luna added. "And there are three barns at the plantation. I'm sure he also has places that we don't know about."

"Luna," Joel said. "Do me a favor. Please write down all the addresses that you know of. I'm going to call for some help."

"Not the police, though, right?"

"No. Not the police. My boss has a network of private investigators throughout the world. He'll hook us up with some good people."

"If you say so," Luna said. "But, I'm telling you, if the police hear anything about this, it'll get right back to Jose. Then, I'll probably disappear, too."

Marianna gasped.

"I'm sorry, baby," Luna said. "I didn't mean to scare you. I just wanted to emphasize how serious I am about this."

"Understood," Joel said. "I promise, the police will not know about this."

Luna raised her brow and shrugged. "I guess I'll just have to trust you."

"I'm sure that's not easy for you. Considering the life you've led," Joel said.

"You've got that right. I trust no one. But, it seems I don't have much choice here." After a heavy sigh, she said, "I really don't feel good about this, but, give me a minute. I'll write down the addresses for you."

"We texted a bunch to you already, Uncle Joel," Casey said.

"What?"

"The addresses. Marianna sent them while you were talking. We started a new group text. You're all in it. It'll be the best way for us all to communicate."

"Very good. That makes it easy for me to forward them to Jay after I explain all this to him. Thanks, Marianna."

Marianna nodded.

As Joel was about to touch the screen of his phone, Luna raised her palm towards him, and adamantly said, "Wait a minute. Since you're expecting me to trust someone I haven't even met. I'd like to know a little about him, *before* you make the call."

"Fair enough," Joel said. "Jay Scott is Reid's personal security director and the Chief of Security for AllSport. He also owns a company that provides security for high level people throughout the world. I served under him in the Navy SEALs, and I work for him now. While Reid and I, and our families are very close friends, I am also here as Reid's bodyguard."

Luna nodded and said, "Tell me about some of these high level people that Jay protects."

"Heads of State, leaders of countries, business moguls, celebrities. The list is quite long."

"Would I know any of them?"

"Absolutely, but, for obvious reasons, we don't reveal their names."

Luna's tightly crossed arms, tilted head, and stare kept Joel talking.

"Look, Luna, Jay is one of the most trustworthy people I know. He's also one of the smartest, and by far the best connected. There is no question that we'll find the women and children faster with his help. I swear to you, you can trust me, and you can trust him."

Reid, Shane, Cindy, Casey and Johnny were all nodding.

Luna silently looked at them all, then turned her head toward Marianna and Juan.

"I trust them, Mom," Juan said.

"I do too," Marianna added.

Luna closed her eyes for a moment and sighed. She looked deep in thought. She opened her eyes, unfolded her arms, and said, "I wish you could all understand how scared I am of Jose. Decisions like this go against all the principles I have set for myself and my kids." Then, after a deep breath and a long exhale, she said, "Go ahead, make your call."

Marianna and Juan approached and hugged Luna as Joel put his phone to his ear and walked away from them all.

A couple of minutes later Joel returned and said, "Jay is reaching out to some of his people down here. He and Stu are coming too."

"I thought they were in Israel, hiring a husband and wife Mossad team?" Reid asked.

"You know him. As soon as I told him what was going on here, his decision was made. He'll probably bring the new recruits with him. What better way to test their skills?"

Reid nodded.

"Wait, did you say Mossad?" Luna asked.

"Yes," Joel said. "It's one of Israel's three intelligence agencies. It's similar to the CIA, and Mexico's CNI."

"Yeah, they're one of the best in the world," Johnny said with exuberance. "I can't wait to meet them."

"I know who they are," Luna said. "I'm just surprised people of that caliber are coming to help."

Joel nodded. "And the husband and wife team that Jay is recruiting were in the Kidon, an elite special operations unit within Mossad, known to be the best of the best."

"Wow, that's so dope!" Casey said.

"When I told him that we can't go to the police for help, he asked if we could put a tracking device on Jose's vehicle. Searching his properties will be easier If we know where he is."

"I already told the kids that that was my job," Luna said. "I will stick by Jose's side for however long it takes to find them."

"That can't be safe for you, considering everything you told us," Joel said.

"As long as he doesn't find out what we're up to, I have nothing to worry about. The fact is, he likes me, he always has, even when I was married to his brother. I've always avoided his advances, but he'll have no problem with me spending time with him."

"And you don't think your sudden change in attitude will raise any suspicion?" Reid asked.

"Well, if it goes on for too long, it will. Hopefully, we'll find them within a day or two, and it will be over."

Joel nodded. "Okay, I need to gather as much information as possible before the troops get here."

"The troops?" Luna's eyes bulged.

"It's just a figure of speech." Joel apologized. "I meant Jay and the rest of our team. Sorry."

Luna nodded. "It's okay. I thought you meant military."

"No. We'll make sure this gets done subtly. That way, even if we don't find them, you won't have any problems with Jose afterward."

"Thank you for understanding."

"Of course," he said with a nod. "Okay, I'd like the four of you to pick whichever locations you feel you know the best and make drawings of them. Include as many details as you can on every level. Include the surrounding grounds too. Then, I'll need you each to describe the drawing to me, so I can inform the others when they get here." Joel turned toward Johnny. "Do me a favor, son. You know where the concierge room is down the hall?"

Johnny nodded.

"I saw a bunch of legal pads and pens there this morning. Will you go get them?"

Johnny looked at Samantha and said, "Come with me."

As they took off out the door, Juan interpreted Joel's request to Antonio.

Twenty minutes later they were studying the drawings.

Juan's and Luna's illustrations of the beach house and hunting camp looked as if young children had created them. Both contained crooked lines and various rudimentary shapes that they explained were rooms, doors, windows and furniture. Their descriptions of the locations were concise, making up for their lack of drawing expertise.

Marianna's depiction of the island cottage was a much cleaner and had the flair of an artist's rendering. She had even added shading behind open doors and under tables. Her explanation was as elaborate as her mother's and brother's had been.

"Holy smokes," Joel said when he looked at Antonio's sketch of the plantation buildings. It resembled an architect's draft. His lines and angles were almost as crisp as if he had drawn them using the edge of a ruler.

"He's always been extremely talented at drawing and drafting," Luna said. "He and Diego often sit and draw together for hours. Antonio has helped Diego become an excellent artist also. I haven't told him yet, but I'm going to offer to pay Antonio's way through architectural school."

Juan translated as Antonio explained his diagram, although his sketch was so detailed it hardly needed any further clarification.

Joel said, "Great job, all of you. Now I want to discuss how we're going to go about the search of each property. But, before that, I want to lay down some ground rules." He looked at Johnny, who was typing on his phone. "Hey, bud, who are you texting?"

Johnny's eyes traveled from his phone across the room to Samantha, who looked up from her phone and grinned at Joel.

"Really?" Joel said. "Texting with someone who's in the same room should be outlawed. You should just talk to each other."

"We were, Dad," Johnny said.

"You know what I mean, you clown. Verbally, face to face."

"This is easier."

"Yeah, well, maybe that's the problem. Being social isn't always easy. Verbal conversation is more appropriate."

"Maybe to you, but not to us," Johnny said as he turned and scanned the room.

All the kids nodded.

"Okay, whatever." Joel looked at his wife. "Losing battle, huh?"

Cindy nodded. "We've tried," she said, looking at Shane, who also nodded. "It's not worth the effort. The term social has a whole new meaning with their generation."

"Alright," Joel said. "Let's just move on. Everyone, please take a seat and pay attention. No talking, no texting. In fact, all phones off, please."

He waited until they were all seated and looking at him. "Okay, this is-" His phone rang, and with a sheepish grin, he reached for it. "Sorry. It's Jay. I have to take it."

Everyone chuckled.

Joel jotted notes on a legal pad as he listened to Jay.

"Okay. See you then. Fly safe." He hung up and looked at the group. "Two of his local guys will get here tonight. Jay, Stu, and the Israeli couple will arrive in the morning."

"We're not going to wait for him to get started, are we?" Casey asked.

"No. That's exactly what I want to discuss." He turned to Luna. "So, which of the properties do you think is the most probable?"

"I'd say the plantation," Luna answered. "There are lots of places to hide them there."

"No way," Juan said. "There are always workers throughout the plantation. We should search the island house first. It's so secluded. It's like the perfect place to hide them."

"Yeah, but it would be tough to move them from there quickly if he needed to," Marianna said. "You can only get there by boat or helicopter. I think he'd probably hide them in one of the houses in town. There are tons of rooms. It would be easy to hide them there."

"Unh-uh!" Juan said. "They're way too busy. There are so many workers living in them, it would be impossible to hide them without someone noticing."

"Okay," Joel said. "You're all making excellent points, but we need to choose a place to begin. So, if Jose is at the plantation, and we need a boat or copter to get to the island, we should head to the houses in town for now."

"Okay, but we need to move fast," Luna said. "Some of the houses are shared by the day and the night shift workers. We'll need to search those as soon as the vans leave. They take the late shift workers to the plantation. Then they transport mid-shift workers from the fields to the estate mansion. Then they bring the early shift workers back to the houses in town."

"What time do the shifts change?"

"The first shift ends at one," Marianna said. "Then, after everyone eats lunch and gets a short siesta, they get shuttled around. The first shift will probably get back to the house around three."

"Are the houses close to each other?"

"The ones in our town are right next to each other, in a row," Luna said.

"How long a drive from here?"

"About ten minutes. Why?" Juan asked.

"Because based on these plans," Joel said, looking at the drawings. "They all have two floors, plus a basement and attic. There are twelve of us, so if we split into three teams of four, we can search three homes in about ten minutes."

"If we leave now, we can be done before they get there," Casey said. "Luna, Marianna, and Juan should each lead a team."

Joel nodded. "What type of vehicle did you drive here?"

"Our Suburban. It's an old rusty thing," Juan said. "But we can all fit in it."

"Good," Joel said. "Let's go. We'll discuss the details on the way."

The kids were at the door in a flash. The grownups were a bit slower.

"I'll be with you in a minute," Shane said. "I need to use the bathroom before we go."

"Oh, mom, come on. You always do this at the last minute," Casey said. "Just hold it till we get back."

"Casey!" Shane scolded. "Be quiet. Everyone just go. I'll be down before you're all in the car." She ran to the bathroom and slammed the door.

Reid smiled and shook his head at his son.

"What?" Casey said. "She does this all the time."

Reid shrugged and said, "Shh. Just move it."

"You know I'm right," Casey said.

"Just go."

Casey ran down the hall, catching up with everyone as they were getting on the elevator. Before stepping in, Casey turned to look back. Reid waved him ahead. "We'll be right down."

Chapter 8

Meanwhile, a phone call to Italy was taking place elsewhere in Colombia

"YOU TELL HIM, if he wants to see them alive again, he better cancel the other order and continue buying from us. Besides the one late delivery, business between us has always been smooth. There is no reason to ruin a good thing."

"Do you really think you can strong-arm him, Pedro? A war between your cartel and my cousin in Sicily would be ridiculous. It would cost both of you a fortune, and the bloodshed would be enormous. It's just not worth it."

"That's why I'm talking to you, Alberto. We don't want a war. We just want things to remain the same. Our relationship has been good for many years. We didn't create the problem, Pasquale did."

"I know, I know. He's not always so smart. But you didn't have to kidnap women and children, did you? And killing their bodyguards? That was unnecessary."

"We ran out of options. He has not returned my calls for weeks. Now, we have his attention, no?"

"Yes. But now he's angry."

"We don't want a problem with him. Just tell him the ball is in his court. If he wants the player's wives and kids released, all he needs to do is call me and say we're good. Business as usual. But if I don't hear from him before the game…"

"You know threats and ultimatums will just piss him off."

"Piss him off? He started this. Either he can end it easily, or we'll do what we have to do."

"I'll call him as soon as we hang up."

"Be convincing!"

"I will try."

"If you want to avoid bloodshed, Alberto? You better try very hard."

Chapter 9

THE SEARCH OF two of the homes was quick and fruitless.

Johnny was the last of the group to exit the third house. He ran to the Suburban and launched himself in through the rear hatch, yelling in a jittery voice, "I think there's a dead guy on the second floor!" Landing on top of Casey, Johnny was winded and shaking with fear.

"Ow," Casey bellowed, pushing Johnny off.

"What makes you think he's dead?" Joel asked.

"'He wasn't moving or breathing, Dad!"

"Are you sure he wasn't just sleeping?"

"Uh, yeah. Kind of."

"Kind of? Come on, Johnny, get serious. This is important."

"Well, he wasn't moving."

"How close did you get?"

"I don't know. Like a few feet, maybe. Then I got scared and ran."

"We have to call the police," Reid said. "No way," argued Juan.

"We can do it anonymously, can't we?" Casey asked.

"Not from our cell phones. They'll track them," Johnny replied.

"I'll handle it," Luna interjected while typing. "Done! Let's get out of here."

Marianna looked at her mother, questioningly. "Carita?"

Luna shook her head. "Her cousin, Shelly," she said as she started the vehicle. "She lives about an hour from here. She'll call it in anonymously." Luna shifted the gears and began driving.

"Very good," Joel said. He turned to face everyone in the vehicle, "So, obviously no one else found anything relevant during your searches?"

All heads turned side to side. A few "No's" were voiced.

"Okay, Luna, do you have any idea what time Jose should be back at his estate?"

"Why?" Johnny asked. "We've already searched there."

"I know, but I think it might be better if they're at home before he gets there," Joel said, sweeping his chin toward Luna, Juan, Marianna, and Antonio.

"I agree," Luna said. "The fewer questions from him, the better. I'll drop you all off at the hotel, and we'll head back to our house."

"Good. And when our other teams arrive, I'll brief them. Then, we'll call you and make tomorrow's plan."

"How about Facetime or Skype?" Marianna asked. "Can we use those?"

"Why do we need that?" Juan asked. "Don't be stupid."

Marianna leaned forward over Juan's seat and punched his shoulder. "Shut up!"

"Hey. That's enough!" Luna said sharply.

Juan sneered at his sister. Marianna raised her fist again and he leaned away.

"I said, that's enough!" Luna looked at Juan in the seat next to her. "No bullying! Sometimes you're just like your uncle."

Juan lowered his head.

Casey ended the uptight moment of silence. "So, depending on where Jose goes tomorrow, we will head to the other locations."

"I will text you as soon as I know where we are headed," Luna said.

"Have you figured out what you will say to him?" Marianna asked.

"I've been thinking a lot about it. I'm going to tell him that I need to talk to him about Diego. I found a school that I think would be perfect for him, so I was planning on talking to Jose about it anyway."

"That will be a good cover," Marianna said. "What made you think of it?"

"I've been researching it for quite a while. That boy needs more help than he gets in that house."

"Wait. You're serious about this?" Marianna's concern grew.

"Honey, he won't be able to rely on you forever. You'll be going to college in a few years, and what then? It's not like Jose will help him."

"But, he's not ready for such a big change. He'll freak."

"That's where you're going to be needed, Marianna. You will be the one to tell him about it and make him comfortable with it."

"No way! Not me."

"We'll discuss it later. You'll like the place, and so will he. It's beautiful."

"You've been there?" Marianna said incredulously. "How could you keep this all from me?"

"I was waiting for the right time. This was not how I wanted this conversation to go. Look, you know I love that boy, and all I want is what's best for him. Jose's home is not a good place for any young boy, especially one with autism."

"So, he can live with us."

"You know your uncle would never allow that."

"Mom, he's gotten so much better with my help. You know he has. Moving him would be so bad for him."

"You have been the boy's savior, my love, but as you get older, you will need more time for yourself. You are not his mother. I won't allow him to hold you back from whatever life you choose for yourself."

Marianna wiped a tear from her eye.

"We'll discuss it later," Luna said.

The last few minutes of the ride were quiet. Casey typed as they drove up to the hotel's entrance. Marianna's phone chirped.

Casey: *Text me when you get home and things settle down.*

He squeezed her hand just before he stepped out of the SUV. She forced a tiny smile at him.

Chapter 10

"WHAT'S WRONG, DAD?" Johnny asked, sitting with the group up in his parent's suite.

"A lot of things, Johnny. To start with, I'm not happy that you and Casey seem to have become magnets for situations like this. I'm not mad, but it worries me. Then, there's the fact that four people's lives may be at stake, and I know next to nothing about how to save them. You know I don't like working a case by the seat of my pants, and that's exactly what we're doing here. And finally, I'm not comfortable that we can't inform the police. While I don't always involve them in my investigations, I've never had to hide something like this from them. I often push the envelope on cases, but I never do anything illegal, and not informing the police, especially while we're in a foreign country, just feels wrong."

"Wow, that is a lot. I'm sorry for putting you in the middle of it."

"No, son. Don't get me wrong. I always want you to come to me with anything you've got. No matter what. Okay?"

Johnny nodded. "Thanks, Dad."

Joel put his arms around Johnny and pulled him in for a tight bear hug. "I love you, Johnny, and I'll always be here for you."

"I love you, too."

Casey gave them a moment, then walked over and stretched his arms around them both. "Me too," he said, hamming it up.

"Go away, you jerk," Johnny said with a forceful shove.

Samantha and Chelsea stifled laughs as Casey fell back with theatrical flair.

"We don't have time for your nonsense right now, Casey," his dad said.

Getting up, he said, "Sorry. I thought it would be funny."

"So, I'm figuring Jay's guys will get here in an hour or two," Joel said. "And as important as this all is, it's still our vacation. I'm going downstairs to work out before my body turns to pudding."

"Ha!," Cindy said. "Your body going soft? There's about as much chance of that as there is of your grandfather walking into this room now."

"Mom! Both of Dad's grandfathers are dead." Johnny realized his error. "Oh."

His mother smiled at him.

"I'll join you, Joel," Reid said.

"Me too," Cindy added.

Johnny flexed his arm and looked at his bicep. "I think I'll go to the gym later. My muscles need to be fed first. Does anyone want to go get a snack with me?"

"Dude," Casey said. "You just finished stuffing your face a little while ago."

"Yeah, really," Chelsea said. "Where do you put it all?"

"There's always room in here for ice cream." Johnny patted his stomach with both hands.

"Ice cream sounds good to me," Samantha said. "I'll come with you."

"Okay, me too, I guess," Casey agreed. "How 'bout you, Chelsea? Can you squeeze some ice cream in that skinny body of yours?"

"Nah, I'm not hungry. I'm going to catch some rays and finish my book."

"I'm with you, girl," said Casey's mom, picking up her iPad. "Except for catching rays, that is."

"Okay," Casey said, looking at his phone. "It's almost four. Let's say we all meet back here at six o'clock."

"Casey, remember, it's everyone's vacation."

"I know, Mom. But there are four lives at stake. That's a little more important, don't you think?"

"Yes, of course I do. Hopefully there will be time to enjoy ourselves after we find them."

"Okay, all, scoot! I need to change my clothes," Joel said. "We'll meet back here at six."

"We should probably have dinner up here again," Reid said. "We can discuss things more openly with Jay's guys here than in a restaurant."

"I'll order while you guys work out," Shane said, doing a quick headcount. "There's eight of us and two more coming, right?"

Joel nodded, "Yeah, so order enough for eleven or twelve."

"Why? We'll only be ten."

Joel grinned and pointed at Johnny.

"Oh, right." Shane nodded and laughed along with everyone else, including Johnny.

Chapter 11

FIFTEEN MINUTES AFTER getting comfortable on a chaise lounge in the shade of an umbrella, Shane's reading was disrupted by the deep, irritating voice of a man speaking Italian. Years prior Shane had taken an online Italian course in order to communicate with the wife of one of Reid's friends on the golf tour.

The man with the deep voice was speaking too fast for her to fully understand him, but she caught snippets of his conversation. After a couple of minutes she rolled her eyes, thinking, *would you please just shut up?* Before giving up on her book, she craned her neck to see what he looked like. Two olive-skinned men were soaking up the rays in lounge chairs a couple of rows back. One was thin and very fit for an older guy. A narrow band of his close-cut, white hair stretched from temple to temple. The reflection of the sun off his mostly bald head made Shane squint. The guy next to him had an ample gut, and lots of dark, curly hair covering his head and his large torso. *Ew*, thought Shane, *it's like built-in sunscreen.* Luckily she didn't mind the smell of their smoldering cigars.

Annoyed that she couldn't concentrate on her book, she closed her eyes in hopes of a quick nap, but the steady drone of the man's gravelly voice prevented that. She turned onto her stomach and lay facing him with her eyes open just enough, she hoped, to send him a subtle message. After another minute, she got fed up and decided to move to the other side of the pool. But, just as she was about to get up, she heard words that caused her to freeze in place.

"Lo uccidero io stesso," the older man said just loud enough for her to hear. Squinting, she saw his angry face and clenched teeth.

Alarmed, she sat up, grabbed her phone, and typed.

Shane: *I'm out at the pool. Just overheard a man say in Italian, "I'll kill him myself." Please, don't come running out here all at once. Let me listen in and keep you updated.*

***

"Should we go out?" Reid asked from the gym floor after he had stopped doing sit-ups to read Shane's text.

"Your wife just said that she can handle it. Trust her!" Joel advised.

Reid nodded. "You're right!"

"Besides, it's probably just an unrelated conversation at the pool."

"You think?"

"I don't know. Give her some time."

***

"Wow! Let's go," Casey said, standing up and shoving his phone in his pocket.

"But your mother said—" Samantha started.

"Whose case is this? Hers or ours?"

"It's ours, but—"

"But, nothing," Casey said. "Let's go."

"Give me a second," Johnny slurred. A trail of melted ice cream was running down his chin as he scooped another huge spoonful into his mouth.

"Stay here if you want. I'm going." Casey walked out of the hotel café.

"Dude, wait," Johnny garbled through a full mouth as he and Samantha caught up just before Casey opened the glass door to the pool area.

"We'll walk out slowly and stop right there," Casey said, pointing. "Next to that big planter. Samantha, you look to the left. I'll look at the people straight ahead. Johnny, you look right."

"Why don't we each just walk in those directions?" Johnny asked.

Casey looked at him, ready to argue, "Dude, you're a mess. Wipe the ice cream off your chin and your shirt."

Samantha giggled.

Johnny opened the door, snagged a towel from the dirty towel bin, and stepped back inside.

"Gross," Samantha said. "Those towels are used."

He shrugged, wiped his chin, and tried to clean his shirt. Looking down at the mess, he said, "Best I can do."

"Okay, let's go," Casey said, pushing the door open.

They walked to the planter and scanned their assigned areas.

"There's Chelsea," Samantha said, waving in Chelsea's direction.

"Stop waving!" Johnny said. "We're supposed to be subtle.

"I am being subtle. I didn't yell her name, did I?"

"There's my mom," Casey said.

"Where?" Samantha asked.

"Under that umbrella," Casey said, scanning the area immediately surrounding his mother.

"Dude, there's like a million umbrellas," Johnny said.

"Oh, right. Hold on. Give me a minute. I'm trying to find the guy she's talking about."

After a few seconds, Johnny asked, "See him?"

"I don't know. There are two guys behind her on the right. And there's a man and woman on her left and another couple in front of her. They're all within her hearing range."

"Do any of them look Italian?" Johnny asked.

"Really?" Casey said, with his face scrunched in disbelief.

"What? Come on, you know what I mean. Some people look like where they're from. Like Asians and Eskimos and—"

"Okay, okay. You made your point. But, it's kind of racist." Samantha nodded.

"I didn't mean it that way."

"Never mind. Listen, this is what we're gonna do."

Johnny and Samantha moved in closer.

"Johnny, you go around the outer edge of the crowd and approach from over there." Casey pointed left. "You do the opposite," he said to Samantha. "Approach from the other side. Find chairs as close as possible to the people I just pointed out and just sit and play games on your phone. Try not to let my mom see you. I don't want to disrupt anything. Listen to everything the people say. If you hear names or places or anything that sounds interesting or suspicious, take notes on your phone."

"Wait, the guy was speaking in Italian, Johnny said. "How will I know what he's saying?"

"Just do your best."

"What are you going to do?" Samantha asked.

"I'm still deciding. I'm going to approach from the rear and then either sit behind my mom or walk right over and sit with her."

"Won't she get mad?" Samantha asked.

"She'll get over it," Casey said. "And besides, she's never done this stuff before."

"Dude, we helped solve one case. That doesn't make us experts, either," Johnny said.

"Hey, that gymnast is alive because of us."

"Yeah, but—" Johnny started.

"Guys," Samantha interjected. "There's no time to argue. Let's just do this."

Casey and Johnny nodded, and they all dispersed.

As Casey slowly approached, he saw a lounge chair just behind his mother that made his decision easy. He could see everything from its viewpoint; Johnny, Samantha, his mom, and all the possible suspects. Johnny and Samantha had already found chairs near the people to the right and left of his mom. Casey looked around, then at his mom. Her eyes were closed. She's sleeping? No way. Casey took out his phone and typed.

Casey: *Mom, don't get mad and don't look for us, but Johnny, Samantha, and I are in lounge chairs surrounding you. You looked like you were asleep, so I texted you. Which guy is it?*

Casey watched his mother pick up her buzzing phone and look at the screen. He held his breath, hoping she wouldn't look for him.

Shane: *So you couldn't just trust me, huh?*

Casey: *Ouch! Yes, we do. Just thought you could use some help.*

Shane: *It would be more helpful if you'd just listen to me! We'll discuss it later. He's mostly bald with some gray hair! Cigar! And NO, I wasn't sleeping!!!*

Samantha and Johnny shot each other quick looks. Then both looked at Casey.

***

"He sure knows how to make her mad, huh?" Joel said to Reid.

"Worse. She's offended," Reid said.

Cindy stepped off the elliptical and said, "Think I should go do some damage control? She's upset."

"No," Joel said. "What's done is done. They'll work it out later." He typed.

Joel: *Do not approach him!*

Casey: *Of course not. We'll listen and follow him (from a distance.) Hopefully, we get to see what room he's in. Then he's all yours.*

Reid: *A looong distance. Do NOT let him see you!*

***

After blowing a few smoke rings, the balding man rested his cigar in an ashtray and stood.

Casey, Johnny, and Shane covertly watched as he made his way through the throng of sunbathers. Casey flinched when Samantha stood. Johnny subtly shook his head, trying to get her attention. The man was not yet far enough away to begin following him.

Casey watched closely, worried that the man would notice Samantha if she followed him into the hotel. Instead of following him though, Samantha surprised them all by taking off her tee-shirt and shorts, then walking toward the shallow end of the pool in her blue bikini. The man walked to the edge of the deep end, dipped his toe in the water, then dove in. Samantha entered the water at the stairs.

After ten agonizing minutes of watching the man swim laps, Casey was contemplating joining Samantha who was now sitting at the edge of the pool with her legs in the water.

Johnny: *I think I'm going to sit near Samantha.*

Casey: *I was thinking the same thing. No, wait. Don't go. He's heading in her direction.*

They watched nervously as the man stopped next to Samantha and said something to her.

Johnny: *Uh oh!*

Joel: *What's wrong?*

Shane: *Everybody calm down. The guy just swam some laps, and now he's talking to Samantha. It looks fine. They are both smiling and talking.*

Chelsea: *Where are you guys? I just woke up.*

Casey: *We're on the other side of the pool. Stay where you are. We'll explain later.*

Johnny: *Chelsea, does Samantha speak Italian?*

Chelsea: *Yeah, a little, why? Hey wait, who is the old bloke she's talking to?*

Casey: *We'll tell you all about it later. Just don't go over there.*

Chelsea: *Okay, now you're scaring me. Who is he?*

Shane: *Chelsea, Samantha is fine. I promise. Just stay wherever you are. We will explain everything in a little while.*

Chelsea: *Okay, thanks, Mrs. Clark!*

***

"How long are you in from Australia," the man asked Samantha.

"We go back the day after the game."

"Bene. Maybe you can meet my grandson while you're here. He's coming by this evening."

"Maybe," Samantha said with a little discomfort.

"You'll like him. He's with the team."

Samantha's eyes lit up. "He plays for Italy?"

"Spero," the old man answered, looking up and patting his heart. "No. He's good, but not that good. He works as a raccattapalle…a ball boy. Not quite as exciting as a player, but it's a great job, and he's on the field during every game. Can't get better seats than that. My son-in-law's cousin plays on the team. He got him the job."

"Nice. What's his name?"

"Tommaso."

Samantha knew all the players' names on Italy's and Argentina's teams. "I didn't know there was a player named Tommaso."

"No. No. I thought you meant my grandson. His uncle is Leonardo."

"Leonardo Sauro?" Samantha's eyes widened.

"Si."

"Wait. So you're related to him? He's amazing. But didn't I hear that his wife and child were…"

Samantha was cut off by the unmistakable thwop-thwop of an approaching helicopter interrupting the serenity throughout the pool area.

She noticed that the old man flinched at the sound, then quickly moved closer to the edge of the pool. He lowered himself so just his head was above the water. He turned, and pressed his back tightly to the wall.

As Samantha looked up at the helicopter, she was startled that the big, hairy guy, who'd been sitting with the old man, was now standing next to her, kind of leaning and hovering over the old man.

A huge round object hung from a long cable under the helicopter. All of a sudden the big sphere opened, and hundreds of small round things fell from it. The wash from the helicopter blades sent the objects in all directions. An air of excitement and anxiety filled the crowd until the first few reached the ground. They were powder-blue and white soccer-ball-sized beach balls. Someone from Argentina knew how to work this crowd. Hoots and hollers followed as bouncing balls flew overhead in every direction. Hotel guests laughed and cheered as they smacked and punched the balls to and fro.

Samantha caught the look of relief on the old man's face when he glanced up at his friend. She also saw him nod his head in the direction of their chairs, then watched the hairy guy turn and walk in that direction.

The old man moved from the wall and turned to face Samantha. He flinched again as a ball hit his head, then bounced into the water. He picked it up, grinned, and hit it to Samantha. She bopped it back toward him.

As he looked at his gold watch, Samantha noticed a sparkle of sunlight reflecting off its diamond bezel. "Well, it was nice meeting you, Samantha. I have to go. Can I give my grandson your room number so he can call you?"

Samantha smiled. "I'm like never there. Why don't you give me your cell number, and I'll text you. Then you can give him my number."

"Hmm. I'll never understand your generation. Text this, text that. Everything is a text. You need to talk to each other more."

"Texting is the same as talking," she said.

"No, mio caro. There's nothing like face-to-face conversation. Think about our discussion here."

"Well, obviously, texting isn't always as good. But it makes things much easier, sometimes."

"Maybe for you, but I'll never get used to it."

She shrugged.

"Forget it. It was a pleasure to meet you. Addio, Samantha."

"Ooroo, Vitorio," she said with a wave.

His baffled look was priceless.

Samantha giggled. "It means goodbye where I'm from."

"Ah, well then, ooroo to you, too," he said with a laugh as he made his way toward the steps.

Instead of returning to her chair and raising his suspicion, Samantha walked over and sat on the end of Chelsea's lounge chair.

"Who was that old curly?" Chelsea asked.

"Give me a minute," Samantha answered, thumbs dancing rapidly on her phone.

Samantha: *Johnny and Casey, follow him. His name is Vitorio. He's related to Leonardo Sauro.*

Casey: *Wow, great job, Samantha. We're on it.*

Joel: *Keep a safe distance boys. We still don't know anything about him.*

Johnny: *Don't worry Dad. We're good at this.*

Joel: *I know. But be very careful. Remember what he said earlier.*

Johnny: *It's pretty hard to forget when someone talks about killing someone.*

Casey: *We'll be careful.*

Joel: *Just find out what room he's in, then come to our suite. We'll be waiting.*

Casey: *They're getting up. We'll see you all in a little while.*

Chelsea: *Good luck!*

Casey and Johnny waited until the two men were halfway across the pool area before they stood. Casey's mom blew him a kiss. Her face was wrinkled in deep concern. His nod was subtle as he walked by and quietly said, "Don't worry, Mom. We'll be fine."

Chapter 12

THE BOYS WERE slowly winding their way through the maze of sun worshipers. As soon as the men opened the door to the hotel, Casey said, "Okay, they're in. Let's move it."

They stepped up their pace, kicking beach balls out of the way as they hurried toward the entrance. As they arrived at the doors, Chelsea and Samantha almost bumped into them.

"We're coming with you," Samantha said.

"No way, Sam. He knows you," Casey said. "Stay here."

"That's exactly why I should come," Samantha said. " Chelsea and I can ride the elevator with him without making him suspicious. You guys run up the stairs. I'll text you the floor number where he gets off."

Casey thought for a second. "Okay, let's go. We gotta hurry."

They ran toward the lobby and quickly slowed to a walk just before making the turn to the hallway that led to the elevators. The two men were standing about twenty feet away with a small group, waiting for the next elevator. Casey and Johnny stopped and opened the door to the stairs.

Johnny turned to the girls and whispered, "Good luck!"

Samantha and Chelsea continued toward the elevators as the boys began running up the stairs.

Taking the steps two at a time, they quickly reached the fourth landing.

"Stay here," Casey said. "I'll go to the seventh floor. That way one of us will be closer to whichever floor they get off on. You know the drill."

"Yeah, stay far enough away not to cause suspicion."

Chelsea: *Didn't see what button they pushed, but we just passed 5*

Johnny started running up.

Chelsea: *Passed 6*

Both boys were sucking wind as they bounded up the stairs.

Chelsea: *7*

"Okay, they're getting off at seven," Casey said through heavy breaths.

"Thank God!" Johnny answered.

Chelsea: *Oops, I meant passing 7*

"Oh no," Casey griped.

Chelsea: *Passing 8*

"Hurry," Casey said, quickening his pace.

"I got nuthin' left," Johnny muttered.

"Just push through the pain."

"This sucks," Johnny said, summoning his last drop of internal fuel. "Okay, move over, slowpoke," he said as he passed Casey.

Chelsea: *They got off on 9*

With no time to catch his breath and a little off-balance from his sapped energy, Casey shoved the push bar on the metal door, expecting some resistance. The door swung away hard and fast, and with Johnny pushing from behind, both boys tumbled through, landing on the carpeted hallway.

"Who do we have here?" exclaimed the balding old man from the pool as they fell at his feet.

"Sorry, sir," Casey said awkwardly, between gasps.

"Let me guess. You raced up the steps?"

"Yes, sir," Johnny said as he stood.

"And?"

"And what, sir?" Johnny wheezed sheepishly.

"Who won?"

"Oh," Johnny said.

"You did, sir!" Casey said, grinning.

The old man smiled and pointed at Casey. "Very good, son. I like to win." He turned to the big hairy guy. "Smart kid, huh, Angelo?"

"Yeah, boss. Very smart," the man grumbled.

"How about you boys race me?"

"Huh?" Johnny said.

"You're kidding, right, sir?" Casey asked.

"I never kid about competition. But," he held up his index finger, "I don't mean a running race. We'll race in the pool."

"In the pool?" Johnny questioned.

"Yes. A swimming race. If I win, you buy me an ice cream sundae. If either of you beat me, I give you each 100 bucks!"

Johnny's eyes lit up. "You're on!"

Casey nudged Johnny.

"I mean, you're on, sir!"

"Not what I meant," Casey said, slightly shaking his head.

The old man laughed and looked at Casey. "How about you? Are you in, or not?" He pulled a wad of cash from his pocket. "Let's see," he said, peeling back bills. "Pesos, lira, ah, here we go." He removed two 100-dollar bills, held them up so both boys could see Benjamin Franklin's picture, then handed them to Angelo. "Hold these for the boys, Angelo."

"Sure, boss." Angelo's eyes rolled.

"Well?" the balding man said, still eyeing Casey.

"Maybe," Casey said.

"Ah, you want to see me swim before you decide. Smart boy. And you," he said, looking at Johnny. "Nuts!"

"What?" Johnny's face twisted in confusion.

"Hot fudge and nuts. That's what I like on my ice cream sundae! Don't forget," he added, waving his finger close to Johnny's face.

Johnny reached for the old man's finger, but the man snapped it away quickly.

"You better be faster than that in the pool!" He looked at his watch and turned to Angelo. "We gotta go. I need to make that call. Addio, boys."

"Bye," Casey said.

"Follow me," Casey whispered to Johnny. They walked slowly in the opposite direction of the men. Casey raised his phone high in front of them as they walked.

"You're taking a selfie, now?"

"Be quiet," he said, adjusting the focus. "Move close to me."

"No, I don't want to be in a selfie. I'm all sweaty."

"Get over here, now." Casey's stern tone got Johnny's attention.

Johnny stepped closer, and Casey adjusted the angle of the phone.

"Dude, you're not even aiming it at us. It's over our…oh. Nice!"

Hearing the door close, Casey turned to confirm the men were gone. He looked at the video with Johnny.

"Last door on the left," Johnny said. "Should we go confirm the room number?"

"Unh-uh. Let's go."

They hustled back to the stairs and started up the last flight.

"So you're really going to race him?" Casey asked.

"Sure. I'd do almost anything for 100 bucks."

"You weren't watching him swim earlier, were you?"

"No, I was busy."

Casey smiled. "Yeah, well, Minecraft is going to cost you an ice cream sundae this time. That guy can swim."

"He's fast?"
Casey nodded and laughed.
"Ah, nuts!" Johnny said.
Casey laughed, "Very good!"
Johnny smiled proudly.

Chapter 13

THE ROAR OF laughter Casey and Johnny heard as they entered the vestibule of their parent's suite was odd. Two distinct voices cut through all the others.

"Must be Jay's guys," Casey said to Johnny. "Sounds like one smokes a lot. And the other one is so loud."

Johnny gave a nod as they reached the end of the entrance hallway and turned the corner into the big living room.

"You must be Casey and Johnny," one of the men said flamboyantly. His short-sleeved, button-down, pink shirt clashed horribly with his purple shorts, bright yellow boat shoes, and powder-blue framed eyeglasses. "I'm Carlo. It's so nice to meet you both. Samantha has had us all in stitches with her story about her new friend, Mr. Bald, old-fart, Sabatini. Did he entertain you fellas, too?"

Johnny glanced at Casey. "Actually, he did," Casey admitted.

"Excuse me?" Shane said. "What happened to keeping your distance? He wasn't even supposed to know you were there."

"Things didn't go quite as planned. It's a long story, but everything is fine. He doesn't suspect anything."

"Yeah, and I'm going race him in the pool for 100 bucks," Johnny said.

"You're what?" Joel said sharply.

"He challenged us to a race. If we win, we get a hundred each. If he wins, we buy him an ice cream sundae."

"He probably meant 100 pesos," Joel said.

"Nope," Johnny emphasized. "He peeled off two crisp American 100 dollar bills from a wad he had in his pocket and handed them to Angelo."

"It won't matter anyway," Samantha said. "He may be old, but he swims like a fish!"

"Yeah, that's what I said," Casey agreed.

"Who is Angelo?" Reid asked.

"The big hairy guy," Johnny said. "You know, the one from the pool. Oh, wait, you weren't out there."

"I think he's Sabatini's bodyguard," Samantha said. "When the beach-balls were released from the helicopter, he ran over to us and leaned over the pool, towering over Vitorio."

Carlo laughed loudly. "Protecting him from beach balls? Now that's some bodyguard!"

Samantha sighed. "No. At first, when they were dropped, nobody knew what they were. It was scary for a moment. Vitorio moved close to the edge of the pool, and practically hugged the wall to get out of the way."

"Did the bodyguard do anything to protect you?" Johnny asked.

Samantha shook her head.

"No?" Carlo exclaimed, throwing both hands in the air. "What nerve! I may have to teach him a lesson!"

The kids laughed. Even the adults were having difficulty refraining. Carlo's extravagance was entertaining.

"Folks," Rodrigo said in his raspy voice. "While Carlo's mannerisms and choice of clothing may be somewhat amusing, he is all business when it comes to security. We trained and served together as Lanceros, Colombia's special forces. The equivalent of the Delta Force in the U.S."

Carlo shrugged and nodded. "Rodrigo and I are an excellent team whether the task at hand is investigation, security, or clandestine operations. I know my actions make some people laugh. I have learned to live with that. So, I won't get offended if you laugh. In fact, I'll probably join you. They say laughter is good for the soul, right?"

After a moment he broke the uncomfortable silence in the room, saying, "Okay, why don't we get down to business!"

"Can we eat while we talk?" Johnny asked. "I'm starving."

"Now there's a surprise!" Casey said, walking to the buffet table.

They all sat and planned the next day's search.

"So, we'll need to split up," Joel said. "Marianna, Juan, and Antonio know the properties best, so they will each lead a group. We need to search both plantation houses and barns, as well as the houses in town, and the island house. We'll need to find out from Luna where she and Jose will be tomorrow."

As Joel spoke, Casey texted Marianna.

Reading her returned text, Casey said, "Luna and Jose are taking Diego to look at a special school tomorrow. They should be gone all day. Marianna, Juan, Antonio, and Luna's assistant, Carita, will come here as soon as Luna and Jose leave the house. They're bringing Antonio's pickup truck, Carita's Hummer, and their Jeeps. Carita is also trying to get us a boat in order to go to Jose's island."

Joel thought a moment.

"I already broke us up into groups, Uncle Joel," Casey said.

"Okay, let's hear them."

"Me, Marianna, and Rodrigo will go in one of the Jeeps. Chelsea, Juan, and Carlo can use the other Jeep. Johnny and Samantha can ride with Antonio in his truck. And you, Aunt Cindy, Mom, and Dad can take the Hummer with Carita."

"Hmm. Jay will probably want to make some changes."

"Why?"

"He typically doesn't want couples working together."

"Couples?"

"Me and Cindy. Your mom and dad. You and Marianna."

"Oh," Casey said. "Wait. We're not really a couple."

Joel smiled. "Let's just see how Jay wants to group us."

Casey shrugged.

"Do Marianna and Juan have licenses?" Joel asked.

"Uh, I don't think so. But they said it doesn't matter. They never get stopped."

"That's probably because their uncle owns," Joel made air quotes with his fingers, "the police force."

"Yeah, I guess. I didn't really think about it."

"That's so cool," Johnny said with brownie crumbs spilling from his mouth. "Hey Dad, why don't you buy," Johnny raised his arms, making big, exaggerated air quotes, "some cops near AllSport, so Casey and I can drive at home?"

"Fat chance," Joel said.

"Don't talk while you're eating, Johnny," his mother admonished.

"Sorry," he garbled, his mouth still full.

"That's gross!" Casey said.

Johnny gave Casey a big chocolate-smeared, toothy smile.

Casey closed his eyes. "Yuck!"

"That's enough, Johnny!" Cindy's tone was serious.

Johnny's mouth snapped shut so fast it made Samantha and Chelsea giggle.

"We should prioritize the order of our search now," Reid said. "So we're ready for them as soon as they get here in the morning."

"It'll be better letting Luna and the others help with that," Joel said. "Their knowledge of the locations and Jose's mindset will help."

"I'll tell Marianna they should start working on it," Casey said as he began typing.

"Good," Joel said.

"I hope we find them early tomorrow," Johnny said. "I really want to go watch the teams practice."

"Yeah, me too," Samantha said. "I almost forgot why we're here."

"This has all been so distracting," Shane agreed. "If we haven't found them by tomorrow afternoon, I think the four of you should take a break and go watch practice anyway."

"No way, Mom. Saving lives is way more important than watching soccer practice."

"Of course it is. I just thought, maybe…" Shane paused, "Never mind."

"They're growing up fast, honey," Reid said.

"Maybe a little too fast," Shane agreed.

Casey looked at his phone and said, "Marianna says they'll list each location by priority and let us know in the morning."

"Okay, why don't we all turn in and get an early start tomorrow," Reid said. "I don't know about any of you, but I didn't sleep much last night. I'm bushed."

"No way," Casey said, looking at his phone. "It's only 8:30." He looked at Johnny and the girls. "You guys want to go down to the pool?"

"Is it open?" Chelsea asked.

"Let's go find out," Johnny said, getting up. "If it's not, we'll go get ice cream."

"What time and where should we meet in the morning?" Carlo asked.

"Did you two get rooms here?" Reid asked.

"Are you kidding?" Rodrigo said. "I don't think there's a vacant room in all of Colombia. We're going to crash at our friend Pablo's house."

"Why don't you just stay here tonight," Reid said. "Both of these couches pull out into beds."

"Nah, we couldn't do that," Carlo said. "We wouldn't dare impose."

"Impose?" Cindy said. "Don't be ridiculous. Our rooms are big, and we each have our own bathroom. We won't even know you're here."

"Ha!" Carlo blurted out. "That's where you're wrong." He pointed at Rodrigo. "This guy snores like a jackhammer."

Rodrigo shrugged and nodded with a grin.

After her quick laugh, Shane said, "I'm used to snoring."

"Oh really," Reid retaliated. "And you think you sleep silently?"

"Well, you ain't heard nothing till you've heard him," Carlo said, waving his finger toward Rodrigo. "I'm serious. He'll make the walls vibrate. We've received complaints in hotels that he kept neighboring guests up all night."

Rodrigo shrugged again.

"I have a solution," Joel offered. "I reserved three rooms for Jay, Stu, and the Israeli couple. I didn't offer it earlier, because I have no idea when they'll arrive. I figured it might be the middle of the night. But it doesn't matter. Jay and Stu can share a room. So you guys can use one of the others tonight?"

"It's still an imposition," Rodrigo said. "I think we'll just head out to Pablo's house."

"Actually," Joel said. "I'd like you to stay. I'm going to visit Mr. Sabatini in a little while, and I wouldn't mind some back-up."

"I'm guessing you've already done some research on him?" Rodrigo asked.

"Just a little. He's connected, kind of indirectly, but connected is connected."

"Well then, that changes everything. We're at your service, sir," Carlo said.

"What's the plan?" Rodrigo asked.

"Don't have one," Joel said. "Just going to knock on the door and wing it."

"Sounds like a plan to me," Carlo said with a laugh.

"Maybe it would help if I went with you," Samantha said. "He already knows me."

"Thanks, Samantha, but no," Joel said. "Besides the fact that it might be dangerous, I think we should keep your new relationship with the guy on the back burner. If our visit tonight doesn't go well, we may need you to get information from him later. It will be better if he doesn't know that you're with us.."

"Yeah, you guys go have some fun," Shane said to the kids.

"Just remember, this is our case!" Johnny said.

"Nobody's forgetting that, Johnny," Reid said.

"If we save them," Joel said. "The press will be all yours."

"If?" Casey said.

"Excuse me, I meant when!" Joel said. "Now get out of here."

"Yeah, mates," Samantha said. "Let's go put our togs on."

"Togs?" Johnny asked.

"Sorry, swimsuits."

"Togs, I like that one," Casey said. "Aussie slang is pretty cool."

Chapter 14

Elsewhere in Colombia

VALENTINA SAURO HAD been pacing with her little boy, Dominic, draped over her shoulder for thirty-five minutes, trying to put him to sleep. Just as his eyelids finally lost their battle and slowly lowered, the roar of engines coming to life woke him into a crying fit.

Sofia, Angelica Marrese's young daughter, also began wailing.

Both mothers were close to tears as well. They had been moved aggressively from two locations already, and had no idea where they were or why they had been abducted. Suddenly, the floor shifted, causing Valentina to lose her balance. Luckily she was close enough to a cushioned white leather armchair to lean and fall into it, in somewhat of a sitting position, without hurting her baby.

Angelica gasped. "Terremoto?" she said, asking if it was an earthquake.

"Si, deve essere," Valentina said, nodding and holding her son tightly.

Chapter 15

JOEL GLANCED AT his watch before giving the door three quick knuckle raps.

When no one answered, Carlo said, "Maybe they're out, or asleep."

Joel put his ear to the door. "No, I hear the TV and some talking." He knocked again. This time the door opened just enough for Angelo, Sabatini's bodyguard, to peer out. Rodrigo and Carlo remained off to the side, out of sight.

"Tu chi sei?" the big man asked.

"My name is Joel Rebah. I believe we have a similar desire that we should discuss." Joel understood a little Italian, but certainly not enough for this conversation. "Can we speak in English?"

"Si. What is this desire you speak of?"

"Rescuing Valentina, Angelica, and their children."

"Give me a second." The man shut the door.

A minute later, Rodrigo said, "He's not coming back. Let me try." The door opened just as he brought his raised fist toward it.

"Who are *you*?" the big man asked. "Where's the other guy?"

Joel stepped into view from the side of the doorframe. "I'm a private investigator from the States, and they," he gestured towards Carlo and Rodrigo, "are local investigators."

The big man's face remained stern as he looked slowly from Joel to Rodrigo, then Carlo. His menacing eyes locked on each for a moment. After his silent analysis, he beckoned them to follow.

Angelo stepped aside and assumed his position by the wall near the door. Three men sat in large upholstered chairs in the suite's living room. Sabatini's chianti-colored, silk pajamas fit him almost too perfectly. *Custom made?* Joel wondered incredulously. Sabatini's bare feet were crossed and perched on a footrest. With his arms folded against his chest, his head slightly tilted, and one foot tapping against the other, he watched as the trio approached.

The other two men, sitting near Sabatini, wore green and red warm-up suits with the Italian team's emblem embroidered on the chest. The room was way too warm for such outfits.

Joel caught Carlo's and Rodrigo's eyes as he subtly patted his leg near his hip. They both acknowledged.

"Yes, gentlemen," Sabatini said. "I'm sure you are not surprised that my boys are packing."

"Not at all, Mr. Sabatini," Joel said.

"Quite frankly, the only reason you're standing in front of me without having been searched is because it's difficult to conceal weapons under golf shirts and shorts."

Joel nodded. "Obviously, we are not armed, and we are not here looking for trouble."

"So, tell me, why exactly are you here?"

"Hopefully, to combine our efforts."

"Explain."

"You were overheard today at the pool saying some interesting things. So we did a little research. When we found that you're related to Leonardo Sauro, we figured we should discuss things with you.

Maybe we can help each other find his wife and child before harm comes to them."

With a shrewd look, the older man said, "So the young girl belongs to you?"

"What girl?" Joel asked.

The old man squinted and thought before speaking. "Tell me who heard me and what I said."

"One of my guys heard you say something about killing him yourself."

"Hmm. I guess I let my guard down for a moment. You never know who's listening. I need to watch what I say in public."

"The only reason we checked you out is that we're already working on finding the women and kids. We have some good leads, and we figured you might be interested in helping."

"Are you working with the police?"

"No. We were warned not to."

"Warned? By who?"

"I'll be happy to tell you everything we know, but first, as I'm sure you can understand, I need to know that we can work together on this."

"If you have information that can help find Valentina and the baby, then yes, I will work with you."

"Very good. But before I tell you what we know, I need to be comfortable that we can trust each other," Joel said.

"The feeling is mutual. As for me, I'm sure your research revealed that I'm not a very dangerous man. I'm a businessman. I don't look for trouble. In fact, I avoid it in every way possible."

Joel nodded. "We did see that. But we also saw that there have been some powerful people that have gotten hurt by you."

"Only when they left me no choice," Sabatini said defensively. "Look, it's pretty obvious that since you have the resources and connections to check me out, you probably don't need my help with your search. So, my guess is that you'd prefer to work together to avoid having us both botch the rescue by working similar angles or searching the same premises simultaneously. Am I right?"

"Somewhat." Joel nodded.

"Nothing is as sacred to me as family. I will do anything to get Valentina and the baby back safely. While I don't typically work with people I don't know, time is of the essence here. Once I verify that you are not working with the police, I will share my resources with you."

"Again, how do I know I can trust you?"

"Let's not waste time on this point. The fact that you're still standing here means that you already feel that you can trust me. I have nothing to gain by crossing you. Your goal is my goal. On top of all that is my word, and frankly, my word is everything to me. In my circles, people know that when I make a promise, I keep it."

"Okay, so let's say I buy all that. Our mutual goal of saving the women and children is the same. But you also have another goal here. Whoever took them obviously did it to accomplish something else. I'd like to know what that is."

"We don't need to discuss that."

"If you want to combine our efforts, we do."

"I don't need your help."

"If you want to find them before any harm comes their way, you do," Joel said.

"You know what, you're starting to annoy me. You come here with all your research done on me. Now you're telling me how much I need you. Give me a reason why."

"We believe we've narrowed the possibilities to only a few locations."

"Who is we?"

"My team," Joel said.

"How about names, anyone I know?"

"Jay Scott. Reid Clark."

"Jay Scott? You work for him?"

Joel nodded.

"He doesn't know you 're talking to me, does he?"

"Why?"

"Let's just say he's not exactly a fan of mine."

"No? Why not?"

"He was working a similar case in Italy, and he thought I was involved."

"Similar? How?"

"A kidnapping."

"Were you involved?"

"Not really."

"Don't play games with me."

"It was ordered by my cousin. I was against it, but an order from a captain is an order that must be followed."

"Did you do the actual job yourself?"

"No. I don't get my hands dirty anymore."

"Anymore?"

"Let it go, please? It's history, and I prefer it remains as such. I wasn't involved, but your boss never accepted it that way."

"So maybe this is all a moot issue," Joel said. "I'll see how he feels when he arrives. If he's okay with it, I'll let you know." Joel turned and motioned to Carlo and Rodrigo to follow him out.

"Hold on a second," Sabatini said. "We're talking about my family. If you know where they are, I want to know."

"We'll see," Joel said, reaching for the door handle.

"Yeah. Well, you tell your boss that regardless of his thoughts about me, I will be searching for Valentina, too. Better that we pool our resources than work separately. We don't want to get in each other's way."

"As I said, we'll see." Joel followed Carlo and Rodrigo out and closed the door.

Chapter 16

WITH ONE SIDE of his head deep in his soft pillow, Casey peered through a barely opened eye at his buzzing phone on the bedside table. Sleep weary, he reached for it. The phone slipped through his tired fingers twice before he slid it to the edge of the table and got a firmer grip. He knew he should have gone to sleep earlier last night. Why did he always let Johnny convince him that staying up late was what vacations were all about? Billiards and darts were fun, but playing till 1 a.m. was just dumb when they had to get up early.

A loud snort from Johnny annoyed Casey as he rubbed the sleep from his eyes and looked at his phone.

Marianna to Casey: *Good morning sleepyhead. Time to wake up and get this party started.*

Some party, he thought. *And how does she know I was sleeping.* He checked the time. 6:42 *Yup, most kids would still be asleep.*

Marianna's text continued: *Mom, Diego, and Uncle J are leaving around 8:30. They have a 2.5 hr ride each way & a 2 hr interview & tour at the school. That gives us 7 hrs. They'll probably stop to eat on the way back. That should add another 2ish hrs*

Casey: *Unless they stop at McDs or someplace fast, like that.*

Marianna: *No way. Uncle J would never touch fast food. He likes long lunches, then usually a cigar and siesta after. Doesn't matter right now. Mom will text us if they stop.*

Casey: *OK. Hey, when this is all over, will you take me for a ride in your Jeep? It's so cool.*

Marianna: *Tee hee. I'll take you four-wheeling on the beach.*

Casey: 👍

Marianna: *See you soon.*

Casey: *What time?*

Marianna: *We'll leave a little after they do. Don't want to leave too quickly in case they forget something and come back. I'll text you when we leave.*

Casey: *Ok. See you later.*

Marianna: 👍

Casey dropped the phone on the bed and sat up.

"Talking to your girlfriend?" Johnny asked.

"I thought you were asleep," Casey said.

"You woke me."

"What? I haven't made a sound," Casey argued.

"Well, something woke me."

"Probably your own snoring."

Johnny laughed. "Maybe it was. I love it when that happens. It makes me laugh."

"You're nuts!"

"Yeah, a little!" Johnny said with another chuckle. "So, what did your girlfriend say?"

"She's not my girlfriend!"

"You like her, right?"

"Yeah."

"And she obviously likes you."

"You think so?"

"Oh, come on, Dude. It's like so obvious. There are the texts." Johnny raised his index finger. "There's the two of you searching together." He raised his middle finger. "There's the constant little smiles." His ring finger went up. "And most of all, there's the flirting." He raised his pinky and smiled.

"She is pretty, isn't she?"

"She's beautiful."

"But she lives down here and…"

"Don't complain. It's a lot closer than Australia."

"You got me there."

"Long-distance love is so difficult." Johnny raised the back of his hand to his forehead.

"Oh, shut up." Casey laughed and threw a pillow at him. "Hey, I have to send a group text about this morning's timing. Want to go down to the gym after that? We have some time to kill." He began typing.

"The gym? Really? No thanks. I'm going back to sleep."

"Oh, don't be so lazy. Come with me. I always work out much harder when you're with me, and I need to burn off that ice cream you made me eat."

"Yeah, like I forced you to eat that huge sundae," Johnny said on his way to the bathroom.

Casey was still typing when Johnny came out of the bathroom. "Are you writing a book? Hurry up, let's go." He picked his shorts up off the floor and pulled them on.

Casey overemphasized the last peck of his finger on his phone's keyboard and stood. "I'll be ready in a second."

Chapter 17

SIMILAR TO MOST hotel gyms near a world championship sporting event, the exercise room was jam-packed at daybreak. Of course, not every soccer fan is an exercise junkie, but many are.

Eyeing the lines of people waiting for the treadmills, ellipticals, and just about every other machine, Johnny said, "This is ridiculous. Let's go for a run instead."

"Okay, but wait a minute," Casey said lifting his phone to take a picture. "This is worth posting on AllSport's Instagram and Facebook pages. He snapped a few shots of Reid, Shane, Joel, and Cindy all next to each other on treadmills. After glancing at his pictures, he tapped on one and uploaded it to both sites. "They're going to be so mad!"

Johnny slid his finger across his screen and tapped. "Oh, yeah, that's going to piss 'em off." The picture showed all four parents in various awkward, sweaty phases of running. Three had wireless earbuds dangling. Joel's headphones were perched over his sweat-soaked headband. Cindy had a steely-eyed look of determination. Reid's eyes were completely closed, either caught by the camera mid-blink, or lost in deep meditation. Joel's and Shane's faces were awkwardly scrunched, revealing their pain. It was not a flattering shot.

"Let's tell them we're going for a run," Casey said.

Johnny followed him and tapped on his dad's shoulder. Startled, Joel managed to keep his pace as he turned his head. "What?" he said way too loudly.

Johnny raised a finger to his lips and another to his dad's ears.

Joel slid his headphones down to his neck. "Good morning."

"We're going for a run instead of waiting in these lines."

"Smart." Joel turned toward Casey. "Good job with the texts." He looked at the clock on his treadmill's digital display. "Come to our room around 8:30. Jay should be ready by then. We'll have a quick meeting before Marianna and the others get here."

"K, bye! And by the way, you better not look at Facebook." The boys hustled away, laughing.

"Samantha just texted me," Johnny said. "They're asking where we are."

"Tell them to meet us outside the lobby for a run."

Staring at his screen, and texting as they walked, Johnny bumped into Casey.

"That's why texting is illegal while driving," Casey said.

"Huh?"

"Forget it. What did they say?"

"They're coming."

"Good."

"You're just happy that they'll keep us at a slower pace than I usually do," Johnny said.

"Did I ever tell you how smart you are?"

Johnny frowned. "Now that I think about it, no!"

"Well, you're very perceptive."

"Thanks." Johnny scrunched his face in doubt. "I think."

Casey chuckled as he pushed open the lobby door.

Chapter 18

On a yacht in a small port near Cartagena

"I WISH YOU had thought more about all this before you had them taken. It's screwing up the betting numbers on the game."

"At the moment I couldn't care less about the gambling nonsense. We have only one business that really matters."

"Yes, but jeopardizing the gambling operation is foolish. It has been growing nicely."

"Don't you dare tell me my actions are foolish. Our business provides a very nice life for you and your family, no?"

"Of course, but—"

"You expect me to just accept it when our business is threatened. They're basically stealing our money. You may be okay with it, but I'm not."

"Of course, I'm not. I just don't like—"

"Enough already, Rafi!," he yelled. "Gambling revenues are a drop in the bucket compared to our real business. I don't want to hear any more about it."

"Fine, I'll stop. But please, tell me you don't intend to kill them."

"We'll see. If they agree to stop buying everything from our competitors and bring some of their business back to us, no one else has to die."

Rafael looked down and shook his head.

"What?"

"Put yourself in their shoes, Pedro. What would you do if they threatened you?"

Pedro's head slowly shook from side to side, and his eyes narrowed as he growled, "Nobody threatens me!"

"That's exactly my point. Your threat isn't going to get the lost business back, it's just going to make them mad."

"No. I've got them where it hurts this time. Not only did we take family members, but this time it's also going to affect the outcome of the Championship. Sauro's and Marrese's minds will be on their wives and kids instead of the game. Without them playing at 100 percent, Italy can't win. Just as we would, our Italian friends will do whatever it takes to win this game. Just watch, we will get confirmation by the end of today or tomorrow. I know we will. It's an easy decision for them. If they choose to do business with us, the women and kids live, and the game will be played fairly. But, if they continue to buy from our competition—well, the results will be less favorable for them, and all of Italy."

"Maybe you're right."

Chapter 19

BOLD STREAKS OF sunlight pierced through the thick Colombian foliage as the sun inched higher in the morning sky. The beams of light cut crisp paths through the heavy, mist-laden air. Kissed by the sun's rays, dew-covered leaves glistened and released an occasional droplet.

When Marianna, Juan, Carita, and Antonio arrived, they joined the others on the hotel bar's secluded flagstone patio. Neither hotel staff nor guests would bother them there this early in the morning.

As expected, the group's headcount had increased by four overnight, and, as Casey and Johnny had anticipated, Jay Scott immediately assumed leadership of the rescue mission. As the owner of the security business that protected Reid Clark, the AllSport Campus, and other high-end clients, he had quite a bit of experience with kidnappings. Joel's colleague and friend, Stu Mann, sat to Jay's left. Joel and Stu had worked with Jay Scott since the inception of his security business. They were his most trusted team and helped him run the business. The Israeli couple, Sun and Tzlil, were seated to Jay's right.

As they were all introduced, Johnny said, "Sun, that's a cool name."

"It was my grandfather's nickname." Sun's Israeli accented English was excellent. "His name was Shimon, but his friends called him Sun. My parents named me in his honor."

"That's nice," Cindy said.

"Okay, everyone," Jay said abruptly. "I have a few things to discuss with you, and then I want to get the show on the road quickly."

Everyone quieted down except Johnny, who was showing Samantha something on his phone.

"Johnny, please turn it off," Jay requested.

"Huh?" Johnny looked up at Jay.

Jay raised his cell phone with one hand and moved his other hand across the front of his neck while mouthing "Off."

Johnny and Jay knew each other extremely well from AllSport. Jay knew that Johnny meant no disrespect, and Johnny knew to take Jay very seriously. He immediately shut his phone off and stuffed it in his pocket.

Jay handed a small pile of paper to Casey. "Please pass these to everyone."

As the pages were dispersed, Jay continued, "Okay, first I want to assign teams and vehicles. As I call out your names, you'll notice a few things; One, all couples, including the newly budding relationship I was informed about, have been split up."

Casey glanced at Joel, who acknowledged with a shrug. The other kids chuckled.

Jay cleared his throat, effectively stopping them. "Sometimes love can get in the way of making the correct decision quickly. I don't want emotions clouding your judgment on this mission."

The word mission widened some eyes.

"Each group will have one local person, who knows the area, as a driver. Drivers, you need to concentrate and be aware of your surroundings. If there's trouble, all passengers must remain calm. Driving while others in the car are excited and noisy is very distracting."

Jay's eyes scanned the group.

"There will also be one of my people leading each group. They have the final say in all decisions. No exceptions!" Again, he scanned his audience. "Am I clear?"

He locked eyes with each person until they nodded or said, "Yes."

"You'll notice the list shows team members, vehicles, and search locations. When I'm done reading it to you, I'd like you to go sit with your group and get to know each other. I'll stop by each table to discuss your search locations individually." He looked at the page and began, "Juan, you're driving with Samantha and Tzlil in the van I rented. Carlo, you're driving the camo Jeep with Chelsea and Reid. Antonio, you're driving your pickup with Casey and Joel. Rodrigo, you're driving your Land Cruiser with Sun and Cindy. Stu, you're driving the blue Jeep with Marianna and Shane. And Carita, you're driving your Hummer with Johnny and me."

Everyone stood, and after a few moments, each team of three was sitting at a separate table, chatting.

Jay visited each group to discuss their search location and introduce himself to those he hadn't met yet.

Shortly after Jay finished, Stu stood and introduced himself to those he didn't know. Sun and Tzlil also visited each table, finishing with Casey and Carita.

As Sun shook Casey's hand, Casey said, "I've been looking forward to meeting you both. It must be so cool to be Mossad agents. And you're in the Kidon. That's so dope!"

"You're not even supposed to know that," Sun said quietly, rubbing his bloodshot eyes. "And, it's not always so cool."

"Sorry, I guess I used the wrong word."

"Don't be sorry. I'm just tired. Long flight and very little sleep."

"Maybe after we're done, and you've had some rest, you'll tell me about some of your missions."

"We're not allowed to discuss them," Tzlil said. "And, as far as the Kidon are concerned, that would be him." She pointed at Sun. "Not me."

Casey nodded. "So there's nothing you can tell me at all?" Casey pressed.

"We'll see," Sun said. "Why are you so interested, anyway?"

"Well, partially because I've heard the Mossad does some really sick stuff, but also because Johnny and I have been working on a book. Ever since we saved that gymnast in Australia, we've had tons of requests from kids on social media to describe cases we've worked. We started putting together an outline, and I'd love to add some of your stuff if that's okay."

Sun's chuckle extinguished Casey's excited look of hope and replaced it with one of embarrassment.

"Casey," Tzlil said. "Sun isn't laughing at your idea. He's amused because we're doing the same thing. The truth is, I don't know of many retired agents who haven't at least thought about it."

Jay had walked over and stood behind Sun as Tzlil finished her statement. "Thought about what?"

"Casey was just telling us about the book he and Johnny are writing."

Casey cringed.

"What's the matter?" Tzlil asked.

"Johnny and I agreed not to tell anyone about it. I only told you guys because I wanted to hear about some of your Mossad missions."

Another chortle slipped from Sun, eliciting frowns from Casey and Tzlil.

"What? Come on, I've never heard a kid talk about Mossad missions. Well, maybe a few Israeli kids, but they're different. They see things most other kids don't. It just struck me as funny. I'm very impressed, though."

"So, you guys are writing a book?" Jay asked, looking at Casey.

"Please don't tell anyone. We want to keep it a secret for now."

"Not a word, I promise. But we'll probably need to compare notes. It wouldn't be good if the cases in your book are the same as the ones I'm writing about."

"Wow, you too?" Casey said.

Jay nodded. "Tzlil is right. It's a pretty common retirement pastime for many in our line of work."

"Well, at least our audiences will be different," Casey said. "Our book is for kids."

"Do you think kids will be interested in reading about murder cases and rescue missions?" Sun asked.

"Definitely. You should see all the comments we get on social media. Kids love this stuff. It's totally cool."

"Wow," Tzlil said. "You guys are brilliant. You're building a fan base to buy your book before it's even finished."

"We are?" Casey coughed. "I mean, of course, we are."

Everyone chuckled as Tzlil typed on her phone. "Maybe we'll trade," she said to Casey.

"Trade what?"

"A few Mossad stories for a crash course in social media marketing."

"You got a deal." Casey stuck his fist out, and Tzlil tapped it with hers.

"I guess I could use some social media marketing help, too," Jay said, looking at Casey.

"What's your offer? I know all your war stories."

"Really? My offer?" Jay sneered. "How about I let you live to publish your book, you little punk."

"Oh yeah, tough guy," Casey said deadpan. "Lay a hand on me, and I'll sic these two on you." He pointed at Sun and Tzlil.

"You forget who they work for, my young friend."

"You forget whose case you're all on right now, my old friend."

Sun and Tzlil laughed as Jay walked around the table and hugged Casey from behind with one arm. "So, you think you know all my war stories, huh? Don't forget, I've been playing this game since long before you were born."

"I know, old man, I know." Casey smiled and patted Jay's arm endearingly.

"Old man? Now, that hurts," Jay said.

"It shouldn't," Casey said. "You're the baddest old man out there!"

Jay snickered and patted Casey's head. Then he said to the group, "Okay, gang, let's get this show on the road. Any questions before we go?"

"Yes," Marianna said, raising her hand high. "I see that all the locations are covered by different groups, except for the Island house. Although it's the toughest to get to, I don't think we should leave it out."

"Good point, Marianna," Jay agreed. "I would have made the Island one of the first locations we searched, but I couldn't get transportation until this afternoon. I have a boat meeting us at noon and a helicopter coming at 12:45. I was told it will take about an hour by boat, right?"

Marianna and Juan nodded.

"Excuse me, Mr. Scott," Carita said quietly. "I have access to a boat too. My friend said it's ready for us whenever we need it."

"I'm sure the one I have arranged for is fine, but I'm curious. Do you know what type of boat it is?"

Carita looked at her phone. "It's a Riverine Barracuda."

"Hooyah," Stu belted out.

"As in high-speed military assault boat?" Jay asked.

Carita nodded. "Do you want to see a picture?"

"Please."

Carita brought her phone to Jay.

A quiet whistle passed Jay's puckered lips. "Who owns this baby?"

"A guy I used to date. He doesn't exactly own it. He's a boat broker. He took possession of it last week and won't deliver it until it's ready."

"And by ready, you mean the buyer wants weapons mounted on board?"

Carita scrunched her face and nodded. "Good guess. Should I tell him not to bring it?"

Jay folded his arms. "No, Carita, it's perfect. Maybe we'll use both boats."

Carita nodded.

"If you'll text me the location where we'll board the Barracuda I'll have the captain of the other boat meet us there."

With another nod, Carita began typing. The clicking of her long, orange, painted nails tapping the screen sounded like Morse code.

Casey looked across two tables at Johnny, smiled, and winked. Grinning from ear to ear, Johnny subtly pumped his fist. This rescue was getting more exciting every minute A helicopter and a military assault boat. Could it get any better?

Jay forwarded the dock location Carita had sent him to his friend, Rich, the captain of the Southern Star, the other boat he'd been talking about. He looked up and said, "Okay, let's roll."

Chapter 20

"WHY CAN'T THEY at least turn on the lights? The darkness is starting to get to me," Valentina whimpered in Italian. Until now she had remained strong, hoping it would keep the children from getting scared. But being held in a pitch-dark room, devoid of windows, was becoming overwhelming. She was exhausted and frightened. The constant drone and vibration of a motor had made sleeping impossible.

Suddenly, the ground shook again, throwing the women and children off their feet.

Angelica Marrese hit the back of her head on a chair as she fell. "Ow," she yelled, raising her hand to the painful spot on her head. It was dry, but a lump was forming quickly.

Both of the children were crying inconsolably now. Valentina groped in the darkness, trying to pick them up. Instead, she tripped over Sofia's legs and landed on Angelica. Angelica grunted and began to cry. Valentina's tears started flowing also. "I'm so sorry." Her words were muddled between sobs. "Are you badly hurt?"

"Yes. I mean, no. I don't know. My head, my arm. Oh, Valentina, this is so horrible."

"I know."

"Just go comfort the kids I will be okay."

Valentina gently climbed off Angelica and crawled toward the crying children. "Sofia, Marco, I'm coming, my darlings."

It took her a moment to untangle the two children, who were clutching each other tightly on the floor. They hugged her fiercely, and amidst their weeping, Marco breathlessly wailed, "Momma?"

"I'm over here, my baby," Angelica whimpered.

Marco pushed away from Valentina, who had no choice but to let him go. He crawled in the darkness, wailing, "Momma? Momma?"

"I'm here, Marco. Come to me."

The volume of Angelica's moan as Marco thrust himself into her arms suddenly increased as the floor lurched yet again.

Chapter 21

JOHNNY: *HEY MARIAN and Jun. You sad Jose has lots of armd gurds. We just reachd th plantatin hous—whoa! its huge. Shuldnt ther b gards her?*

Chelsea: *Excellent typing Johnny! LOL*

Johnny: *Sut up! Wer on bmpty drt rod*

Chelsea: *No you sut up! LOL*

Casey: *LOL*

Samantha: *LOL*

Jay: *Enuf!*

Juan: *Uncle J has 3 full-time guards who are almost always with him. There are a few others occasionally at different locations. He hires more when he's at war.*

Reid: *WAR?*

Marianna: *With other cartels, drug enforcement, or gangs. He hires more guards when he's worried about people coming after him.*

Stu: *But if he's hiding kidnap victims, he'd put guards at that location, right? We're at the plantation barn, and there are no guards outside here either.*

Reid: *None at rental house either*

Chelsea: *None here at apt building*

Cindy: *Wer not at hnting cmp yet—yes wer on bumy rd too*

Joel: *We see guards at the tobacco barn.*

Juan: *They're always there. Besides curing tobacco, they process coca there.*

Joel: *Great! Guess you guys just forgot to mention that earlier?*

Juan: *Sorry*

Marianna: *Me too*

Joel: *It's okay. I just like to be better prepared.*

Marianna: *Don't worry, the guards all know Antonio. It shouldn't be a problem.*

Joel: *Unless they're holding the victims here.*

Marianna: *Yeah, I guess*

Jay: *Joel, feel out the situation with Antonio. If the guards let you in without a problem, the women & kids are probably not there. If the guards give you a hard time, just leave. We don't want word getting back to Jose. We'll form a plan, and all go back together. Try to get a head count of guards if you can.*

Joel: *Copy that!*

Jay: *Everyone else, stay in your vehicles until we hear more from Joel. STAY ALERT!*

Reid: *Casey, please be careful*

Casey: *I will*

Reid: *Why don't you stay in the car*

Casey: *No way!*

Reid: *That's my boy! Always so respectful.*

Shane: *Casey, please.*

Casey: *Mom, Dad! I'm not being disrespectful. I'll be safer with Joel vs being alone in the car.*

Jay: *Everyone else remain in your vehicles—be alert and ready whether you see guards at your location or not!*

***

Joel began lifting the handle on the vehicle's door.

"Detener. Voy primero," Antonio said.

Joel removed his hand and looked at Antonio.

"I think he said he should go first," Casey explained.

"I know. I'm just not sure I agree. If he goes first, it may look suspic..."

Antonio opened his door and was out before Joel finished his statement. He walked with confidence toward the closest guard. Joel watched closely, while removing his gun from his holster. Casey's eyes bulged as the guard gripped the handle of the automatic weapon slung from a strap around his neck and waved the barrel toward the pickup while speaking to Antonio.

Antonio answered without skipping a step.

As the muzzle of the guard's weapon swept toward the windshield, Casey gasped, and dove under the dashboard. Gun now in hand, Joel pushed his door open and quickly slid from his seat to the ground, keeping most of his torso behind the open door.

A moment later, he said, "Hm. Would you look at that."

"What?" Casey's voice was shaky as he saw Joel peering around the edge of the door.

"Just look. It's okay."

Casey slowly raised his head and peeked through the windshield. Antonio and the guard were disengaging from a hug and patting each other on the shoulder. Antonio turned toward the pickup and waived Joel and Casey over.

"Should we go?" Casey asked nervously.

"Yes, but stay alert." Joel holstered his gun.

"Duh!"

"Be serious, Casey."

"Sorry."

As they slowly walked to Antonio, he introduced them to the guard.

"Miguel, Joel y Casey."

The guard turned toward them. "Antonio tells me that you are good friends with Luna and you want to see how we grow and cure tobacco. Come, I'll show you."

"Gracias, Miguel," Joel said.

As Miguel turned toward the double barn doors, Casey noticed that Joel kept his hand low and close to his gun while his eyes remained fixed on the guard. Casey quickly pulled out his phone, typed as fast as he could, and shoved it back in his pocket.

Casey: *We are getting a tour from one of the guards. Could mean that vics are not here. Or that guard wants to keep an eye on us. Gotta go.*

Shane: *Please be careful.*

As Miguel swung the barn doors open, a multitude of odors infiltrated their nostrils. The faint smell of ammonia and other pungent, slightly sweet off-gases from drying tobacco leaves poured over them from the cavernous room. Row after row of yellow, and brown leaves dangling from long wooden poles formed tunnels that ran the length of the soccer field-sized structure. Racks of wrinkled leaves hung above one another all the way up to the barn's roof.

Several large openings throughout the building provided ventilation. Beige burlap billowed in the warm breeze that flowed through the large wall openings. Heavy, dark-green canvas coverings were propped up at each roof opening.

As they walked the length of the barn, Miguel described leaves in different stages of the drying process.

After removing a leaf from its rack, he rubbed it between his fingers, sniffed it and said, "This is a ligero, it grows at the top of the plant. It contains more oils and is stronger than the lower seco, viso, and volado leaves." He passed the leaf to Casey.

As Casey brought the wilted, brown leaf to his nose, his eyes wandered from Miguel to Joel, and he relaxed a little, thinking, *Joel looks pretty calm and his hand is no longer near his gun.* With a slight grin he thought, *Miguel doesn't seem suspicious at all.*

As they approached the wall at the far end of the building Casey tensed. Armed guards sat at small tables that were adjacent to various doors, including large, double barn doors similar to those they had entered. The guards each looked up from their card games and gave

Antonio a slight nod as he passed. The last guard smiled, stood, and embraced Antonio.

The guard took a quick step back and drew his handgun. Pointing it at Antonio's waist, he flicked the barrel twice and said, "Saca tu arma."

Casey's heart skipped a beat. He glanced at Joel, whose hand was once again down by his gun while his eyes were fixed on the guard.

Antonio raised his hands and said, "Todo bien." He slowly reached behind himself and removed his gun from the waistband of his jeans. He held it up, pinching the end of the grip, letting the gun dangle from his fingers. "Tranquilo, mi amigo."

All were silent as the guard stared at Antonio. Casey held his breath.

"Todos en la familia de Jose llevan una pistola," Antonio said.

Casey understood enough—Jose's family carries guns.

After the longest seven seconds Casey had ever experienced, the guard nodded and lowered his weapon.

Antonio reached back and returned his gun into the waistband of his jeans.

Casey finally exhaled loudly. The guard looked at him and laughed.

Frustrated at his own display of emotions, Casey stared at the guard with as bold a face as he could muster.

The guard grinned, let out another chortle, then turned his attention back to Antonio.

"Continua," he said with a flick of his pistol, indicating that they should move on.

"Gracias," Antonio said.

As they slowly walked by the closed door, Casey noticed movement in the light emanating from the gap between the door and the floor. A shadow moved one way, then the other, then back again. *Women and children, or drug processing?* Casey wondered.

As they walked toward an exit at the rear of the building, Miguel reached into a wooden bin filled with dark, fully aged leaves. He sniffed the brown, paper-thin frond and passed it to Joel, saying, "Bien."

Joel smelled the leaf, nodded, and passed it to Casey.

Casey's face scrunched. He was so repulsed by smoking, that it was difficult for him to bring the leaf to his nose. He despised cigarettes and pipes, and especially hated when his dad lit an occasional cigar. He sniffed. It smelled different than Casey expected. *Not terrible,* he thought. *Not good, but not so bad.*

Joel put his palm out, and Casey returned the leaf. Joel smiled as he folded it and put it in his pocket. "I'm going to try to roll a cigar later and smoke it."

Hearing Joel, Miguel grabbed a few leaves from another wooden crate as they walked out of the building. He handed them to Joel. "You need at least three to roll a decent cigar. It's not so easy. I'll get you a few already rolled sticks before you leave." He laughed, "Funny, I'm giving you leaves before you leave." He laughed again.

Casey laughed politely, thinking, *This guy's humor is as bad as Jose's.*

Miguel continued their tour down a long row of tobacco plants. Casey was losing patience quickly as Miguel droned on and on about the acidity of the earth and how tobacco is less water-intensive than some of the other plants they grow.

Finally, they turned at the end of the row and made their way back to the barn. Miguel stepped inside and then returned a moment later. He handed Joel a few cigars and said, "Adios, gringos."

"Gracias, Miguel. Adios," Joel said.

Once they settled into Antonio's pickup, he started to drive down the dirt road they had arrived on.

As soon as they were out of sight of the barn, Joel said, "Antonio, we should –"

Antonio raised a finger to his lips, cutting Joel off. He soon turned off the dirt road and drove down a narrow path between two rows of tobacco plants. Leaves whipped against the truck's side mirrors. Casey and Joel remained silent as Antonio changed direction twice, driving along row after row. He finally passed the end of a row and continued into the woods that bordered the plantation. He stopped in an area dense with trees and underbrush and cut the engine. After gesturing for them to follow, he exited the truck and began walking rapidly.

As they followed him out the woods, Antonio pointed to the far side of the long field they were approaching. The back of the barn was visible over the rows of tobacco. Casey quickly understood what Antonio was doing. They needed to go back and see if the women and children were in that back room.

"Mira," Antonio said, pointing with two fingers first towards his eyes, then past the fields to their right. "Cana de azucar."

"Ah, sugar cane," Joel said, nodding. "Bueno."

"Y uvas." Antonio pointed in the opposite direction.

"And grapes," Joel translated.

"We're in the middle of all three plantations, aren't we?" Casey asked.

"Exactly," Joel said. "We can approach all three on foot without alerting any guards.

Casey reached for his phone and began to type.

"What are you texting?" Joel asked.

"Just telling everyone, especially my mom, that we're out and safe."

"Good."

"Should I also tell them there's no sign of the women and kids yet?"

"Yeah, go ahead."

Casey typed.

Antonio started walking toward the barn.

"Antonio," Joel said.

Antonio looked back, and Joel pointed at his watch. "We should run, uh, correr."

A smile stretched across Antonio's face. He turned and took off like a jackrabbit, sprinting toward the barn.

"Holy cow," Joel could barely speak as he and Casey did their best to keep up.

"Yeah. Careful what you ask for," Casey gasped. "And I thought Johnny was fast."

Antonio stopped and ducked low into the rows of vegetation before getting too close to the barn. Joel and Casey were gasping for air when they reached him. Antonio smirked without even a heavy breath.

Unable to speak, Casey gave Antonio a thumbs up. Antonio winked.

Waiting for his breathing to return to normal, Casey studied the surrounding area. A bunch of big blue plastic barrels were stacked near two doors. "Chemicals?" he asked Joel.

Joel nodded. "Fifty-gallon drums for drug processing."

"You've seen them before?"

Joel nodded, still breathing heavy.

They all quickly knelt in the dirt as a guard came around the corner of the building. He walked casually along the back wall of the barn holding a cigarette in one hand and an automatic weapon in the other. He flicked the remnants of his lit cigarette into the tall weeds near one of the stacks of barrels, then stopped to light another.

Joel, Casey, and Antonio remained still until the guard turned the corner at the far end of the building.

"He threw his lit cigarette near those barrels," Casey said. "You think they're flammable?"

Joel nodded. "Some of the chemicals used for processing drugs are. If it's acetone or kerosene, yes. Then, it depends on whether the barrels are full or empty. A barrel full of liquid is flammable. A barrel of vapor is explosive."

"Explosive?"

"Chances are it would have blown already."

"So, we should be safe?"

"Interesting choice of words, considering our situation at the moment."

"Yeah, well, I was only talking about the barrels."

Joel nodded as Antonio stood and dashed toward the barn, staying clear of the line of sight of the window. As soon as he reached the building, he pressed his back against the wall and waved for Joel and Casey to follow. It would take some time for the guard to make his way around the entire building. But the question was, how long?

Regardless, they needed to move quickly.

"Go," Joel whispered.

Casey took off with Joel at his heels. Both reached the barn and, just like Antonio, turned and pushed their backs to the wall.

Wasting no time, Antonio crouched low and made his way under the first window opening. Similar to those in the front of the barn, there was no glass in the window frame, just light brown gauzy cloth. The air was hot and still. The fabric hung limp.

Antonio raised from his crouch just enough to peer over the window ledge. After about ten seconds, he ducked down and moved to the far side of the opening. He looked back at Joel and Casey, shook his head, and motioned for them to follow, then he darted toward the next window frame.

Joel inched his way below the opening, peeked through, then continued toward Antonio.

It was Casey's turn. He crept under the window, settled his nerves, then lifted his head to look in. He froze in place and stopped breathing. A guard inside was now standing with his back to the window. The butt of the guard's weapon was inches from the tip of Casey's still sore nose. Casey could clearly see each turn of the coils of twisted rope that spelled Wrangler on the faded leather patch of the guard's blue jeans.

Luckily the sound of a motor inside the room drowned out the snap of the twig Casey had stepped on as he lowered himself and slinked away. His heart was racing as he edged up next to Joel, lightly bumping into him.

Joel turned his head and looked at Casey. Concern immediately engulfed Joel's face. He mouthed, "Are you okay?"

Casey did his best to nod, and a rush of air passed from his lips. He hadn't even realized he was still holding his breath. There was no time to discuss it, and they had to remain silent anyway. Casey closed his eyes and breathed deeply, trying to quell his fear.

Antonio had already looked through the next opening and was gesturing for them to follow him.

Holding another big breath under the next window, Casey snuck a quick look over the ledge. His view brought on a relieving sigh. There were no guards in the room, but to Casey's surprise, three cement mixers were churning round and round. Casey's brain was loaded with all kinds of facts and information, but drug processing wasn't in his wheelhouse. He was baffled, not only by the cement mixers but also by the row of washing machines next to them. They obviously weren't washing clothes.

He turned to ask about the washers and saw that Antonio and Joel were already halfway to the final opening. Running toward them, he thought, *That guard is going to come around the corner soon. We need to hustle.*

By the time Casey had caught up, Antonio had already assessed the last room. As he motioned for Joel and Casey to start running for the truck, they heard a loud raspy cough coming from the corner of the building. Their only possible hiding spot was the pile of barrels about thirty feet away. Casey's heart sank. They were going to get caught.

A loud shout from around the corner of the building snapped their attention back toward it. The barrel of the guard's rifle appeared past the edge of the building, then was quickly pulled back, out of sight. They heard the guard yell, "Que?"

"Correr!" Antonio hissed.

They all ran and dove behind the barrels just as the guard appeared from around the corner. They watched him repeat his earlier routine, but this time he stopped and spoke with the guard through the last window. As the guard passed his lit cigarette to his colleague, Casey whispered, "That guard wears size thirty-two jeans."

"What?" Joel asked.

"When I looked in, right after you guys did, the guard's butt and the stock of his gun were about an inch from my nose. Luckily, he was facing inside the room, and those machines were running, so he didn't see or hear me."

"I'll bet that was scary!" Joel said, craning his neck to look behind Casey.

"What are you doing?" Casey asked.

"Checking to see if you made a mess in your pants." Joel grinned. Casey punched Joel's arm.

As soon as the guard turned the far corner of the building, the threesome bolted to the pickup truck. Antonio chuckled again, watching as Joel and Casey tried to catch their breath. He turned the ignition and began driving toward the sugarcane barn.

Chapter 22

CARITA KNEW EVERY inch of the plantation house. She had worked there as a caretaker, along with her brothers, Alonzo and Santana, long before becoming Luna's assistant. The brothers maintained the exterior of the house and grounds while their cousin, Elena, had taken Carita's place cleaning and managing inside the large farmhouse.

Alonzo parked the tractor he was driving close to his sister's Hummer. He bounded off the machine and greeted Carita with a big hug as she stepped from her vehicle. Santana approached them slowly after he had climbed down a long ladder from the roof. Johnny noticed Santana's eyes moving back and forth between Carita and the Hummer.

Alonzo's and Santana's skin-tight tank tops revealed their massive muscles. Full sleeves of colorful tattoos adorned Santana's arms. The red bandana tied around Alonzo's head was soaked with sweat. His dripping ponytail glistened in the sunlight. As Santana picked up Carita with one arm, Johnny noticed a bulge in the side pocket of his cargo shorts.

While Carita and her brothers spoke, Johnny nonchalantly nudged Jay with his elbow and nodded toward Santana while subtly patting his own pocket. Jay's eyes remained fixed on Alonzo and

Santana as he gave Johnny a slight nod. He smiled as Carita and her brothers approached.

"Jay, Johnny, these are my brothers, Santana and Alonzo. We call him AJ, short for Alonzo Jadiel. As I mentioned earlier, they maintain the house and grounds with my cousin, Elena. At least two of them are here daily, and they all take turns staying overnight. The boys said the only activity during the last few days was a visit from four men in a black Mercedes. They spoke Italian, so neither the boys nor Elena understood much. Santana said the men acted similar to Jose and Pedro, and they all carried concealed guns. He assumed they were mafia." Johnny noticed Santana's hand slide slowly into the pocket containing his gun.

"There was an older guy who acted like the boss. He kept repeating the words donne y bambini, and he got mad when they wouldn't let them enter the house. The old man finally got so mad that instead of returning to the back seat of their car, he sat in the driver's seat and yelled for his men to get in. He drove off with the wheels spinning in the gravel before his men had a chance to shut their doors. Instead of slowing down when one of his men almost fell out of the fishtailing vehicle, the old man hit the gas."

Jay nodded. "So, you're convinced the women and children are not here?"

"Absolutely!," she said, gesturing toward her brothers. "The boys would know it if they were."

"They wouldn't lie to you, would they?"

"What?" she yelled. "How dare you! Their loyalty is to me, not that monster they work for!"

Santana pulled his hand from his pocket. He kept his arm straight by his side with his gun pointed down.

Jay's hands went up, palms forward. "Please don't get mad, Carita. I have to ask these questions. I don't know your brothers, or really even you, for that matter."

"So, you don't trust me either?"

Jay closed his eyes and shook his head, looking frustrated. "That's not what I meant."

"So why did you say it?" she seethed. Her arms were spread wide, questioningly. Her fingers splayed.

Johnny's eyes darted back and forth between Carita and her brother's gun, which was still at Santana's side.

"Come on, Carita," Johnny pleaded. "Jay was just stating an obvious fact. You don't know him any more than he knows you, but we're all here to do the same job. You want to save the women and children as much as we do, right?"

"Of course I do. But I can't work with someone who doesn't trust me."

"Maybe he used the wrong words. But, he never said that he didn't trust you! Come on, give him a break. He can be an idiot, just like the rest of us."

Jay tilted his head in Johnny's direction with his eyes blinking wide.

A snort slipped from Carita, and she covered her mouth trying to stifle her amusement. Johnny's squeamish face and Jay's look of shock won out, and she began to laugh.

Jay's dismay was quickly replaced with a smile, then laughter. Then, Johnny, Alonzo, and Santana caught the bug too. Johnny was relieved when Santana repocketed his weapon.

As the tension dissipated, Jay said, "Carita, I'm sorry. Johnny is right, I can be an idiot." Jay glanced at Johnny, whose smile evaporated into a comical look of concern.

"Leave it to you to diffuse an awkward situation with a little abusive comedy," Jay said.

"I'm sorry," Johnny responded.

"Don't be. It was necessary, and, frankly, it worked rather well."

Johnny smiled and said, "So, should we search the house?"

Jay scanned the eyes of Carita, Santana, then AJ. "No. We're good here. Let's check in with everyone else." He glanced at his watch.

"Then, we'll head to the dock. I want to meet with the captain before everyone boards."

"You're assuming no one has found them yet?" Johnny said.

"If they had, I'm sure they'd have informed us."

"Duh." Johnny smacked his forehead with the heel of his palm.

"Don't be so hard on yourself. If it wasn't for you, we'd probably be staring down the barrel of his gun right now," Jay nodded toward Santana. "Or maybe worse."

"True. Guess I'm good for something."

"Johnny, I can't even imagine what it would have been like to be as intuitive as you and Casey when I was your age. You guys amaze me, and you know I'm not easily impressed."

Johnny smiled. "Thanks, Jay!"

Jay nodded, pulled out his phone, and typed.

Jay: *No women or kids at plantation mansion. Heading to the boat. Team leaders, send status update.*

Carlo: *Townhouses 3 & 4 r clear. No Ws or Ks. C U @ boat.*

Stu: *Plantation barn & stables clear. No Women or Kids, just horses. To the boat we go.*

Sun: *Still on way to hunting camp.*

Tzlil: *2 more floors to search at apartment bldg. will text when done.*

Joel: *Tobacco and sugarcane barns clear. Heading to vineyard.*

***

A couple of minutes after the group texts had stopped, Casey received one more from Marianna with pictures of two beautiful horses.

Marianna: *The pretty blonde one is my horse, Mare (yes like the sculpture you saw) but I call her Belleza—it means beauty.*

Casey: *Nice! What's the other horse's name?*

Marianna: *Tequa—short for tequila. She's Juan's. He named her—dumb, huh?*

Casey: *Nah, it's kinda cool.*

Marianna: *When we're done with all this stuff, you and I will take them for a ride on the beach or in the mountains. Your choice.*

Marianna: *Oh wait, can you ride?*

Casey: *I'm not very good. But yeah, I can ride. And how bout both.*

Marianna: *Both what?*

Casey: *Beach and mountains*

Marianna:

Chapter 23

JOHNNY, JAY, AND Carita were the first to arrive at the marina.

The docks were filled with power boats and sailboats of all sizes.

"Do you know where they're docked?" Jay asked, looking at Carita.

"No, but I can call and ask."

"I got it," Jay said, scrolling through his contact list. He tapped on a number and pressed the speaker button.

"You're here already, Jay?" the captain asked.

"Hi, Rich. We're in the parking lot. How do we find you?"

"We're at the end of pier five. Go to the gate. I'll have Lauren meet you there.

"Thanks."

"Hey, that's some backup boat you've got here. You never cease to amaze me."

"Well, you never know when you may need a little speed."

"Yeah, I guess, and firepower too."

"Oh yeah?" Jay said.

Rich laughed. "Oh yeah. Wait till you see this baby."

"Can't wait," Jay said with a hint of sarcasm.

"If I remember correctly, you said there would be no violence on this little jaunt. The owner of Southern Star won't take kindly to bullet holes or blood on his boat, and, quite frankly, if anything hits the news at all, I'll have hell to pay. He likes to keep a low profile."

"Let's discuss it when I get on board."

"Just be truthful with me, and you know I'm your man."

"I know that, Rich. The truth is, there are two women and two children whose lives are at stake. We are doing whatever we can to save them. And, as long as I'm being completely honest, I haven't had the time to fully prepare, so I'm kind of shooting from the hip on this mission."

"Well, that's the Jay Scott I remember best! Back in the day, we ran most of our missions in that fashion."

"We certainly did."

"See you in a minute. Lauren should be at the gate by now."

"Yeah, she's here."

While Jay was on the phone, Stu, Marianna, Shane, Carlo, Chelsea, and Reid arrived.

Jay: *Do not discuss your searches while walking on the dock. Wait till you're on the boat.*

They all walked through the wrought-iron gate, held open by a tanned, barefoot, twenty-something brunette wearing shorts and a navy blue Southern Star polo shirt. She followed them down the ramp to the dock and said with a big smile, "Hi everyone, I'm Lauren. Please follow me."

"Wait, I know you," Carlo said pointing at her. "You were on that T.V. show, *Below Deck*."

Everyone turned to look.

"I've seen that show," Shane said.

"I love it," Carlo added. "It's one of the best reality shows on T.V."

"That's not saying much," Reid said.

"Oh, come on," Carlo continued. "Housewives, the Kardashians, the Bachelor, and, of course, Drag Race. I love them all."

"There's a reality show about drag racing?" Stu asked.

"It ain't about cars," Carlo emphasized.

"Then, what is…" Stu covered his face with one hand. "Wait. Are you telling me there's really a show about drag queens?"

"I sure am. RuPaul is the best."

The owners and crews of other yachts watched curiously as the team laughed hysterically as they walked by.

"Very nice," Reid said as Lauren stopped at the stairs to the Southern Star.

Magnificent as it was, as they boarded the gorgeous yacht, Johnny couldn't rip his eyes from the boat docked next to it. Its sleek black hull and carbon fiber frame made the Barracuda stealthy and fast on high seas. Johnny's eyes shifted to the bow, taking in the entire boat. On the front deck, sure enough, was the hatch he had read about. His lips curled as he imagined what was underneath.

Johnny reached the top of the rounded, highly polished wood stairway and stepped onto the teak floor of the open-air, covered aft deck.

Captain Rich approached and shook Johnny's hand. "Nice to meet you, Johnny. Jay told me about you and Casey. Couldn't help noticing your eyes glued to the interceptor over there." He nodded towards the Barracuda. "Pretty awesome boat. Watch this. You'll like it."

Then, as if Captain Rich had been reading his mind, Johnny heard him say into his phone. "Captain Enrique, would you please raise the cannon for our guest's viewing pleasure?"

Johnny stared as the forward hatch on the Barracuda's deck slowly opened. The double- hinged cover raised from the center. Once fully opened, a platform began to rise. Large, intertwined, stainless steel, curved pipes anchored to the rising turret were both intimidating and awesome.

Subtle whistles emanated from Jay and Stu.

"Whoa," Reid said.

"Oh my God!" exclaimed Shane. "That gives me the chills, even though I have no idea what it is."

"Sweet!" Johnny exclaimed. "Thanks, Captain. You read my mind. That's the Force 50 anti-pirate, robotic water-cannon, isn't it?

Captain Rich smiled and nodded.

"That's so dope," Johnny continued. "Hey, I know the boat is running twin 600-horse engines, but are they tied to screws or waterjet propulsion?"

Rich laughed. "First of all, call me Rich. Second, I'll introduce you to Enrique and Tito, the captain of that vessel and his brother. I'm sure they can tell you what's under the hood."

"Cool."

"In the meantime, Lauren, why don't you give our guests a tour of the Southern Star. Jay, do you want us to put lunch out while we wait for the rest of your team?"

"Sure, thanks. Nothing elaborate, though. I want to be ready to head out as soon as the next group arrives. The following group will board the Barracuda. And the last group will fly over on the chopper."

"Copy that. Don't worry. You can eat as we cruise."

"Good. Hey, can we talk in private for a minute?"

"Sure, follow me." Rich began walking.

Noticing Johnny following him, Jay turned and said, "Johnny, I just need to speak with Rich for a moment."

"Come on, Jay. You know this is our case? You're here to help us, right?"

Jay returned a skeptical look.

"It's only fair if I'm included in everything. You would expect the same courtesy."

Jay grinned and looked at Rich. "Hard to argue with this guy, especially when he's right." Jay put his arm over Johnny's shoulder as they followed Rich to the helm.

As soon as they stepped into the wheelhouse and closed the door, Jay turned to Rich. "So, here's the deal. I have no idea who we're up against, or how messy this could get. I can't guarantee anything, including no damage to your boat. I don't want you getting fired over this, so if you want to, you can back out now. We can get by with the other boat and the chopper. No hard feelings either way."

The captain looked at Jay for a moment, then said, "Brother, we've been through a lot together, and we've always had each other's backs. I don't know two other guys who can claim that they took a bullet for each other."

Johnny's eyes bulged. "Wait, what?"

Jay looked at Johnny, nodded, and put his finger to his lips.

Captain Rich continued, "Years ago, we made a pact, and I'm not going to break it now. Especially because there are women's and children's lives at stake. I already explained it to my boss, and he agreed. So, let's go do this thing."

Jay stepped forward and put his arms around Rich. Their hug was brief but clearly heartfelt. Johnny rarely saw Jay get emotional over anything. In fact, sometimes he thought Jay, while very kind, was cold as ice. Watching him now made Johnny smile.

With glassy eyes, Jay said, "Okay, let's do it."

Once the emotional moment ended, Johnny's eyes swept over the yacht's control center. Some of the gadgets and gauges were obvious: multiple levers that controlled the two motors, depth gauges, and a couple of radar displays. There were rows of labeled buttons and switches, a big, beautiful compass housed in a brass case, and a couple of full-size computer displays with keyboards.

"Maybe you can take the helm for a few minutes once we get going," Captain Rich said.

"Actually," Johnny said. "I was kinda hoping to go on the Barracuda. I hope you're not offended."

Captain Rich laughed. "Offended? Dude, if I had my choice, I'd be on it with you. I love this baby, and I'm glad it's my home base, but that sucker would be my idea of the ultimate joy ride!"

Jay laughed. "You'll never change, will you? Just an overgrown kid!"

"Like you're any different?" Johnny said with a grin.

They all had a good chuckle as they walked aft to the others. Juan, Samantha, and Tzlil were now aboard and were helping themselves to the buffet lunch the chef had laid out.

"Wow, nice spread," Jay said.

"Yeah," Rich said, patting his stomach. "We eat well onboard." He laughed and walked away from the group.

As Johnny stepped to the rear of the buffet line, Jay typed on his phone.

Jay: *Team leaders check-in.*

Joel: *plantation barns all clear. ETA 15m*

Rodrigo: *Just arriving at hunting camp.*

Jay: *We are departing. Joel, the Barracuda is waiting for your team. Rodrigo, your team will fly in the chopper.*

Joel: *copy that*

Rodrigo: *Copy*

While all the texting had been going on, Captain Rich had brought the yacht's engines to life.

Jay: *Captain—depart when ready.*

Johnny: *I'm going to wait for Casey and go on the Barracuda.*

Jay: *Okay, but hustle off the boat.*

Cindy: *No, it's not okay.*

Johnny: *What? Mom, why?*

Cindy: *Because I don't want you out there waiting by yourself. It's dangerous.*

Johnny: *But I won't be alone. I'll be with Captain Enrique and Tito.*

Cindy: *No. You're going to stay with Jay.*

Johnny: *But, that's not fair.*

Cindy: *Maybe not, but that's the end of this discussion. Stay with Jay.*
Johnny: *Dad?*
Joel: *Don't drag me into this. Just do what your mother says.*
Johnny: *Fine. But not fair!*
Cindy: *That's enuf Johnny*

Johnny sighed, stepped away from the buffet line, and sat with Samantha.

"Want me to get you a plate? It'll make you feel better."

Dismayed, Johnny said, "No. I'll get it in a minute, but thanks."

Samantha smiled and winked.

One of the crew members quietly scurried past the group and down the stairs to the stern deck. Johnny thought about following him to help, but his stomach was growling loudly. He could always lend the crew a hand later and possibly even go for a ride on the Barracuda.

He finally filled a plate, and as he carried it to the table, Johnny looked to the side, toward the dock. Walking toward the rear of the yacht while it was moving forward created an illusion that he was moving faster than he was. A little unbalanced and completely zoned out, Johnny almost walked into Samantha.

"Earth to Johnny." She put her hands up, ready to fend him off.

He snapped to attention and stopped abruptly before making contact.

"Sorry."

"Is that for me? Thanks. You're so sweet." She gave him a peck on the cheek and took the plate from his hands.

Johnny's jaw dropped. "Huh?"

He hadn't moved an inch as she sat at the table with his plate. "Would you get me a Coke too?"

"Uh, sure," Johnny said, still wondering what had just happened.

As he turned to go back for her drink, Samantha said, "Come back here, silly."

He turned. "Huh?"

"I was kidding, mate. I can't eat all this." She pointed at the mound of food on his plate.

Juan and Chelsea laughed.

"Oh," he said, lowering his head.

"Come back and sit. I'll go get my own plate," Samantha said.

Johnny sat and said, "That was embarrassing."

"No," Tzlil said. "It was cute. She's sweet."

"Yeah, she is." He smiled just before taking a huge bite of his sandwich.

Chapter 24

CASEY: *HEY, MOM & Dad, just wanted to tell you I'm okay.*

    Shane: *Thank you, I was worried.*

    Reid: *Good to hear. Hope you got me a cigar?*

    Casey: *No, sorry!*

    Reid: *Just kidding…well, kind of. Glad you're safe.*

    Casey: *Yeah, all safe—except for guns and drugs.*

    Shane: *What????*

    Casey: *Just kidding…well, kind of. Sorry mom!*

    Joel: *Don't worry. Everything is fine.*

    Johnny: *Dude wait till you see the boat you'll be riding on. It's dope times 10!!!!*

    Casey: *Cool! What's yours like?*

    Johnny: *Like a floating 5 star hotel, but better. Even great food.*

    Casey: *Cool. Save me some, will ya?*

    Marianna: *Too late, he ate it all!*

    Casey: *Figures*

    Johnny: *No way—there's a ton!*

    Captain Rich: *Casey this is Captain Rich. I had a platter of sandwiches placed on board the interceptor for you guys.*

    Casey: *Thanks Captain! Interceptor? I thought it was a Barracuda.*

    Captain Rich: *Barracuda is the model of the boat, interceptor is the type.*

Casey: *Gotcha. Thanks. Prop or waterjet?*

Captain Rich: *Ha—You and Johnny are two of a kind. Not sure. Enrique—Tito?*

Tito: *Screws on twin 600s. Jets are gas & horsepower hogs. They're only better in very shallow water.*

Casey: *Cool, thanks!*

Tito: 👍

Chapter 25

DRIVING MORE THAN a mile with the Land Cruiser's tires fighting through almost a foot of dense mud and rocks on the rainforest trail had left Rodrigo exhausted. His forearms burned from lactic acid buildup as he opened and closed his aching hands repeatedly, trying to loosen them after his long battle with the steering wheel. He was in no mood for their less than cordial reception at the hunting lodge door.

Cindy yelped as the door creaked open just enough for the muzzle of a shotgun to poke through, pointing directly at Rodrigo's head. The only thing visible was the bluish-black steel gun barrel. The room behind was completely dark.

Rodrigo's arm shot up. His palm hit the bottom of the barrel, knocking the gun upwards. The resulting blast was deafening as the discharge of lead pellets passed over their heads.

Sun immediately threw all his weight at the door, crashing through it. The shooter dropped the shotgun and fell backward, pinned to the wood floor by Sun's prone body.

When Rodrigo flipped the light switch, the long, curly, auburn hair and attractive face of the woman Sun was on top of somewhat surprised both men.

"Who are you?" Sun asked forcefully.

"Me? Who are you?" the woman screamed, squirming to get free, her slender body trembling.

Listening from out on the porch, Cindy quickly typed.

Cindy: *Marianna or Juan, is there a hidden key to hunting camp?*

Juan: *Under rear leg of bench on front porch*

"We're Jose's friends," Rodrigo said.

"How come he didn't tell me you were coming?"

"Because he didn't know," Rodrigo said. "He lets us use the camp when he's not here."

"Why should I believe you?"

"Because he gave us this," Cindy said, walking in the door while displaying the key.

The woman looked at Cindy and then at the key. "Would you get off me already?" She sneered at Sun, their faces only inches apart.

"You haven't told us who you are yet," Sun said.

She stared at him through piercing eyes. "Israeli?"

"Perceptive," he said.

"I dated an Israeli years ago. Most arrogant man I ever met."

"Until now," Sun answered, slowly allowing a grin to soften his steely face.

She chuckled. "Let me up."

Sun looked her in the eye without budging.

"Come on. Get off. Without that shotgun, I'm completely harmless."

Sun laughed.

"What?" she said, toying with him.

"The gun didn't make much difference, did it?" he said with a grin.

"Fine. Point made. Will you get off me now? Please."

Sun slowly stood, then offered her his hand.

She frowned and stood on her own.

"So much for detente," he said.

She turned, walked to the refrigerator, opened it, and said, "Anyone want a beer?"

"No thanks," Sun said.

"How about you? You look like you could use one." She held a bottle toward Cindy.

Cindy shook her head, looking very rattled.

"Prefer some wine?" the woman asked.

"Please." Cindy's voice was shaky.

The woman removed another bottle from the fridge. "White okay?"

Cindy nodded.

"What's he doing?" the woman asked, looking at Rodrigo as she sat and poured a glass of wine.

Rodrigo was closing the fourth and final door of the cabin after he had quickly searched two bedrooms, two bathrooms, and a pantry closet. "I'm checking to see if you have any friends here with you."

"I'm alone."

Rodrigo's head tilted skeptically.

"What?" she said, raising her hands in question.

"How did you get here?" Rodrigo asked.

"How do you think? I drove."

"Drove what?"

"My Jeep, why?"

"Because I didn't see it outside."

"Of course, you didn't. It's out back, in the garage. "

Rodrigo raised an eyebrow at Sun.

Sun nodded, and Rodrigo rushed out the back door.

"Wait a minute. If you guys had been here before, you'd know there's a detached garage. Who are you?" she said, reaching for her phone.

Sun quickly seized it from the table.

"Hey."

"I'll give it back, but first, we talk."

"Give it to me, now!" She tried aggressively to get it from him. Finally, after multiple unsuccessful attempts, she sat in frustration and took a gulp of beer.

"Are you done?" Sun asked.

"Shut up!"

As Rodrigo walked back into the cabin, he said, "All clear."

"What's that supposed to mean?" the woman asked. "What are you looking for?"

"I'll explain, but first, tell me your name," Sun said.

She looked at him angrily and crossed her arms in silence.

"Fine, don't. My name is Sun, and we're here looking for two women and children that we think were abducted by Jose."

"Abducted?"

"Kidnapped."

"I know what it means, you idiot." Her irritation flared. "I'm just surprised."

"So, we're—" Sun began.

"Tamara," she said softly, cutting him off.

"What?"

"My name is Tamara."

Sun nodded. "Thank you, Tamara."

"You're wrong. Jose is not a kidnapper."

"Okay, let's say you're right. Do you know what he does for a living?"

She rolled her eyes. "Obviously. Everyone knows."

"And you're okay with that?"

She shrugged. "I try not to think about it. He treats me nicely."

"Nicely enough that you're okay with all the violence he causes in the drug trade?"

"As I said, I don't think about all that?"

"How can you not when people die every day because of him?"

"He doesn't kill people!"

"He may not do the actual deeds, but believe me, between murdering his rivals, and supplying drugs to addicts who overdose, he has a lot of blood on his hands."

"Look, of course, I don't approve of the things he does. They disgust me. But, if you knew what I've lived with all my life, you'd understand."

"Try me," Sun said.

"I grew up with nothing. My father picked coffee beans. At least, when he was sober, he did. We lived in a dirty, old shack without plumbing or electricity. There was never enough food. I didn't own shoes until I was around ten. Life sucked, but I didn't know any better back then. Then, when I was about sixteen, I started working on Jose's plantation. When I was nineteen, he pulled me aside one day and offered me a better life. Who was I to say no?"

Sun nodded. "I'm sorry to hear that," he said somberly. "So now you live here?"

She nodded. "Over the garage."

"Okay, it's understandable that you'd avoid thinking about his faults when he has made things so much better for you. But, let me ask you a question."

"What?"

"Would you be able to live with yourself if you knew that you helped him hide and possibly hurt or even kill innocent women and children?"

"Help him? Are you crazy? I'd never do that!"

"Good. So, let me make you an offer. I want you to come with us without letting him know. I'm going to hold onto your phone just to make sure. If you tell him about us, he'll probably have them killed. If you help us, we'll give you a better life."

"Better? How?"

"Sun, may I?" Cindy asked, standing up from the couch and approaching the table. She sat and looked at Tamara. "Have you heard of AllSport, the professional sports training facility in New York?"

Tamara nodded curiously.

"Our friends and family run the camp, and we live there. You can live and work there too."

"What would I do?"

"There are lots of jobs. We can figure that out later, but I promise you'll enjoy it. It will be a good life. Much better than living here, all by yourself. The campus is beautiful, the food is excellent, and there are lots of good people there. You'll make a ton of friends in no time."

Tamara remained silent. Knowing it was a lot for her to digest, Cindy gave her a moment to think while searching for a series of AllSport pictures on her phone.

"These may help convince you." Cindy passed the phone to her.

As Tamara swiped from one picture to the next, a smile slowly cracked the rigid indignation on her face. "It looks nice. Could I train there?"

"Of course, the facilities are open to everyone who works there."

"I mean, could I train to compete?"

"In what?" Cindy asked with a curious look.

"Running, swimming, biking, I'm good at all three. I've always dreamt of competing in a triathlon."

"How good are you?" Cindy asked.

"I've only competed locally in running and swimming, but I always win…usually by a lot. I'm good at biking too, but I've never had the chance to race."

"Then you have to come with us," Cindy said with a smile. "Maybe you'll become the next AllSport champion?"

Tamara's eyes widened. "You think?"

"Why not?"

"Okay, let's go." Tamara put her beer down on the table with fervor and stood.

Cindy, Rodrigo, and Sun laughed, then followed Tamara out the front door.

Halfway to the Land Cruiser, Tamara said, "Oh wait, I need to get a few things." She turned and quickly went back in.

Rodrigo looked at Cindy. "I knew that was too easy. Go with her."

"What if she's getting a gun?"

"I'm on it," Sun said, turning quickly and bolting toward the door.

A couple of minutes later, they both came out laughing. Tamara had a leather backpack slung on one shoulder. As they climbed into the Land Cruiser, she said to Cindy and Rodrigo, "So, you guys thought I was getting a gun?"

Cindy shrugged. Rodrigo looked at her in the rearview mirror and nodded.

"Let me explain something. Yes, Jose offered me a better life. No, I don't love him. The truth is, I don't even like him. Call me a hypocrite or whatever you want, but when someone offers to change your life when you've been living like I was, it's difficult to turn down. But, what you are offering me now is like the chance of a lifetime. Whether I can compete in a triathlon or not, living somewhere like AllSport, where I can do honest work, meet nice people, and not have to hide or be ashamed of who I am, that's a dream come true for me. So, if Jose is truly the monster you say he is, let's go save those women and kids and put an end to his reign of terror."

It was Sun's, Cindy's, and Rodrigo's turn to be quiet.

After a moment of stunned silence, Cindy said, "Whoa. That was powerful."

"Yeah," Rodrigo said. "How long has that been brewing inside of you?"

Tamara giggled. "I didn't even realize it was. It just kind of spewed out."

"Well, bravo!" Cindy quietly clapped.

Sun: *Hunting camp is clear. We have a new member of our team. We'll explain later. Jay, we have over an hour to drive. Can the chopper come get us?*

Jay: *Yes—I'll send the pilot toward the hunting camp. Let me know when you have coordinates for a landing spot.*

Sun turned to Tamara. "Can a helicopter land anywhere near here?"

"Of course. Jose's pilot usually lands in a clearing at the top of a mountain, or, if it's too windy, down in the valley at a farm. The mountain clearing is closer, but the dirt road is pretty rough. How's the four-wheel-drive in this old thing?"

"This old thing is tough as nails, girl!" Rodrigo grumbled as he drove through the mud.

"We'll see." Tamara snickered. "Turn around and go back toward the cabin."

"Where is the clearing in relation to the cabin?" Sun asked.

"It's close. The cabin is over there, and the mountain is there," she said, pointing. "Why?"

"Because I need to send the pilot coordinates, or an address."

"I don't know the coordinates."

"Didn't expect you to."

"The clearing is pretty obvious. Tell him to look for the cell tower."

"Cell tower, really?" Sun said as he typed.

"Yup, there was no reception or WiFi out here, so Jose had towers installed. Turn left up ahead, just after that big rock."

"Gotcha," Rodrigo said, turning onto a narrow, rocky trail. "Wow! Buckle up, everyone."

After a slow, twisty, jarring ride up the steep trail, the Land Cruiser climbed its way over the edge of a cleared plateau. Once they all disembarked, Rodrigo locked the doors.

"Good idea," Tamara said with a laugh. "The wildlife up here loves to steal vehicles."

Sun and Cindy laughed.

"Hey," Rodrigo said defensively. "This baby's a classic. You never know."

The sound of an approaching chopper ended their banter.

Chapter 26

LUNA: *FYI—WE'RE done at the school. Stopping for lunch, then stopping at the plantation before going home.*

Marianna: *Thanks mom! Be careful!*

Luna: *Me? I'm just eating lunch. You be careful!*

Juan: *We're fine!*

Luna: *Gotta go. Jose is coming back to the car.*

Jose sat in the driver's seat and slammed his palm on the steering wheel.

"What's wrong?" Luna asked.

"I just read a message that Javier sent me earlier. There are people looking for me."

Luna's body stiffened. "Who?" she asked, barely able to breathe.

"I don't know. He said that they sounded and acted like the mafia."

Luna relaxed a little. "Why would the mafia be looking for you?"

Jose looked at her. "I've told you a hundred times, don't meddle in my business."

"Don't you dare play that card again," she seethed. "You tell me the mafia are looking for you, and you don't want me to ask any questions? Don't be an idiot, Jose. I've been a prisoner of your stupid business for years. My life, and, more importantly, my kids' lives, are constantly in peril due to your business. I deserve to know about anything that may bring danger to us."

Jose looked at her silently while removing a cigar from the inside breast pocket of his sports coat. He slowly put it to his lips, bit off a tiny piece at the end, and spat it out his open window. He put the cigar in his mouth, took a lighter from his pocket, and raised it to the cigar.

"Do not light that with Diego and me in the car."

He turned just enough to look at her with one eye. Then, with a defiant grin, he ignited the flame and puffed repeatedly until smoke began to fill the vehicle.

Enraged, Luna opened her door, stepped out, turned, and opened the rear door. She held her hand out to Diego and said, "Come with me, Diego."

As Diego got out, Jose demanded, "Get back in the car, both of you!"

Luna slammed both doors shut, took Diego's hand, and began walking.

Jose started the engine and slowly drove up next to them. "Stop this nonsense and get in."

Luna attempted to quicken her pace but her body lurched as Diego stopped dead in his tracks, squeezed her hand hard and tugged her back. She turned and saw Diego uncharacteristically staring at Jose.

Stopping the car, Jose growled, "I said, get in."

"Get rid of that cigar, and maybe we will."

He took a long puff, blew a large plume of smoke into the windshield, and threw the cigar out the window. "There. Now get in!" He stopped the car.

She looked him in the eye, shook her head, and opened the rear door. "Go ahead, Diego. Get in."

With detest engraved in her face, she opened the front door, sat, and slammed it shut. She leaned forward, cranked the air conditioner to full blast, then sat back, crossed her arms tightly, and stared out the windshield.

After about a minute of driving, the silence in the car was broken by the steady tapping of Diego's finger on his window. As the tapping continued, Luna turned to see Jose looking in the rearview mirror and biting his lip. "Don't you dare yell at him. You've upset him enough already."

"Me? You're the one who got him upset. Don't ever show me disrespect like that in front of him. I don't need him becoming as defiant as you. He's tough enough to deal with already."

"Ha! I disrespected you? Are you crazy? You lit a cigar inside the car with us in it. It's one thing if you want to give yourself cancer, but subjecting us to that smoke is downright insulting. You want his respect? You want my respect? Well, maybe you should show us some."

The silence resumed, except for the consistent tapping.

Chapter 27

THE OCEAN WAS rough. The Barracuda, although built to handle high seas with speed and agility, was riding the swells like a roller coaster. Its bow surged beyond every crest, and periodically, bigger waves would launch the entire boat into the air.

Somewhat nervous when the boat smacked down into the water after its first quick flight, Casey quickly followed the captain's order to, "Buckle up!"

Casey saw Joel nod after Enrique looked at them and pointed at the throttle levers. *Guess he's going to slow it down*, Casey thought with relief. Then, to his shock, Captain Enrique pushed the levers forward. Casey quickly tightened the straps of his harness, then clenched his hands on his armrests. His timing was perfect as the boat pierced through the top of another big wave. Casey heard the engines scream when the propellers left the water.

He glanced at Joel, who was looking back at him and Antonio.

"Are you guys okay?" Joel asked loudly.

Casey raised his thumbs without letting go of the armrests.

Antonio grinned.

"Feel free to crank it up, Captain," Joel said, tightening his harness.

Captain Enrique pushed the levers further forward.

"How much longer?" Casey yelled.

Tito glanced at the dashboard and said, "About fifteen minutes. The other boat will get there in about five."

"Joel, will they wait, or will they start the search before we get there?" Casey yelled.

"They'll probably start without us."

"Oh man, that's not fair," Casey moaned. "Well, I guess it doesn't matter as long as we save them."

"Exactly. But I know how you feel. Being part of the actual rescue always feels good.

"Especially because it's Johnny's and my case."

"And you should be proud of that."

Casey nodded.

Chapter 28

"HMM, I WONDER who that is," Captain Rich said, looking at the ship's radar.

"What do you see?" Jay asked, glancing over the captain's shoulder.

"Two boats are leaving the island." He pointed at two green blips on the screen that were moving away from the island in the opposite direction of the Southern Star's approach.

"You think they know we're coming?" Johnny asked, craning his neck to see from the captain's other side.

"If someone is watching a radar, they do. Unlike the Barracuda, this baby is not exactly stealthy. They can see us just like we see them."

"I wonder who it is. I mean, it's obviously not Jose," Johnny said.

"Right," Jay agreed. "It could be his staff. Somebody has to maintain that place."

"Yeah," Johnny said. "Or it could be those mafia guys that were at the plantation."

"Mafia?" Captain Rich groaned.

"Don't worry," Jay said. "We're just speculating. They are probably just Jose's employees going on a supply or fuel run."

"Why would they use two boats on a supply run?" Johnny asked.

"It's not a supply or fuel run. They're heading in the wrong direction for those," Captain Rich added.

"I was just trying to ease your mind, Rich," Jay said. "How quickly can you get us to the dock?"

"A few minutes," he said, giving the throttles a nudge forward. "I need to evaluate the dockage and depth when we get close."

"How about the speedboat, or the jet skis?"

"It'll take too long to lower them into the water from up top."

"Where are your binoculars?" Jay asked.

Captain Rich pointed down. "Middle drawer."

As Jay pulled two pairs of binoculars from the draw and handed Johnny one, he said, "Rich, can you ask my team to come up here. Marianna, too, please."

"I don't have a PA system if that's what you mean. I talk to my crew on two-way radios."

"I just sent them a text," Johnny said.

Rich radioed his crew, "Prepare for docking!"

Johnny: *Jay's team up to the wheelhouse—NOW!*

Johnny: *Marianna too.*

Jay glimpsed at his phone, then shook his head toward Johnny. "Wise guy!"

Johnny returned a big smile.

A couple of minutes later, Carlo, Tzlil, Stu, and Marianna gathered around Jay and Johnny.

"We're going to dock soon," Jay began. "Two boats just left the island, heading in the opposite direction of our approach. They could be Jose's people, but who knows? Rich will keep an eye on them on the radar." Jay looked at the captain, who gave a quick nod.

"We treat this the same as any other search and rescue. Carlo, you search the grounds. As far as I can see there's a boathouse and the main house. Is that it, Marianna?"

"There's also a small cabana by the pool."

"Tzlil, you're with me. We'll search the house. Stu, you check the cabana, then come help us with the house. Rich, would you mind searching the boathouse, then, getting back on board to watch over everyone here?"

"No problem," Rich said as he kneeled and removed his handgun from a small safe that was inside a polished mahogany cabinet.

"You don't have to do this, Rich," Jay said.

"You think I'm going to let someone else protect my house? Not a chance. Besides, it feels good to have a reason to hold this again. The only thing I've done with it lately is clean it. I've got something more powerful locked up down below if you think you might need it."

"Hooyah," Jay said quietly, with a nod.

"Hooyah," Rich repeated.

Captain Rich smiled, holding his Sig Sauer pistol with pride. Then, standing and looking out the windshield, he picked up his two-way radio, pressed the button, and said, "Prepare for port side docking. Amanda, controls are yours till I'm back at the helm."

"Copy that, Cap'n," Amanda, Rich's First Officer, said.

As Rich dashed out of the cabin, Jay lifted the binoculars and scanned the island. "There's no one in sight."

"You'd think…" Tzlil started, then let her voice trail off as she noticed the whole team nodding.

"Yeah," Jay said. "If they were holding them here, they'd probably have guards posted. On the other hand, if they're locked up somewhere inside, maybe the guards are staying inside too. After all, what are the chances that anyone would come out here looking for them?"

"Wait," Johnny said. "That's stupid. It's exactly why we're here."

Everyone smiled.

"Oh, gotcha. That was your point."

A minute later, Rich returned and handed Jay a Bergara, high-power, long-range rifle.

"For pirates?" Jay asked

"You never know," Rich said.

"Have you ever had to use it?"

"Not yet. Thank God! You better get ready. Here, take these radios," Rich handed Jay a small duffle bag. "They'll be easier to use than your phones. We'll be docked in a minute. Head to the stern deck."

Jay handed the radios out to his team. "Let's roll."

As they passed through the main salon, Jay turned to Johnny and said, "You're going to hate me, but you have to stay on board."

"No way!"

"'I'm afraid so, my friend."

"Come on! It's our case."

"I know it is, and when we find them, you and Casey will get all the credit. In the meantime, your parents would prefer that you don't get shot at."

"But you said that you didn't see anyone."

"I also said that they might be inside the house."

"It's not fair."

"Would it help if I told you that the chef is making a big plate of chicken parmesan so that you won't starve during the ten minutes we're on the island?"

Johnny's eyes lit up. "Really? That's my favorite!"

"Why don't you go to the galley and see for yourself."

As he hurried away, Johnny said, "Thanks, Jay. I take back all the things I was just thinking about you."

Jay chuckled.

"I thought he was going to put up much more of a fight," Tzlil said. "That was way too easy."

"He is more passionate about food than anyone I know."

"When did you speak with the chef?" Tzlil asked.

"I got worried when we saw those boats leave the island. I knew Johnny would give me a hard time. He loves being part of the action, but his stomach usually rules his thoughts. I had Rich radio the chef then."

"Well done!"

"Yeah, sometimes it's the little things that matter most. Let's go."

Jay and Tzlil followed the rest of the team, who were already ashore and running to their assigned locations.

Within minutes Captain Rich radioed. "Boathouse, all clear!"

Stu quickly followed with, "Cabana—clear except for a smoldering cigar in an ashtray. I'm heading to the house."

"Grounds are clear. I'm at rear entrance to house," Carlo announced.

"We're at the front door," radioed Jay. "Carlo, do you see any surveillance cameras? There are none visible here."

"Negative."

Winded due to his sprint from the cabana, Stu joined Jay and Tzlil.

"Need a moment to catch your breath?" Jay asked.

Stu breathed deeply and said, "I'm good."

Jay turned the doorknob, then radioed, "The front door is unlocked. Check the back."

"It's locked, but entry won't be a problem. The door frame is frail."

"Okay, Stu, you head upstairs. Carlo, first floor with me. Tzlil, if there's a basement, it's yours. Everyone ready?"

Stu and Tzlil nodded as Carlo radioed, "Ready"

"Okay, we'll enter on three. One, two, three."

After the loud crash of the back door, the house was silent except for their footsteps as they opened door after door. Slightly less than a minute later, Stu yelled, "Second floor, clear."

Tzlil belted out, "Basement, clear."

"Living room, office, and kitchen, all clear," Jay shouted.

"We've got bodies in the den," Carlo yelled.

The others ran to the den where two men were slumped over on the couch. Each had a game controller in his hand and a bullet hole in the back of his head. The TV had a bullet hole in it, too.

"The one on the left has an empty holster," Carlo said.

Jay sighed, handed Tzlil the rifle, pulled out his phone, and typed.

Jay: *Enrique, do you see the two boats that left the island earlier on your radar?*

Enrique: *Yes*

Jay: *Is your boat fully armed?*

Tito: *Besides the remote control water cannon, we've got 4 pintle mount stanchions in the rear. 2 facing stern, 1 port, and 1 starboard. We're fully stocked with guns and ammo below deck. Mostly automatics.*

Jay: *How close are you to us?*

Enrique: *Docking now*

Jay: *I want Casey & Antonio off the Cuda and on the S Star by the time we arrive. Sorry Casey, no time to argue. Please get off now. Joel, start mounting the machine guns. Enrique, there will be 4 more of us boarding—total of 6.*

Enrique: *Ready when you are.*

Jay: *Rodrigo, what's your ETA?*

Receiving no answer from Rodrigo, and having no time to wait, Jay started running toward the boats, thinking, *they're over the water in a chopper—hopefully just bad reception.* He stopped running a moment later and resent the text.

Rodrigo: *4 mins*

Jay breathed a sigh of relief and typed. Jay: *Do you have weapons on chopper?*

Rodrigo: *2 Glocks*

Jay: *OK. Land on island near boats. Drop off Cindy. Pick up 2 automatic rifles. Then tell pilot to follow the Barracuda.*

Rodrigo: *Copy that*

Jay pocketed his phone and ran. He reached the dock just as the helicopter landed. Stu was running towards the chopper with two automatic assault rifles. Joel, Enrique, and Tito were mounting machine guns on the rear stanchions of the Barracuda. The water cannon was above the bow deck.

Rodrigo jumped from the chopper, helped Cindy and Tamara step out, then ran to Jay.

"I forgot that you mentioned having a new team member," Jay yelled over the noise of the chopper. "Who is she?"

"Jose's girlfriend. She was living at the hunting camp. She's on our side. I'll explain later."

"You trust her?"

"I'm pretty sure, but we have a bigger problem right now. The pilot is young and scared. He's responsible for the aircraft. He won't follow."

"Stu!" Jay yelled, waving him over.

Stu ran to Jay's side.

"Rodrigo, tell the pilot Stu is going to fly his bird. Explain that he's licensed and flew for the SEALS. Tell him we'll pay for any damages, and we'll replace his Raven I with a Raven II if anything extreme happens. Make sure he understands that the lives of women and children are at stake here. If that's not enough, tell him he'll be well compensated. But only offer money if necessary. Just make sure he gets out of the chopper and onto the big boat."

"And if he declines?" Rodrigo asked.

"Force the issue!" Jay said.

Rodrigo raised a thumb and ran off.

"You got this, right?" Jay said to Stu. "It's been a long time since you've flown a chopper,"

"Sure. It's been a while, but it's like riding a bike, right?"

"Exactly!" Jay yelled. Then, he quietly added, more to himself than Stu, "Glad I'll be on the boat."

"What?" Stu yelled.

"I said, good luck!" Jay shouted with a quick salute before he turned and ran to the Barracuda.

***

Jay's team was waiting on the dock near the stern of the Barracuda. Joel and Tito were almost finished mounting the guns. Rich and his crew stood on the lower rear deck of the Southern Star. Casey, Johnny, Marianna, Juan, Carita, and Antonio stood on the dock nearby. The others were in the main salon. Casey and Johnny were sullen.

Jay handed his phone to Marianna. "I'd like you, Juan, and Carita to look at these photos of the two men we found in the house. Tell me if you know who they are, and whether they work for Jose, or not. Mind you, they're a little unpleasant." The pictures were close-ups. There was no visible blood, but the eyes had an empty look.

Marianna pointed at one. "This one is Carita's cousin. He's the island caretaker. The other guy is one of Uncle Jose's guards."

Taking Jay's phone and expanding the picture, Carita cringed and asked hesitantly, "Wait, they're not dead, are they?"

Jay sighed and quietly said, "I'm afraid they are. I am so sorry, Carita."

She lowered her head and began to cry. Marianna hugged her.

"Marianna, please take her back on the yacht," Jay said. "She doesn't need to hear this."

"No," Carita said while wiping her eyes with the back of her hand. "I want to hear it. Especially now," she seethed.

Jay nodded. "I understand. I have one more question for you guys. The boathouse only has a small power boat in it. I'm guessing that's your cousin's. Did the guard use a different boat?"

"Yes, he used Uncle Jose's race boat. It's a cigarette. It's really fast," Juan said.

Jay nodded. "I guess it's one of the boats we're going after."

He turned toward his team and began his briefing loudly enough for everyone to hear over the racket of the helicopter, "We found two male bodies in the main house. Both were executed with one shot in the back of the head. One was security, the other was Carita's cousin, the island caretaker. We still don't know who we're dealing with, but obviously, they're willing to kill. We also know that one of the boats is a cigarette that can easily outrun the Barracuda in smooth seas, but probably not in these waters. Stu is piloting the chopper. Rodrigo is with him. Tito, can I control the water canon from inside the cabin?"

"Yes, I'll show you how."

"Good. Joel, when we get close, I want you on the stern gun. Carlo, port. Tzlil, starboard. Sun, take this," He handed Sun the long-range rifle. "We may need your marksmanship."

Sun nodded.

"If they have the women and kids, my gut tells me that they're not holding them on the cigarette, but obviously, I can't be sure. Enrique, do you know the approximate size of the second boat from your radar image?"

"No. I haven't had a chance to study them. I didn't even know that we were going after them until a few minutes ago."

"I have," Rich said. "The cigarette is probably around fifty feet, the other boat looks to be a little more than double that."

"I'm going to guess, if they have the women and kids, they're probably on the yacht, along with the boss. I could be wrong, but the yacht is a more comfortable ride for the boss, and I'm sure he would want to keep an eye on his prisoners."

"The boss?" Joel asked. "Why do you think he's on board?"

"Stu found a smoldering cigar at the cabana. My guess is that the boss, whether he's cartel or mafia, had his soldiers do the dirty work while he waited at the pool. I'd say he probably left the cigar intentionally, to make a statement."

"You mean kind of like his calling card?" Casey asked. "Did you look at the label? If it was a cartel boss, maybe he grows tobacco and makes his own cigars, like Jose does. Maybe he was sending Jose a message."

"Good point," Jay said, scrolling, then tapping on his phone. He put it to his ear, then rolled his eyes and put it down, mumbling, "What am I doing? Stu's not going to answer."

He looked at the group. "Who's the fastest runner here?"

"I'm pretty fast," Tamara said.

"Antonio is like lightning," Casey said.

"Marianna," Jay said. "Ask Antonio to run as fast as he can and bring back whatever is left of that cigar. And, if the label is not on it, please tell him to look for it and bring it too."

As Marianna spoke with Antonio, Jay turned to Tamara and said, "Don't take it personally, but I really don't even know who you are yet."

They all watched Antonio run down the dock, up the ramp, and through the open gate.

"It looks like you chose the right person anyway," Tamara said. "He's fast." She turned her head toward Cindy, "You should probably explain who I am."

"Good idea," Cindy agreed. "Tamara is, or rather was, Jose's girlfriend. She lives at the hunting camp. She is here to help us."

"Oh my God." Marianna smacked Juan lightly, on the shoulder. "Did you hear that? I can't believe it."

Juan looked at Marianna and laughed.

"Wait. You knew?" she said, hitting him harder. "How could you not tell me?"

Juan just smiled.

Marianna looked at Tamara with wide eyes and arms spread, questioningly.

"Don't you dare judge me," Tamara said defiantly. "You had everything. I had nothing. Not food. Not even shoes when I grew up. You know how I was living. Jose offered me a change that I couldn't refuse. I'm not proud of it."

"Tamara, Marianna, I'm sorry, but please talk about it later." Jay turned toward his team. "I need everyone to listen up. If we end up in a gunfight, don't fire into the hulls. I don't want our bullets hitting the women or kids if they're down below deck. Hopefully, these guys are not heavily armed. Maybe, if we're lucky, between the chopper and this," he pointed at the Barracuda. "They'll get intimidated and allow us to board without a fight."

"You're kidding, right?" Joel asked.

"No. Just optimistic."

"A bit," Joel said sarcastically.

"Look," Jay continued. "We have no idea who we're dealing with or if they even have the women and kids. The only element we have going for us is surprise, and that's only if the Barracuda is as stealthy as it's supposed to be."

"It is," Casey said. "The radar cross-section is really low. Radar needs large flat surfaces to ping off of. If you look at the Barracuda, you see lots of small surfaces and angles. They deflect the radar beams away from the source. And there is no metal exposed anywhere above the deck."

His statement brought impressed looks.

"Thank you, Casey," Jay said.

Marianna looked over at Casey and mouthed, "Wow."

Casey blushed.

"So, things won't get interesting until they can see us," Jay said. "Sun, I want you situated somewhere securely with the long-range rifle." He turned to Tito. "Can we mount it somewhere?"

"No, but we can harness him onto the rear deck right here." He pointed just behind where the cabin enclosure ended. "These loops and steps are on both sides of the boat." He unfolded a peg-like step that was hinged to the rear edge of the cabin. "It should work well as a gun rest. I've got flak jackets for everyone that double as harnesses. They can be attached to the weapon stanchions or the shock-absorbing seats. Sun can latch his harness to one of the loops."

"Good," Jay said. "Sun, while I'm hoping for no gunfire, if they shoot at us, take the shooters out immediately."

"Will do," Sun said with a quick nod.

"Okay. Let's do this."

As everyone began boarding their respective boats, Jay walked over to Rich. "I don't want you to take any chances. Just follow us and stay at a safe distance until we're done. If they're on board and we rescue them, I'd prefer to transfer them to your boat for the ride back. Okay?"

"I'm ready when you are, but you're going to get there long before us. You'll probably be done with the rescue before I get close enough for a visual."

Jay nodded. "Do me a favor, protect your passengers. I'm sure you've noticed they're like family to me."

"They'll be safe."

Jay leaned in and quietly said, "Keep an eye on Tamara, the curly-haired one they brought back from the camp. I don't know her story. Not sure if she's trustworthy."

Rich nodded. "Will do."

"Until later, my friend," Jay said patting his heart twice with a closed fist.

"Hooyah," Rich expressed, performing the same gesture.

"Hooyah."

They didn't have to wait long for Antonio to return. He handed Jay the cigar stub. A quick look at the black label revealed two crossed machetes above the word Rebanada.

He showed his team. "Anyone know of Rebanada cigars?"

"Never heard of them," Joel said.

Jay: *Does anyone know of Rebanada cigars?*

Carita: *That's Pedro Abila's brand. He's another cartel boss. Rebanada is his nickname. It's Spanish for slice.*

Casey: *Another Pedro!*

Juan: *I told you it's a common name.*

Carita: *Very common.*

Jay: *Okay. Let's go pay Mr. Abila a visit.*

Chapter 29

THE SEA WAS choppier than it had been earlier. The Barracuda bounced and shook. Again and again, the craft jettisoned into the air off the large cresting waves, only to hit each trough with a jarring thwack.

"Thank God for these shock absorbing seats," Tzlil's voice chattered. "Can you imagine how this ride would feel without them?"

"This ain't nuthin, honey," Carlo said.

"It's going to be tough when we're manning the guns," Joel said.

"Got any tips for a first timer?" Tzlil asked.

"Strap your harness in as tight as possible," Joel said. "Keep your finger off the trigger till you're ready to fire. Try to absorb the bouncing with your legs."

"Thanks." The word coughed out of Tzlil as the boat slammed hard in the water. She turned toward Sun. "You better go hook up at your position soon, so you can get used to it. Getting a steady long distance shot off is going to be difficult."

Sun nodded, unhooked his flak jacket harness from his seat, and slowly stood, holding the rifle in one hand and one of his armrests tightly in the other. After unsuccessfully attempting to strap the rifle sling over his head with only one hand, he said, "Can't do this with one hand."

"Let me help." Tzlil reached for the rifle just as Sun let go of the armrest. At the same moment the boat crested another wave and dropped fast. Unprepared, Sun was lifted off his feet, then crashed hard to the floor when the boat smacked the bottom of the wave.

Sun's grunt as he hit the floor was loud, yet, in spite of any pain, he grabbed hold of the closest chair and hoisted himself immediately to his feet.

"You okay?" Joel asked.

"Yeah, but where's the gun?" Sun said, looking around the floor.

"Here," Tzlil said, holding the weapon out to him.

"How'd you do that?" Sun asked.

"I was reaching to help you just as you fell. I had to choose, you or the gun. Sorry."

Sun chuckled. "Gee thanks."

"I hope you're being sarcastic?"

"You know I am. You made the right choice. It would have been a disaster if the gun hit the floor and discharged." He walked over, gave her a quick kiss, and let her help him strap the rifle sling over his head.

"Thank God," Carlo said. "We're bouncing a little less. The water is calming down."

The boat then rocketed off another wave and landed hard. This time Sun was holding Tzlil's armrest and managed to remain upright.

"I guess I spoke too soon," Carlo said. "But at least the choppiness is gone. Smoother water with an occasional big wave is way more tolerable than that constant shaking."

After Sun made his way up the steps from the lower forward cabin, Jay stuck his head down through the hatch. "About ten minutes till we have visual, then another five or so till we catch up to them. Come up and get comfortable at your weapon positions."

As Joel, Tzlil and Carlo stood, Jay continued, "We won't know which side we'll be able to approach the yacht from until we get close. The cigarette complicates that decision. I'll let you all know as soon as we figure it out. Then, whichever one of you is on the opposite side will be the one to prepare for boarding. We'll try to pull up wherever boarding is easiest, but that may not be possible."

Enrique and Tito glanced quickly at each other and nodded; they had no need for verbal communication, as is often the case with siblings.

Tito looked at Carlo. "Give me a hand."

Tito opened a cabinet and removed lines for securing the boat, and a rope ladder with grappling hooks. "Stow a couple of these on the forward deck and a couple at the rear."

"Copy that," Carlo said.

Tito opened a second cabinet, looked at Joel and Jay, and said, "Give me a hand before you go to your weapons. I want fenders all around the boat. We'd rather not have to pay for repairs, or replace this baby."

"If anything happens I'll get it taken care of one way or another," Jay said. "If we rescue them, I'm sure I can get the Italian team, and their government to help pay."

"Maybe, but I'd still like to keep damage to a minimum. We need to deliver this boat soon."

"I'm firing a test shot," Sun yelled just before shooting the long-range rifle in the direction of a distant red buoy.

"One more," he yelled, then pulled the trigger. A moment after, they all saw the red glass lamp near the top of the buoy disintegrate.

"Nice shot," Joel said. "Not sure I could have hit it with all the movement."

"I missed." Sun's voice depicted his frustration.

"No way, we all saw it!" Carlo said.

"I was aiming for the smaller top part of the lamp, I hit the larger globe."

Everyone chuckled, except Sun. He was dead serious.

Joel gave Tzlil a look of surprise.

"He's the consummate perfectionist," she said.

"Guess that's why he chose you," Joel said with a smile.

"Obviously," she said, throwing her hair back with a sarcastic smirk.

Suddenly a thunderous whooshing sound coming from the forward deck grabbed everyone's attention. A heavy torrent jettisoned fiercely from the nozzle of the water cannon, and out over 150 feet from the boat. The massive blast of water was similar to that from a firehose, only much stronger. As Jay moved the toggle stick on the remote control from his chair inside the cabin, the intense high-pressure jet swayed to and fro, then up and down. Even at long distance, the powerful stream of water was strong enough to knock over the largest of men. As Jay adjusted a dial, the jet became a wide spray, which, at close range, could decrease their adversary's ability to see the Barracuda, and simultaneously create panic and confusion. It was an extremely effective, non-lethal weapon.

"We have visual at eleven o'clock on the horizon," Enrique announced over the public address system.

The previously high cresting waves had now settled into more manageable rollers. While the waves were still too large for full throttle, Enrique increased the speed without the boat taking air.

The faster they could approach the yacht, the better. The question was, would they begin shooting from the yacht before they even knew who was aboard the Barracuda. A boat armed to the hilt would pose a threat to any captain, regardless of their vessel's inhabitants.

As they approached, Jay asked. "Enrique, if you were Abila or the captain, what would you be thinking?"

"That we're probably pirates."

"But pirate's aren't very common in these waters, right," Jay said with a head tilt.

"True, but they have been known to attack private yachts."

"Okay, yet, the Barracuda isn't your typical pirate boat, although, of course, it could be booty from a recent attack."

Enrique nodded. "They might think we're drug runners, this is a perfect vessel for it."

"Right, in fact I'll bet your customer is probably just that."

"Smart bet," Enrique said.

"But why would a rival drug runner approach Abila's yacht?" Jay asked. "That would be absurd, unless the runner works for Abila. Hmm?"

As the Barracuda got within Sun's firing distance, everyone listened for the sound of gunfire from the other boats. Suddenly the engines of the cigarette roared, and the boat raced away.

"Chase the cigarette, or head for the yacht?" Enrique asked.

"You can't catch the cigarette, can you?"

"No."

"Then, head for the yacht, but track the cigarette on your radar."

"Copy that," Enrique said, maintaining his course.

Nerves were taut, yet, trigger fingers remained stable as the team prepared for battle. Soldiers' emotions differed when heading into hot zones. While anxiety and adrenaline were inevitable, in some soldiers, the mixture raised acuity, while others had to quell those feelings in order to remain calm.

Minutes later, without gunfire, they were close enough to the yacht to communicate via the PA system. Jay picked up the microphone, looking at Enrique, who nodded his approval.

"On second thought, you should make the announcement. My Spanish is okay, but my accent is pure gringo."

"What should I say?" Enrique reached for the mic.

"This is the captain of the International Coast Guard Interceptor requesting permission to board the, what's the name of the yacht?"

"Rebanada de Cielo."

"Slice of sky?" Jay questioned. "I guess it's like slice of heaven. Slice cigars, slice of heaven. Maybe the guy is talented with a knife."

"Nice thought," Enrique said, furrowing his brow. "So, what do I say if he doesn't respond, or more likely turns the request down."

"Say that this will be a peaceful search as long as he cooperates. However, if he does not allow us to board, we will be forced to use weapons and confiscate his yacht."

"You think he'll believe that?"

"That's up to you, my friend."

"Oh, great." Enrique shook his head. "He'll probably ask if we have a warrant."

"The Coast Guard doesn't need one," Jay said. "Probable cause is enough. But if he asks, just tell him, yes."

"What if—" Enrique was cut off by Jay, who gestured toward a man with a rifle, who was now on the top deck of the yacht.

"Time's up," Jay said to Enrique. "You got this. Just take a deep breath and say it."

Enrique brought the microphone to his lips. "Este es el capitan del Interceptor de la Guardia Costera Internacional, que solicita permiso para abordar."

After an uncomfortable moment of silence, the captain's voice boomed from his PA system, "Permisio concedido."

Enrique lowered the mic. "Wow, that was easy!"

Head atilt, Jay said, "Too easy."

Enrique nodded.

"What side do you want to tie up on?" Jay asked.

"Our port to his starboard."

Jay yelled, "Sun and Tzlil, pull the fenders from starboard and place them between the ones we already have on the port side. Carlo, prepare lines for tying up on port, and be ready with the rope ladder. Joel, stay near your weapon, but keep your hands off of it. We don't want to spook them. I'm staying here with the water canon control."

Watching everything through the bulletproof cabin window, Jay expected to see more of the yacht's crew join the armed man at the top railing. He briefly turned and caught Joel's skeptical eye. A quick scan of the rest of his team's faces revealed similar doubt on each.

The Barracuda moved steadily toward the rear, starboard corner of the yacht. The only visible movement on the yacht was the lone man on top. Jay scanned the dark tinted windows of the vessel through the binoculars, stopping at the wheelhouse. Dismayed, he said, "Between the sun's glare and the tint, I can't see anything through those windows."

"Yeah, that tint is very dark," Enrique said. "Obviously, it's intended to keep more than just the sun out."

"All the more reason to be suspicious. How big do you think the crew is?"

"Captain plus two, maybe three."

"And unless the crew members double as security, there should be more."

"Everyone on a cartel boss's staff doubles as security, no matter what their day to day job is," Tito said.

"How do you know that?"

"When your clientele is the likes of ours, knowing stuff like that can save your life from time to time."

"How are you with a gun?" Jay asked.

"Why?" Tito asked skeptically.

"Don't worry, I'm not going to ask you to board the yacht with us."

"I'm pretty good with most firearms. As you can see, we deal with all kinds of weapons in our business. And, like I said, with clients like ours, we need to know how to protect ourselves."

Jay nodded without taking his eyes off the yacht.

"So, why'd you ask?"

"Because I like the way you and Enrique handle this vessel, and I'm always looking for the right type of people for my business. As you can see, I need people with many types of expertise. I get jobs all over the world, so I like to have people available everywhere. I pay very well. My full timers have become wealthy, and my part-timers, like Carlo and Rodrigo, make a handsome sum when they're on a case."

"Is that an offer?" Enrique asked.

"No, not yet. If you're interested, we'll talk later."

Enrique looked at his brother. They both nodded. "We are."

"Good."

The yacht had slowed to little more than a drifting speed as they neared it.

"Everyone, stay alert. They're making this way too easy. I don't trust it at all. I'm boarding first, then Carlo, then Tzlil, then Sun. Joel, stay at your gun post."

"I can take his post once we're tied up, then he can board with you," Tito offered.

Jay looked at him inquisitively before saying, "Alright, that will be good." He turned back to his team. "Joel, once we board, come with me to speak with Abila. You three, search the boat. But, stay together. Work as a team. They are really making this way too easy. I don't like it."

The waters had settled enough to make the final approach easy. The rear deck of the Barracuda was just over a foot away from the aft deck of the yacht.

Following Jay, each team member made the long step from the Barracuda's gunnel to the yacht's. Guns in hand, they hastily made their way up the short flight of stairs to the next level. That no one was waiting to confront them was strange and unsettling. Jay pointed to Carlo, Sun, and Tzlil then swept his arm toward the front of the boat. They moved forward quickly and quietly.

Joel followed Jay through the main salon, and they continued forward in search of the wheelhouse. The boat was eerily devoid of activity. Guns raised, they moved cautiously. Curious about a consistent tapping noise, Jay gestured for Joel to follow him towards it. As they turned the corner into the galley, a large man turned toward them wielding a long knife.

Jay and Joel pointed their guns at him.

Without even flinching, the man slowly laid the knife on his cutting board and raised his hands in surrender. "Soy solo el chef."

After a quick scan of the chef's work area they lowered their guns. He picked up his knife and resumed his work, chopping carrots.

A few steps from the galley, the men saw two steep, side-by-side, narrow staircases—one went up, the other down. Both were wide enough for only one person. Joel motioned upward with his chin. Jay started up the steep, polished wood stairs. His rubber soles silently gripped the non-slip tread strips on each step. He stopped near the top of the stairs, remaining within the tight confines of the walls and closed hatch cover. A small door was open below the hatch cover. With his eyes just above floor level, he could see only part of the room. The rest was blocked from view by an adjacent wood cabinet. He was facing what he figured was the rear wall of the wheelhouse. Book shelves separated by a large video screen were built into the wall. The screen was split into two views. Half showed a radar view of the area surrounding the yacht. The other half was divided into nine smaller boxes, each showing different areas of the yacht. Jay's heart sank seeing Tzlil's face on one view, then it skipped a beat as he saw the top of his own head on another section. Irritated, he thought, *How could I have missed the cameras?*

Seeing no movement and hearing only two voices in the room above, he sighed, climbed the last few stairs while lifting the hatch cover, and stepped into the wheelhouse. Joel scrambled up, stood beside Jay, and they both lowered their guns to their sides without holstering them.

"Gentlemen." The deep, raspy voice came from the guy sitting next to the uniformed man at the ship's stainless steel wheel. Each sat on white, high-backed captain's chairs that kept their heads hidden from view from behind. Pushing his leather sandals against the instrument panel cabinet, the man swiveled his chair to face Jay and Joel. Sitting casually, his thick mane of slicked back, ebony hair contrasted intensely with the white leather chair. "I would say welcome aboard, but you are not." The man's eyes hid behind mirrored aviator sunglasses. His nose, moustache and mouth twitched repeatedly. His stocky body was wedged tightly between the chair's armrests.

"I don't know what you're looking for, nor do I really care. You will find nothing of interest here, and I'm not looking for trouble. So, search all you want, and then get off my boat."

Jay stared at the man for a moment. "Mr. Abila, we saw this yacht leave Jose Camarillo's island as we were approaching it."

Abila smiled. His perfect, brilliantly white teeth stood out against his dark, leathery face. "Ah yes, I was looking to visit with my friend, Jag, but as you probably know, he wasn't there. So we left."

"Your friend?" Jay asked as he felt his phone vibrate. He read Carlo's text.

Carlo: *All clear. Women and children are NOT onboard.*

"Mr. Abila," Jay said. "Thank you for your time, and please excuse our interruption. We will leave you now."

Abila spun his chair forward. Looking out the windshield, he said, "Por fin!"

***

As the Barracuda left the yacht's side, Jay asked, "Did you see where the cigarette went?"

"Rich was able to follow it on his radar," Enrique answered. "It docked at a small hotel in Magdalena. Rich and Stu are on their way now."

"How long before we are there?"

"About thirty five minutes, unless everyone buckles up, and we nail it."

"You heard him," Jay yelled. "Strap in."

After tightening his crossover seatbelts, Jay typed a text, constantly correcting with each bounce of the vessel.

Jay: *Stu/Rodrigo, don't fly or land near hotel. Don't want to spook cigarette captain. If you need to save fuel, land elsewhere. Rich, cruise by the dock at a distance. Casey and Johnny, grab the binoculars and report whatever you see on the dock, and at the hotel.*

Rich: *Copy that*

Rodrigo: *Copy*

Casey: *Copy that.*

Johnny: *Ditto*

A few minutes later. Stu: *Landed on nearby soccer field. Waiting for orders.*

From his seat behind Jay, Joel said, "I was surprised you didn't ask Abila about the women and children, or killing the guys on the island, or stealing the cigarette."

"It would have been a waste of time. He would have denied everything, and we'd have tipped our hand. If he's got the women and kids and we let him know that we're looking for them, who knows what he'd do. Hide them deeper? Kill them? Believe me, I thought about it all. I just figured the less said, the better."

Joel nodded. "I'm just disappointed. We've achieved basically nothing so far."

"Me too."

Casey: *Sign on dock reads Rebanada de la Buena Vida—Privado. I guess that means he owns hotel? No guests on beach. No movement in hotel windows. Two men sitting at table on patio near pool. Both smoking & drinking—looks like brown, beer bottles. Lots of bottles on the table & ground surrounding them. Both have handguns. One also has bigger gun (looks auto) hanging by a strap on the back of his chair. They are laughing a lot.*

Johnny: *The cigarette is docked next to another big boat. No one in view. There's a gas pump on dock. There's a smaller power boat also docked. There are three more open spaces at dock.*

Casey: *A curtain was just opened on the first floor. Windows are big—look like sliding doors? Wait—I see someone. Looks like a woman. Wow—I think she's waving—really fast. She stopped. Curtain was just closed.*

Marianna: *Sorry to interrupt. I just got an alert on my news feed. The police just raided one of Abila's houses in Cartagena where they think the women and children are being held. They received an anonymous tip.*

Rodrigo: *I got the feed too. I'm calling a friend to see what he knows. He's a cop.*

Jay: *Casey—tell me more.*

Casey: *Didn't see anyone else in room. But didn't really have chance to look.*

Jay: *Do you think the woman was waving at the men on the patio or trying to get attention for help.*

Casey: *Don't know.*

Jay: *We'll be there in a couple of minutes. Rodrigo let us know the minute you talk to your friend.*

Rodrigo: *Copy*

Stu: *You want us to stay here? Fly to hotel? Or move on foot to help at hotel?*

Jay: *Stay where you are. May need air support.*

Stu: *Copy*

Jay: *Rich, wait till we dock, then dock next to us. Everyone on Southern Star, stay put!*

Rich: *Copy*

Reid: *Copy that*

"Really?" Shane said, shaking her head.

"Oh, come on. I keep seeing it in their texts. I just wanted to say it myself."

Cindy and the kids laughed. Shane rolled her eyes.

"Okay, everyone," Rich bellowed. "We're going to need some help putting fenders out. Then I want you all to stay out of the way as we dock."

"Follow me everyone," Lauren said, then turned and hurried down the stairs to the lower deck. She pulled big, blue, inflated rubber fenders from various storage compartments. "Hook these," she explained, holding a leather encased, metal hook lined with sheep's wool on the interior side, "over the handrail at the spots I assign each of you."

Johnny approached and picked up the first fender.

"Port side rear," Lauren said in a serious tone.

"Aye aye, Captain Bligh," Johnny said, grinning.

Lauren chuckled as she pulled out another fender and handed it to Casey.

"Sorry you have to put up with him," Casey said. "I know how tough it can be."

"He's funny," she said.

"Ha," Johnny exclaimed, giving Casey a light push. "In your face, jerk."

"Well, I guess someone has to like you," Casey said with a laugh.

"I like him too, you big bully!" Samantha said, smiling.

"Me too," Chelsea added.

"So do I," Marianna said.

The smile on Johnny's face was priceless. Arms held wide, he hammed it up, saying, "Yeah, baby! Me and my girls! Come huddle up for a big hug, ladies."

"You had to take it one step too far, didn't you mate?" Chelsea remarked.

Casey laughed.

"Oh, come on, one quick group hug?" Johnny pleaded.

"Hug this!" Chelsea said, raising the fender she was holding.

Everyone laughed, even Johnny.

"Okay, that's enough," Lauren ordered. "Time to get serious. If you already have a fender, go place it where I told you. If not, grab one."

As they finished setting out the fenders, their phones all chirped.

Rodrigo: *Police raid revealed nothing.*

Rich pulled the yacht into a slip between the Barracuda and the other large, docked yacht, named, Otra Rebanada de Cielo.

"Wow, he's got two yachts!" Johnny said, standing on the dock. "How much money does this guy have?"

"Obviously, more than he knows what to do with," Joel answered, walking over to his son. "I'll bet he has more boats and other homes too."

"You think?" Johnny asked.

Joel shrugged. "Just guessing."

"Chances are, your dad is right, Johnny," Jay said, as he approached from the Barracuda. "We've already seen a bunch of Jose's properties. These guys have so much cash they don't know what to do with it all. But don't let it fool you, it's dirty, and it comes at a hefty price."

"What do you mean?" Johnny asked.

"You heard Marianna and Juan. They live in constant fear. They can't trust anyone."

"He's right," Marianna said, taking the big step from the yacht to the dock. "I would trade all our stuff in a minute, my Jeep, the big house, everything, just to have a normal life where I didn't always have to look over my shoulder."

"Yeah, it sucks," Juan agreed, vaulting over the yacht's handrail and landing on the dock with a loud thud.

Looking up at the building through binoculars from the mid-level deck of the yacht, Casey interrupted, "Hey, the two guys that were on the patio are gone. Did anyone see where they went?"

"They're a little tied up at the moment," Carlo said with a grin.

"What do you mean?" Johnny asked.

"He means that they came down here to pay us a visit, and we took care of them," Tzlil said as she and Sun approached from the Barracuda.

The kid's faces revealed shock and horror.

"Don't worry, we didn't kill them," Sun said. "They're sitting comfortably, down in the Barracuda's lower cabin. Bound and gagged, but comfortable." Sun turned to Jay. "I checked their phones. Neither sent any texts, emails or calls during the last hour."

"Good job," Jay said. "Okay, Carlo, Sun, go check around the building, one go around the left side, the other, the right, then, go in the front entrance and check the rooms on the second floor. Joel, Tzlil, we'll go in the rear entrance, by the pool. Casey, which room did you see the woman in?"

"Come with me, I'll show you." Casey turned and ran the length of the boat's outer deck toward the rear.

"Stay where you are, Casey," Jay ordered. "Just tell me which room it was."

Casey continued running down the steps to the lower deck, grabbed the railing and vaulted over it, just like Juan had. But, momentum got the better of Casey as he landed on his feet. He tucked and rolled nimbly on the dock, as he had done hundreds of times during his martial arts training. Luckily Carlo was close enough to grab a fist full of Casey's shirt just as he was about to go over the edge of the dock.

"Oh man," Johnny moaned, holding up his phone, catching everything on video. "Did you have to stop him, Carlo. This video would have gone viral in like a minute."

"I could drop him in, if you'd like?" Carlo grinned, holding Casey by his shirt at an awkward angle over the water, like a leaning tree.

"Enough, we have no time for this," Jay said sternly. "Casey, which room was it?"

Regaining his balance and composure, Casey answered, "I'll show you."

"No, you won't. Just tell me."

Casey's pleading puppy dog look annoyed Jay.

"Save the cute stuff for your parents and friends. You know it doesn't work with me."

"But—"

"Enough!" Jay said sharply. "Casey, this is no joke. These people are killers. Just tell me the room, and then I want you and everyone else to get back on the boat and stay inside. End of discussion."

"Third on the right from the rear pool entrance," Casey said in defeat.

Jay: *Stu, start the bird, but stay where you are. We are going into the building. Be prepared. Are you close enough to hear if shots are fired?*

Stu: *Not with the blades turning.*

Jay: *Right—dumb question. If there's gunfire, one of us will text you. Then, hover over hotel in case we need protection while getting women & kids back to boat. Rodrigo strap in near the opening with the automatic.*

Stu: *Copy*

Rodrigo: *Copy!*

Jay's eyes roamed the hotel property, then he typed.

Jay: *Correction. We need a distraction. We'll be open targets when we run from dock to building. Bring chopper now. Hover near front of building. Not too close—not too far.*

Rodrigo: *On our way.*

Moments later, they heard the reverberating sound of the helicopter's blades slashing the air. The team's eyes were glued on Jay, waiting for his signal.

When the chopper stilled itself above the parking lot just long enough to get the attention of anyone in the building, Jay yelled, "Go!"

Casey and the other kids stared out the windows in the lower rear salon while the adults who were still onboard made themselves comfortable in the mid-deck, main salon. Casey watched sullenly as the team dashed up the hill and split up just before reaching the pool.

"What's the matter?" Marianna asked.

"I hate it when they take over. We should be up there too." Casey's eyes never left the window.

"Are you crazy? You're not trained for that stuff."

"I know. But still, it's just not fair."

Marianna reached for Casey's hand. His face softened, and his pout converted into a slight smile.

All eyes except Samantha's were fixed on the building.

"Hey, look! There's someone in the window on that boat." She yelled, pointing at Abila's yacht.

They all looked.

"Which one?" Johnny asked

"Lowest row, middle window!"

"You're right," Chelsea said. "It's a woman. She looks scared."

"She's writing something on the window," Juan yelled.

"Quiet," Johnny said in a loud whisper. "We don't want the adults to know."

"Why?" Marianna asked.

"Because they won't let us go," Johnny explained. "They'll just text Jay, and he'll make us wait till they come back from the building."

"Exactly," Casey agreed.

"A-I-U-," Marianna read the letters as the woman continued to write. "Ew, I think she's writing with her own blood. It's red and dripping down the window."

"She's writing something backwards," Chelsea said.

"OTUIA," Johnny said. "What does that mean?"

"Oh my God, it's them," Samantha said. "AIUTO is help in Italian. She's writing it forward. It's backward from this side."

"Let's go. Be fast and be quiet," Casey said scurrying out and down to the dock.

Marianna, Johnny, Chelsea, Samantha, Juan and Antonio all chased after him.

"Wait," Chelsea whispered loudly. "What if there are armed guards on the boat?"

Casey looked at Antonio. "Pistola?"

Antonio nodded, reached behind his back, and brought out his gun.

"Oh, great. Now I feel much better." Chelsea's voice was drenched in sarcasm.

Before stepping from the dock to the boarding deck of the yacht, Casey turned back toward the group. "If any of you don't want to come, go back now. Everyone else, take off your shoes and socks. We need to keep quiet, but I don't want anyone to slip." He looked Antonio in the eye and waved him forward. "Keep your gun out and stay next to me."

Juan translated, and Antonio nodded.

Slowly and quietly, they followed Casey up to the next level and through a door that led into a large salon. The air conditioning was set very low. They walked around chrome-framed, white leather couches and chairs, and black enamel tables. Despite the extreme Caribbean heat, the white tile floor felt cold as ice.

Dark hair was visible over the top edge of a high back chair facing away from them. As Casey slowly moved toward the chair from behind, quiet, steady snoring grew louder and louder. Casey, Antonio, and Juan stopped abruptly as the man let out a loud snort, and then, as he adjusted his position, he released a loud fart. Casey grinned at Antonio and Juan, and held a finger to his lips. When the snoring resumed, Casey lowered himself to his knees and crept to the side of the chair.

He saw a handgun and a cell phone within reach on a black table. There were also two empty beer bottles and another with some beer in it. Peering further around the edge of the chair, Casey saw that the man's eyes were closed, and wireless earbuds hung from his ears. Casey picked up the gun and phone, then slowly backed away. Handing the gun to Juan, he whispered, "Stay here with the gun pointed at him. If he wakes up, make sure he stays put."

"What if he tries to get up?" Juan asked sheepishly.

"Shoot him in the knee, or foot, or something like that. I don't care. Just make sure that you scare him. Let him know you're serious."

"I don't want to shoot him," Juan said.

"Give me the gun," Marianna said as she approached with her hand held out, palm up.

"You're kidding, right?" Juan asked. "You won't shoot him."

"Give me the gun," she repeated. "He's holding kidnapped women and children hostage, and he's probably the one who just killed the men on the island. If he moves, I'll be happy to shoot him."

Johnny let out a quiet whistle through his teeth.

Juan handed Marianna the gun.

"Are you sure about this?" Casey asked.

"I'll be fine," Marianna said, taking a seat in the chair facing the sleeping man and pointing the gun at him. "Just hurry up."

"I'll stay with her," Samantha offered.

"Good," Casey said. "Okay, everyone else. Let's go find them."

Casey, Johnny, Chelsea, Juan and Antonio dashed across the room and down the nearest flight of stairs. Antonio clasped his gun with both hands at chest-height, ready to fire, while they rapidly checked each of the three staterooms and bathrooms.

"Where are they?" Johnny whispered, pointing at the wall in one of the rooms. "That's the window facing our boat. They should be right here."

"Unh-uh," Casey said. "Look out at the dock. The window we saw the women in was closer to the water and more forward than this one. There has to be another staircase that goes to the lower floor. Antonio, stay next to me."

"Quédate a su lado," Juan told Antonio.

Antonio nodded and climbed the steps next to Casey.

At the top of the steps Casey looked toward Marianna and Samantha. When he got their attention, he shook his head. He turned back toward Antonio, pointed forward and hustled through another doorway. They passed two open doors, then saw another staircase down. This one was much steeper, and its thin treads were only wide enough for one person. As Casey took the first step down, Antonio put his free hand on Casey's shoulder. Casey stopped and turned his head.

Antonio tapped his pistol barrel against his own chest, then pointed it down the steps.

"Are you sure?" Casey asked.

Antonio nodded, nudged Casey over and stepped down in front of him.

Carefully, they all followed Antonio. Gun raised, he turned the corner at the bottom of the tight staircase wall, and froze. Casey bumped into him.

Another man was lying on a bed just a few feet away. Fear surged through Casey, seeing the handle of the man's pistol slightly exposed under the corner of his rumpled pillow. Shifting his eyes, Casey expelled a sigh of relief. The man's eyes were closed.

A loud thud on an adjacent closed door caused the man to stir. As he rolled over, an empty liquor bottle rolled off the edge of the bed and hit the floor, luckily without breaking. The man's eyes sprang open. Adrenaline surging, Casey and Antonio rushed forward. Antonio pointed his gun at the man's face while Casey and the man simultaneously reached for the gun under the pillow. As Casey tightened his hand around the gun's handle, the man gripped Casey's wrist, and squeezed. Their faces were close as they struggled. Luckily for Casey, alcohol had dampened the guy's strength, but his boozy breath on Casey face was sickening. Casey pulled hard but felt his sweaty palm slipping from the grip. Repulsed by the smell and panicked that he'd lose the gun, Casey clenched his free fist and slammed it into the man's nose. They heard a crack, and the man's bloodshot eyes instantly widened. His intensely scary look sent a chill through Casey. Then, just as quickly as his eyes had flared, they closed, and his body went limp. With another burst of adrenaline, Casey pulled the gun from under the pillow, and along with Antonio they pointed their barrels at the man's head. Casey's hands were shaking.

Chelsea and Johnny ran to the door that the noise had come from. She reached for the handle and turned, but her sweaty palm slipped off. Johnny took a step back and loudly said, "Move away from the door."

He lunged forward with his leg raised and kicked his heel near the handle with all his might. Wood cracked, and the latch gave some, but the door remained closed. After regaining his balance, he placed his hand on the knob and slammed his shoulder into the door. This time the lock broke free from the splintered door jamb enough so that Johnny could slowly push the door open.

The two women were squatting in the far corner of the room with their backs against the wall. Both held their children tightly. All four were crying.

Chelsea rushed toward them. "Are you okay? We're here to help you."

Fear remained in their eyes. Their crying became louder as they cowered even tighter against the wall and each other.

"Aiuto," Johnny said, approaching slowly with a subtle smile.

Both women looked skeptically into Johnny's eyes. It took a moment for their fearful looks to soften. "Grazie," one of the women cried out softly.

"Grazie Dio," the other woman said, child in one arm, crossing herself with the other.

Johnny and Chelsea bent low and offered their hands. The women each took a hand and stood, still clutching their children. Tears continued to flow as Chelsea opened her arms and gave both women comforting hugs.

"We need to get them off the boat now," Johnny said.

Chelsea released her embrace, and backed away from the women. "Venire," she said, waving them toward the door.

Johnny followed, giving Casey a wink as they moved quickly out the door and toward the stairs. Casey smiled, and took a deep breath. He looked at Antonio and, with emphasizing hand gestures, said, "I'm going with them. You stay here with your gun on him. I'll send someone to help you. Okay?"

Antonio nodded, and Casey went up the stairs behind Johnny.

As Chelsea led the group through the main salon, Samantha gave her a smile. Casey thought he saw a slight smile on the face of the man in the chair, despite having Marianna's gun pointed at him.

"Samantha, you go with them," Casey said. "I'll stay here with Marianna."

"Why? I'm okay staying with her."

Casey held up his gun. "Cause I've got this, and you don't."

"That's good enough for me, mate."

Casey sat in the chair that Samantha had vacated and aimed his gun at the man.

Marianna smiled. "Thanks."

"I couldn't let you have all the fun. Besides, two guns are better than one, right?"

"Uh, yeah, I guess. But Alberto, here, won't give us a problem. He's actually happy that we're saving the women and kids."

"He told you that?"

"Uh-huh."

"So why was he guarding them?"

"Because when you work for someone like Abila, you do what you're told, whether you like it or not."

Casey nodded. "And when you say someone like Abila, you mean—"

"Yes, like my uncle too," Marianna finished his statement.

The loud stomping of approaching feet on the outer deck's stairs quieted them. The crash of breaking glass as the French doors swung open too hard and fast made everyone cringe. Joel, Sun, Tzlil, and Jay entered the salon with guns pointed in the kid's direction. "Are you alright?" Joel asked loudly.

"Yup. You should check on Antonio. He's back that way." Casey pointed backwards with his thumb. "Go down the stairs. He's holding another guy at gunpoint in the crew's cabin."

"Anyone else on board?" Sun asked.

Casey's eyes widened. "We never checked."

"Joel, Sun, go search the boat," Jay said. "Tzlil, stay with Casey and Marianna. I'll go help Antonio."

Minutes later, the men walked back into the salon. Antonio was helping Jay drag the other guard, leaving a trail of blood that was gushing from the guard's broken nose.

"Antonio told me this was your work," Jay said to Casey, gesturing toward the man's face.

"You did that?" Marianna asked. Casey shrugged with a slight nod.

"Did you hit him with the gun?"

"No."

"What did you use? He's a mess."

"Just this." Casey raised his fist.

"Really?"

Casey nodded.

With a nudge of her gun, Tzlil convinced Casey's and Marianna's prisoner to stand and walk out with everyone. Marianna followed them, with Casey next in line and Jay at the end.

Jay leaned over Casey's shoulder. "Dude, you've got a keeper. Not only is she cute and tough, but most girls hate it when their boyfriend hits another guy. She thought it was cool!"

"Will you be quiet," Casey whispered. "She can hear you, ya know."

"No, she can't," Jay said with a chuckle.

Marianna's giggle caused Casey to blush.

***

Twelve minutes later, the water below the Southern Star churned as the last of the lines was detached from its cleat on the dock, and the yacht slowly reversed. The rescued women were bathing their children in two of the staterooms. Abila's two men were securely bound, cuffed and locked in the captain's quarters. Sitting in the wheelhouse, Jay was making calls, sending emails, and texting those who needed to know about the successful rescue.

Tito was at the helm of the Barracuda, floating idly nearby in the still waters of the harbor. Carlo stood alert and ready, behind the port side gun stanchion with his eyes locked on the hotel property, scanning for any sign of trouble.

The loud, throaty engines of the cigarette growled steadily behind the Southern Star with Antonio seated next to Juan, who was at the wheel. Both were laughing as their heads shuddered slightly against the vibrating headrests while they waited to follow the larger yacht out of the harbor. With Carita's help, Juan and Marianna had convinced Jay that taking back Jose's cigarette might help reduce his upcoming tirade. He was going to be furious with them when he found out that his entire day was just a setup to get him out of the way. He was not one to be scammed.

It wasn't that the race boat really meant that much to him amongst all his possessions, but it would be one less infuriating factor among many. He was going to be upset with Luna for lying and keeping him away for the whole day. He would be furious with Juan, Marianna, Carita and Antonio for rallying against him. He would be beside himself now that his relationship with Tamara had been uncovered. And finally, of course, there was Abila.

So many things were yet unknown. Had Abila taken the women and children from the island where Jose had been holding them? Or, was Abila responsible for the kidnapping in the first place? Did Jose have anything to do with it at all?

There were many questions that needed answers. But first, the women and children needed to be returned to the men who loved them. Then there was a World Cup Championship game to attend.

Chapter 30

The World Cup Match

THE CORNER KICK was on target. Although not the tallest player in the pushing and shoving melee in front of the Italian goal, Arnaldo's vertical leap rivaled that of many NBA players. It was as if he had springs in his muscular legs. Not only was his head towering above his defender's at the peak of his jump, but his timing was absolutely perfect. He snapped his forehead toward the goal just as the ball made contact. It careened off his head like a bullet and rocketed past the goalie's reach into the upper right corner of the net.

"Gooooaaallllllll!" The long bellow from the announcer was mimicked by half of the fans in the stadium. Outside the arena, in fact, throughout Cartegena and most of Latin America, horns honked, and people cheered on the streets.

With only twelve seconds left in regulation time, the goal drove the crowd into hysteria. If ever there had been a perfect matchup of two teams in a championship, this was it. The entire game had been fierce. As the clock ticked off the last seconds, sending the game into overtime, the stadium was bustling. Adrenaline surged through players and fans alike. Aggressive shoves on the field were benign compared to the flare-ups in the stands. Fights had to be stopped by security guards everywhere.

Luckily, Casey, Johnny, and their rescue team colleagues were sitting field-side, far from any of the clashes in the bleachers.

Prior to the game, when the news of the rescue had gone public, the group had been swarmed by the media. Casey, Johnny, Samantha, and Chelsea were worldwide heroes once again. Of course, Marianna, Juan, Antonio, Carita, and Luna were too, but they needed to avoid the limelight, at least until Jose's fury waned.

For some reason, there was much more fanfare and publicity now than there had been after the Australian Olympic gymnast rescue. It seemed that everyone involved in the World Cup Championship was looking to show their gratitude; Italy, Argentina, Colombia, the South American Futbol Confederation, and even FIFA wanted to congratulate the young crime fighters. And, of course, the USA felt the need to be in on the action. After all, the boys were now two-time American heroes.

Everyone they came in contact with wanted to shake their hands or hug them. People were even showering them with gifts.

Earlier, during halftime, Casey had joined his dad and Jay as they went to the bathroom. Walking under fluorescent lights in the crowded, concrete stadium hallway, a thin, slightly hunched older man with a cane approached the trio. He held out a $100 bill to Casey and said, "Grazie, figlio."

Surprised, as he accepted it, Casey looked at his father for guidance. Reid shook his head, but as Casey reached to place it back in the elderly Italian man's wrinkled hand, Jay quietly interrupted, "Keep it, Casey. Not only did you earn it, but you'll offend this nice gentleman if you give it back. Just put it in your pocket and thank him."

Receiving a conceding nod from his dad, Casey smiled and said, "Thank you."

"No, no," said the old man with a smile and a wave of his gnarled finger toward Casey. "You deserve it." He patted Casey's shoulder, then turned and subtly winked at Jay before hobbling away. His worn, wooden cane produced a rhythmic tap with each labored step.

Casey and Reid both looked at Jay with questioning eyes. "You know him?" Casey asked.

"Fuhgeddaboudit," Jay said with a slight grin.

Casey's and Reid's eyes shifted curiously from Jay to each other.

"Wait," Casey said. "Are you saying he's—"

Jay put his palms up. "I said forget about it, and I meant it. Just put the money in your pocket, and let's go."

"Jay." Reid's voice was laden with concern. "If he's in the mafia, I don't want Casey taking his money."

"Did I say anything about the mafia? But, now that you mention it, if he is connected, you absolutely would not want to turn down his gift."

Casey looked at his father, who shrugged again and said, "I guess we'll open a bank account for you. You'll share it with Johnny, Samantha, and Chelsea, right?"

With an ear-to-ear smile, Casey said, "Of course, I will. Can we open the account in the name of our business?"

"I don't see why not. What is it?"

"Johnny said it should be Casey's Cases, but I decided it should be Cajosach Investigations."

"Cajo what?" Reid asked.

"Cajosach, it's the first two letters of each of our names."

"Hm, Cajosach," Reid said. "It doesn't roll off the tongue as easily as Casey's Cases, but I'm proud of you. You always seem to do the right thing, lately." He wrapped his arm over Casey's shoulders and pulled him into a tight yet playful headlock.

Casey grimaced. "Ow. Dad. Stop!"

"I love you, Bud!"

Casey smiled. "I love you, too."

A series of clicks caused Reid to release Casey and turn toward the photographer who had appeared out of nowhere. "Please don't," Reid said calmly.

"Sorry, Mr. Clark, but Casey is hot news right now. Might as well get used to it, at least for a while. But don't worry, the word is out to go easy on him. We all know how you get when photographers push you too far."

Jay snickered. "Sounds like they've got you pegged, Reid."

"Hey, I only snap when they get too aggressive."

"Don't worry, Dad. A few pictures might be good for Cajosach business."

"Listen to you, my young entrepreneur." Reid re-clenched his arm around Casey's neck. They heard more rapid clicks. Reid turned his head slightly toward the photographer and gave him the stink eye.

The photographer lowered his camera, raised two fingers in a V, and quietly said, "Peace." Then he backed away and disappeared into the nearby crowd.

Reid looked at Casey. "Guess it's your turn for fame now. Better get used to it."

"Get used to it? It's cool."

"Nice to know that at least one of the Clark men is reasonable," Jay said. "As far as the paparazzi are concerned, anyway."

"That's not fair, Jay. You know it's different for Dad. He's so famous they hound him everywhere he goes. But it's all new for me, and if the publicity brings in business for my team, all the better."

Jay furrowed his brow. "Isn't your team part of my team?"

Casey took a moment to think. "Well, yeah, we'll still work with you. But I think we'll work some on our own too. I guess we'll evaluate it case by case."

"Oh, we will, will we?" Jay smirked. "So you get to pick and choose when you need me and when you don't?"

Casey frowned and thought for a moment. "No. Well, maybe."

"Really?" Jay scowled. "Getting a little full of yourself, aren't you?" He shook his head.

"I didn't realize it would make you mad. I'm sorry."

The corners of Jay's lips rose just a touch.

"Oh, you're just busting my chops."

Jay smiled and nodded.

"You're a jerk."

***

Half the stadium ignited in a frenzy as Sauro's kick sent the ball in a fast arching flight just past the gloved fingertips of Argentina's goalkeeper. The decibel level doubled as the ball smacked into the white, metal, top post and ricocheted up into the stands behind the goal.

The near-miss was Italy's second, compared to one for Argentina during overtime play. There were only four minutes left of the second, fifteen-minute half. Although a game-winning goal could be scored at any moment, murmurs throughout the stadium were now of the pending shootout.

Johnny leaned toward Casey to say something, the greasy kabob Johnny was eating came way too close for Casey's comfort.

"Yuck. Keep that thing away from me."

"Sorry."

"The meat looks weird. What is it?"

"I don't know, but Colombians love it."

"How come I haven't seen anyone else eating it?"

"I don't know."

"How did you know they love it?"

"Because there was a heart next to its description on the menu board."

"What's it called?"

"Corazo or something like that."

"Corazon?" Samantha asked from Johnny's other side.

"Yeah, that's it."

"Ew, that's gross." Samantha stuck her finger in her open mouth.

"Why, what is it?" Johnny asked.

"Heart! You're eating a heart."

"Oh, that's so gross," Casey said.

Johnny held the skewered meat up and inspected it closely. After a moment of skeptical contemplation, he shrugged and took another bite. "It's pretty good."

Samantha returned Casey's horrified look.

The crowd screamed as an Argentinian player was tripped from behind and fell hard just as the overtime clock hit 00.00. The yellow penalty flag was retrieved by the ref who had thrown it, and he and his colleagues gathered at the sideline to review the play. As the refs stepped back on the field and announced their decision, the stadium erupted once again. The shootout was about to commence!

Johnny leaned in towards Casey and said, "I hate shootouts."

"What?" Casey raised his arms, palms up.

"I said, I hate shootouts!" Johnny yelled, way too close to Casey's ear.

Casey pushed him away.

"Don't push me!"

"Don't scream in my ear!"

"Dude, you just said you couldn't hear me."

Casey looked skyward and shook his head.

"Shootouts stink!" Johnny said.

Casey rolled his eyes. "I guess you're not going to let this go. Okay, tell me, why do you hate shootouts?"

"Well, I don't really hate them. Actually, they're kinda cool, but a game shouldn't be decided based on penalty kicks. I mean a shootout contest can be exciting, but…"

Casey was watching the field as both teams gathered in front of their respective benches.

"Hey, are you even listening to me?" Johnny asked, knocking his knee hard into Casey's thigh.

"Stop it, you jerk. What's the matter with you?"

"Me? You asked me a question then didn't even listen to my answer."

With his eyes glued on the five men from each team making their way back onto the field, Casey raised his palm toward Johnny's face. "Can you just be quiet until this is over?"

"But—"

Hand still held high, Casey leveled four fingers together horizontally with his thumb hanging at an angle under them. He then snapped them together like an alligator's mouth. "Just watch without talking for a few minutes, please."

Johnny sneered and returned his eyes to the field.

One by one, five players from each team took turns shooting on goal. Pandemonium grew throughout the stadium with every shot.

The shootout score was now 3-2 in favor of Argentina. The goalies had blocked one shot each. Sauro was next up for Italy, with Marrese taking their last shot and Arnaldo would be Argentina's final shooter.

Looking and leaning left as he moved toward the ball, Sauro fired his shot to the right. Reading his body language, just as Sauro had intended, Argentina's goalie dove to his right as the ball flew, unobstructed, into the opposite rear corner of the net. Tied at 3-3, the entire game was now riding on the shoulders of Marrese, Arnaldo, and the goalies. As Arnaldo stood facing Italy's goalie, they both, almost simultaneously, raised their hands to their foreheads and crossed themselves. Inspired by the players, hands everywhere throughout the stadium mimicked the ritual.

As Arnaldo took his first step toward the ball, the crowd hushed. The ball left his foot like a gunshot, and the goalkeeper read the shot perfectly. He leapt high to his right. The ball hit the goalie's fingertips, careened further right, banged into the goal post, and into the goal.

Arnaldo screamed while his fists punched wildly at the air. He turned and ran, dropping down for a long knee slide, right into the center of his cheering fellow players. Their celebration quieted quickly as Marrese placed the ball in front of the goal and prepared for his shot.

If he scored, Marrese's goal would extend the shootout into a sudden death finish. A miss would give Argentina the win. With the weight of his nation laying heavily on his shoulders, Marrese held his head high and took a few steps back. He then stood, looking from ball to goal and back again. The crowd watched as he drew a deep breath and blew it out while rubbing his hands together in front of his face. Finally, he lowered his hands, took one last look at the goal, then focused on the ball as he took a few quick steps and gave it the kick of his life.

His shot was almost a duplicate of Arnaldo's. The goalie's reaction was similar too. But this time, redirected by the goalkeeper's fingers, the ball sailed to the right, outside the post, missing the goal completely. Marrese fell to his knees and buried his face in his hands, as did many of his teammates.

Arnaldo and his shootout team colleagues were hoisted onto the shoulders of their screaming teammates.

Jubilated Central and South Americans hugged, screamed, and danced throughout the stadium while downtrodden Italian fans slowly exited with heads hung low, many in tears.

"Hey, look who's coming," Casey said.

"Arnaldo. How cool," Marianna said.

"Why would he bother with us in the middle of the team's celebration?" Johnny asked.

"Wait, look who he's with," Chelsea said.

Flanking Arnaldo on his right, blocked from view by other players, coaches, and journalists, were Erminio Marrese and Leonardo Sauro. As the three superstars' destination became apparent, the surrounding media pushed their way over to capture the moment.

"Here they are," Arnaldo said to Marrese and Sauro, sweeping his arm down the aisle. "Your rescue team." Arnaldo gave the kids a quick wave, then dashed back to his teammates.

Marrese and Sauro made their way down the line, hugging and thanking each member of the rescue team. Photographers and TV film crews caught everything as tears streamed heavily down the two men's faces.

When they finished thanking everyone, Sauro walked back to Casey. "You're Casey, right?"

Casey nodded.

"From what I've seen on the news, you are the leader of this team, yes?"

"Well, not really. My team is part of—"

"How do you like that, he's not only the leader, he's humble too," Marrese interrupted, stepping next to Sauro.

"I'm sorry about the game," Casey said.

"Thanks, Casey. But although losing hurts," Marrese said. "What you and your friends gave us put things in perspective for me. The past few days have been very difficult. It made me realize that my wife and child are my life. Losing them would be like having my heart ripped out. I didn't realize it until now, but I've always placed soccer ahead of my family. I'll never do that again. Family always comes first."

"Yes," Sauro agreed. "This whole thing has changed me too. I realized that I can live without soccer, but not without my family."

"Wait, you guys aren't going to quit playing, are you?" Casey asked.

The camera clicking stopped, the TV cameras zoomed in, and microphones were shoved closer to the men. Then, all activity around them completely stopped—waiting for their answer.

Marrese and Sauro looked at each other in silence. When they turned back toward Casey, Marrese let out a boisterous laugh as Sauro exclaimed, "Us quit? Never!" The men's infectious laughter spread quickly through the rescue team, and others in the immediate area.

Cameras clicked away as the two men pulled Casey in for a tight, three-way hug.

Chapter 31

THE FOLLOWING EVENING, stretch limousines were sent to bring the rescue team to Argentina's team celebration.

While Johnny worked hard on making a dent in the buffet table's offerings, Casey, Samantha, and Chelsea posed for umpteen pictures with the players. The media spent almost as much time with the rescuers as they did with the soccer players.

The rescue squad left the party early to attend a ceremony that team Italy and other Italian officials were holding in their honor. The adults rode in one limo, the kids in another.

A few minutes into the ride, Chelsea looked up from her phone and said, "I posted some of the pictures we just took on our CAJOSACH Instagram and Facebook pages.

"Since when do we have those?" Johnny asked

"Sam and I created both pages this afternoon, after Casey told us about CAJOSACH. I thought you guys would be excited. They're both blowing up."

"What did you name them?" Johnny asked, looking at his phone.

"Just CAJOSACH. CAJOSACH Investigations was too long. I wanted to keep them short and simple."

"CAJOSACH is simple?" Johnny chuckled. "I mean, I guess it'll catch on, but simple? No way! Casey's Cases would have been simple."

"Hey, don't knock it," Samantha said. "Casey named it for our benefit. The more you say it, the easier it gets, anyway."

"Cajosach, cajosach, casojach," Johnny repeated. "Nope, it's not working. Maybe we should hold a tongue twister contest. Anyone that can say it three times fast wins."

"Hm, that may be a good idea," Samantha said. "We'll get people to post videos of themselves trying to say it. It'll be funny, and it should bring more people to both sites."

"I was kidding. That sounds ridiculous," Johnny said. "CAJOSACH is a business, it should be serious."

Casey laughed. "Ha, now that's ridiculous. We laugh at everything, even serious stuff most of the time."

"Yeah, I guess. But I still think the contest sounds dumb."

"Oh, stop complaining," Chelsea said.

"Whatever!" Johnny's eyes went back to his phone. "Holy cow! This last shot of the four of us with Arnaldo has like 1200 likes already."

"You see. It's working," Chelsea said. "When I posted the first few pictures today, I tagged each of us. Oh yeah, Casey, I also tagged your dad. That's probably helping the page also. He won't get mad, will he?"

All eyes went toward Casey when he didn't answer. He was gazing out the window, not paying any attention to them. Johnny and the girls looked at each other and shrugged.

"Hey," Johnny nudged Casey lightly. "You okay?"

"Hm," Casey said, turning to see them all looking at him. "What?"

"What were you thinking about?" Samantha asked.

"Nuthin'"

"Oh sure," Chelsea said coyly. "It's Marianna, right?"

Casey nodded.

"Yeah, mate," Samantha added, "She should be here with us. Juan and Antonio too."

"And Diego, Luna, and Carita, also," Chelsea said.

"Yeah," Johnny said. "We were all in this together."

"I just hope Jose isn't too mad at them," Casey said. "They were all kind of scared when we left them."

"It's gotta be so tough to live that way," Chelsea said.

"I wonder if Jose had anything to do with the kidnapping," Casey said. "If he did, it's going to be really bad for them. But even if he didn't, he's still going to feel betrayed. It's going to be bad, either way."

"Yeah, you're right," Samantha said.

"Well," Johnny said. "Not to be mean or anything, but there's nothing we can do about it right now, so why don't we talk more about CAJOSACH. It'll help take your mind off them."

"Casey, take a look at our pages on Instagram and Facebook," Chelsea said. "The picture of you with Arnaldo is going crazy."

"Whoa!" Casey said, looking at his phone. "That's so bad. I look like a total dork."

"That's not what all the girls are saying, Dude." Johnny let out a silly guffaw. "Look at the comments. Adorable, cute, gorgeous. Wait, oh, you gotta see this one." He passed his phone to Samantha.

"They're talking about Arnaldo," Casey said. "Girls love him."

"Nope, they're talking about you, mate." Samantha laughed. "This one says, 'Casey can investigate me anytime!' And Casey, she's beautiful and very exotic looking. She's Hawaiian."

"Look at you," Johnny said. "You've got a Colombian girl and now a Hawaiian. Aren't you a man of the world." Johnny, Samantha, and Chelsea cracked up.

"Oh, shut up!" Casey said, grinning and reaching for Johnny's phone. His eyes lit up when he clicked on the Hawaiian girl's comment and it took him to her page.

"Told you!" Johnny said.

Casey scrolled down, looking at the screen.

"Can I have my phone back?" Johnny asked.

"Oh, sorry." Casey handed Johnny his phone. His tone became serious as he said to Chelsea and Samantha, "The pages are really good. Nice work."

"They'll probably start bringing in some business once the hype dies down. We all need to start responding to the comments. The more personal we make it, the better."

"Like, how personal do you mean, lover boy?" Johnny asked with a smirk.

"Will you shut up!" Casey snarled. "That's not what I meant, and you know it."

"Alright, take it easy. I was just kidding."

"Well, stop."

"Fine."

"Hey, look," Chelsea said. "Here's a comment from a guy that says, 'I need to hire you guys.'"

"Wow! Really?" Samantha said.

"Yeah." Chelsea clicked onto the guy's Facebook page. "It's a guy in Florida. He looks like he's around twenty-five."

"Well, that's good," Johnny said. "He's old enough to have a job, so at least he should have some money. I mean we're not going to work for free, right?"

"I guess that will depend on who's asking, where they live, and what they need," Casey said.

They all nodded.

"You better update our profile to say, please PM or email all business requests," Casey said. "We'll evaluate and respond ASAP. I guess we need to set up an email account now too. Let's keep it simple."

"Already done. It's cajosach at gmail." Chelsea said with a smile.

"Wow," Casey said. "I'm impressed. I guess we know who the business manager should be."

"We'll need a phone number, too," Samantha said. "Should we get a dedicated phone?"

"I think we better wait and figure out everything we need before we buy anything," Casey said.

"Yeah, and I think we should tell our parents about this first, right?" Johnny said.

"Yup," Casey agreed. "And we'll need a piglet."

"Wait, what? A piglet?" Johnny asked.

"You mean like Izzy, right?" Chelsea said, smiling.

"Exactly. If you think we're getting likes now, post a few pictures of Syd, our mascot, and people will go nuts."

"Great idea," Samantha said.

"Syd?" Chelsea asked.

"Yeah. It's short for Sydney, where the four of us met."

"I love it," Samantha said.

"Me too," Chelsea agreed, typing on her phone. "Oh, how cute! Here's a website called Teacup Piggies. Look at them. They are so adorable."

"How much are they?" Johnny asked.

"Oh, look how cute they are," Samantha crooned.

"How much?" Johnny repeated.

"They really are cute," Casey said.

"Okay, okay, they're cute. Now, how much do they cost?" Johnny demanded.

"Chill, mate," Chelsea said. "They're around $1000."

"Oh, that's all," Johnny blurted sarcastically.

"What?" Chelsea said, looking at Johnny's frown.

"They're cute, and I agree, it would help build our following on any social media site, but we don't have any money."

"True," Samantha said sullenly.

"Well, we have this." Casey pulled the $100 from his pocket and explained about the old Italian man.

"That's so cool," Johnny said. "Our first official payment. We should frame it."

"Frame it?" Casey said. "I think we should put it in the bank."

"Definitely," agreed Chelsea.

"We need to make a To-Do list," Casey said.

"You mean like this?" Chelsea said, holding up her phone for them all to see.

<u>CAJOSACH INVESTIGATIONS</u>
1. Buy Syd, the pig—mascot/marketing

"Nice. Add open bank account as number two," Casey said.

"Number three should be, get business cards," Johnny said.

"And if we're going to have business cards, we all need titles. Make that number four," Samantha said.

"Titles will be easy," Johnny said. "Let's just do that now. Obviously, Casey is President."

The girls nodded.

"Okay, Mr. President," Samantha said with a giggle. "Your first job as head of CAJOSACH is to give us our titles."

Casey smiled. "Alright, give me a second." After a moment, he added, "What do you think of this. Picture it on a business card. The top line is Chelsea D'Agostino. Next line, Vice President. Then, the next line should be, Investigations/COO/General Manager."

Casey noticed Johnny's smile disappear, so he quickly added, "Johnny's should say, Johnny Rebah. Next line, Vice President. Next line, Investigations/Secretary."

Johnny smiled, then frowned again. "Secretary?"

Casey said, "Okay, forget secretary. Make it Investigations/ CFO."

"What's that?" Johnny asked.

"Chief Financial Officer," Samantha said.

"Cool." Johnny's smile returned. "What about Samantha?"

"Samantha Westmoreland, Vice President, Investigations/CMO"

"CMO?" Johnny asked.

"Chief Marketing Officer. I like that," Samantha said.

"Good," Casey said. "Now that that's settled let's go have some fun."

"Fun?" Chelsea said. "Are you serious, Mate? We're going to a boring ceremony. It's not going to be fun."

"Yeah," Samantha said. "But I bet we'll get some more great pictures to post."

Johnny nodded. "And maybe we'll get more reward money. That would make it fun!"

"Spoken like true marketing and financial officers," Casey exclaimed.

Samantha and Johnny were beaming proudly as the limo pulled up to the entrance of another hotel.

Barraged by camera flashes and microphones, they politely made their way through the media onslaught to the main doors, where the adult portion of the rescue team awaited.

Once inside, they followed a red carpet path to the end of an ornately appointed hallway where two men slowly opened oversized, French-style, mahogany doors. Silence within the tremendous ballroom was instantly broken by raucous applause as soon as the group stepped inside. The red carpet was centered between two rows of dress-suit adorned Italian players. Maresse and Sauro, along with their wives and children, were facing the rescue team at the end of the line. Behind them stood their coaches and managers, Italy's and Colombia's presidents, the presidents of FIFA and the Italian Futbol Federation, Cartagena's mayor, and some other government officials.

After lots of handshakes and hugs, everyone sat. Maresse, Sauro, and their families, as well as the four presidents, and the mayor, were seated on the podium behind the lectern. The rescuers, the Italian team, the media, and the other guests took seats in the rows of chairs facing the stage.

The ceremony was brief and extremely emotional. Each of the presidents thanked the rescue team for saving the women and children. After their speeches, they asked Casey to approach the lectern. Each shook his hand and gave him an envelope.

Maresse, Sauro, and their wives each said a few words and handed Casey envelopes as well.

As Sauro put his envelope in Casey's hand, he leaned in close and quietly said, "I can't thank you enough for what you've done. You and your friends are doing great work. I read about the gymnast you saved. I wanted to give you more than what's in the envelope, but I was asked not to. I put a note with my cell number in with the check. Please call me if you need more money in order to help others. I really want to give more."

"Thank you very much, Mr. Sauro."

"It's my pleasure, Casey, and please, call me Leonardo."

"Okay."

Sauro's wife approached, holding their daughter in one arm and a black nylon duffel bag with an embroidered FIGC logo, in the other. She handed Casey the bag and hugged him.

"What's this?" Casey asked, looking at the bag.

"Official team jerseys for your whole group," she said.

"Wow, thank you!"

"This one is especially for you, though," Sauro said, handing Casey the jersey he had worn during the championship game."

Casey's eyes widened. "Really?"

"Why don't you put it on and join us for a family picture."

Casey quickly threw the jersey on over his shirt. He pulled a Sharpie marker from his pocket and held it out to Sauro. "Would you mind signing it?"

As Sauro signed the jersey he said, "Looks better on you than it did on me. I hope it works better for you too," He then put one arm over Casey's shoulders and his other around his wife. The frenzy of clicks and flashes multiplied as Maresse joined them with his wife and son.

***

Back in the limo on the way to their hotel, as Chelsea was digging through the bag of jerseys, looking for the number she wanted, Samantha swiped and tapped on her phone. "Now that should bring in like a zillion likes and followers." She raised her phone and showed them all the pictures she posted of Casey with the Sauros and Marreses.

"Dude, you are so lucky," Johnny said. "I can't believe Sauro gave you his game jersey. You know what it's worth?"

Casey smiled and reached for another bag that had been given to him. "Probably about the same as this one." He pulled Marrese's game jersey out of the plastic bag and tossed it to Johnny. "Put it on. Let's see what it looks like on you."

"Wait. Are you giving this to me?"

"We're in this thing together, right?"

"Wow, you bet!" Johnny's smile was ear to ear as his head poked through the neck of the jersey.

"Move closer together, you two. I want to post a picture with the jerseys on," Samantha said, holding her phone up.

The girls also put on jerseys. They all took turns posing, snapping pictures, and posting them.

"Oh my God!" Casey blurted out as he opened one of the envelopes he'd received. His eyes were huge as he stared at a check, took a deep breath, and repeated, "Oh my God."

"Tell us already," Johnny begged. "How much is it? Bet ya it's like a thousand bucks, right?"

"Try fifty," Casey said in disbelief.

"That's it, fifty bucks?" Johnny asked.

Casey slowly shook his head, looking like he was in a trance. "Fifty thousand," he said quietly.

"What?" Samantha shrieked.

"You heard me. Leonardo Sauro gave us a check for fifty thousand dollars."

"Oh my God," Chelsea said. "That's crazy!"

"Yeah, and totally awesome," Johnny said. "Open the others."

With trembling hands, Casey handed them each an envelope.

They opened them simultaneously.

"This one's for twenty-five thousand from FIFA," Samantha said.

"We got the same from FIGC," Chelsea said.

"And also from the Dipartimento del Tesoro," Johnny said slowly.

"That's the Italian Treasury," Chelsea said. "That's pretty cool."

"Oh wow, Marrese gave us fifty grand too," Casey said. "That's $175,000. And I forgot to tell you, when Leonardo handed me his envelope, he whispered that he had wanted to give us more but was asked not to." Casey pulled Sauro's note out of the envelope and held it up. "He gave me his cell number and said if we need more money to help save people, I should just call him."

"That's sick," Johnny said.

"I guess we've got enough to buy Syd now," Samantha said.

They all laughed.

"Do you think we can keep it?" Johnny asked.

"I don't know. We'll have to ask our parents and Jay," Casey said. "Some of it will probably have to cover the expenses from the rescue."

"I thought the boats were loaned to us," Chelsea said.

"Yeah, but I don't know about the helicopter. And what about the flights and hotel expenses for Jay and his team?"

"Ohh," Samantha moaned with a pout.

"Don't worry, there will be plenty left," Chelsea said. "If they let us keep it, that is."

"Well, we'll find out soon enough," Casey said, looking at the text they all just received from Jay as their limo pulled up to their hotel.

"Oh man," Johnny complained. "Another meeting? That sucks!"

"He says it'll be quick," Chelsea said.

"Oh sure," Casey said. "A quick meeting for Jay is like an hour."

"Ugh," Samantha groaned.

After another frenzied round of paparazzi photographs, the group walked into the hotel. As they made their way through the lobby, a twenty-something-year-old girl wearing a Team Argentina polo shirt approached. "Hi, Casey. These are for you and your friends from Arnaldo and the team." She handed him a duffel similar to the one he received from the Italians but much bigger. "And this one is specifically for you." She handed him a small, wrinkled, brown paper bag.

"Thank you," Casey said with a smile.

As she walked away, he opened the paper bag, brought it close to his face, and looked in. "Oh man, that stinks." Cameras clicked away, catching his hilarious expression as he looked up from the bag,

"What is it?" Johnny asked amidst all the laughter.

"Must be his unwashed game jersey," Casey said, putting his finger in his open mouth. Again the cameras clicked away.

"I guess he saw the posts of us wearing Italy's jerseys. Let's look in the other bag.

"Go ahead, I'm not opening that one!" Casey said squeamishly.

Chelsea bent down, unzipped the big bag, and rifled through the contents. "Wow, lots more jerseys and some warm-up jackets and hats. She held a jersey up to her nose. "Nice and clean."

"Toss me a jersey, will you, Chelsea?" Casey said.

Casey caught the jersey and walked away from the group, over to a young boy in a wheelchair, holding his father's hand. Casey had noticed the boy watching him with wide eyes and a crooked smile. Lowering himself to his knees, Casey said, "Hi, what's your name."

The boy's expression became pained as he tried to speak.

"Julio," said his father. "His name is Julio, but he can't speak. He's very sick."

Casey nodded, and his eyes went from the father back to Julio. "Hi Julio, my name is Casey. It's nice to meet you. Here, I have something for you." Casey offered the jersey to Julio, but instead of Julio reaching for it, his dad leaned over and helped Casey put it in Julio's lap. Casey noticed that Julio's wrists were bent awkwardly inward.

"He has muscular dystrophy. He has no control of his muscles, so he can't move his arms very well," the father said.

"I'm so sorry."

"Sorry? Casey, you just made him happier than he's probably ever been in his life. We're from Argentina and he, well…we, are big fans of our team. Earlier, when I asked him if he wanted to go back home so we could attend the team's parade tomorrow, he said no, much to my surprise. Instead, he wanted to come here to see you and your friends. He was very impressed with the way you saved the women and children. I think you may have just taken Arnaldo's place as his hero."

Julio made a noise, and when Casey looked at him, he was trying hard to nod at Casey.

"Can I give him a hug?" Casey asked.

"Of course, you can," Julio's father said.

Casey leaned over, putting one arm around Julio's shoulder and his other arm lightly across the boy's chest. After a brief hug, Casey slowly stood and saw a woman and a young girl at the father's side.

"Casey, this is my wife, Marguerite, and Julio's sister, Sofia. My name is Julio also."

After shaking their hands, Casey turned toward Johnny, Chelsea, and Samantha. He waved them over, saying, "Bring the bags."

After introductions, Casey reached into the bag, removed two jerseys, and handed them to Sofia and Marguerite. Then, he reached for the brown paper bag and removed Arnaldo's game jersey. He bent down to Julio and said, "Julio, this is the jersey Arnaldo wore in today's game. I want you to have it. Just don't smell it. It stinks!"

As everyone laughed, Casey put the jersey on Julio's lap, removed the one he had given him earlier, and handed it to Julio's father.

"Sorry to interrupt, but we need to go," said Casey's dad, who had walked over. Casey said, "This is my father, Reid—"

"I know who he is," Julio senior interrupted, with his eyes bulging. Julio took a deep breath. "Excuse me, Mr. Clark. I am a little overwhelmed at the moment. I am a big fan of yours."

"Very nice to meet you," Reid said. "I don't mean to be rude, but we have to get to a meeting."

"Can we please get a picture with all of you before you go?" Julio said.

"Of course," Reid said.

As they bunched together for a few quick shots, Marguerite said to Reid and Casey. "You have made our family's day. Mr. Clark, you wouldn't believe how big a fan of yours my husband is. He cried when you were shot years ago."

"Really? Me too," Reid said with a touch of sarcasm.

"And Casey, what you just did for our son with your hug and giving him Arnaldo's jersey. I don't know how to put it into words," she said with a sniffle. "You just gave a boy with an incurable disease the thrill of his life."

Casey smiled. "Are you staying in this hotel?"

"No," she said. "We could never afford this. We are staying with friends."

"Oh." Casey turned to his father and said, "Can you give me just a minute, Dad?"

"Sure."

Casey turned to the Cajosach team, "Why don't you all go to the meeting. I'll be there in a second."

"Fine," his father said. "But hurry, everyone is waiting. We're meeting in one of the conference rooms on the second floor. I'll leave the door open so you can find us."

"Thanks. I'll be quick, I promise."

As Reid, Johnny, Samantha, and Chelsea walked away, Casey swiped and tapped the screen of his phone. A moment later, Arnaldo joined him on Facetime. "Hi, Arnaldo. Thanks so much for the jerseys."

"Glad you liked them, but, I must admit, it was kind of selfish."

"Selfish? How?"

"When the team saw your posts with Italy's jerseys, it kind of pissed everyone off."

"Oh, sorry about that."

"Don't be sorry. Just give our jerseys equal time, and we're good."

"Well, that might be a little difficult, but I think you like what I've done even more."

"What are you talking about?"

"I have a new friend next to me who I want you to meet. Please don't be offended, but I gave him your jersey."

"You what?"

"You'll understand when you meet him. I think Julio is like your biggest fan ever. And your jersey has made him a very happy boy. I'm going to turn around and kneel next to him in his wheelchair so we can both see you. Okay?"

"Okay," Arnaldo said.

The next few minutes were very emotional as Casey, Julio, and Arnaldo Facetimed. When the call was over, Julio senior and Marguerite both gave Casey tear filled hugs.

"You're a special boy, Casey Clark," Marguerite said. "I can never thank you enough."

"I was happy to do it. Hey, before I go, would you type your name, address, and phone number into my phone while I say goodbye to Julio?"

He handed her his phone and bent down to Julio.

"Hey, dude. It was great to meet you. Enjoy that smelly jersey. I will be in touch, I promise." Before he stood, Casey noticed tears rolling down Julio's cheeks.

Marguerite returned his phone.

"I'll text you soon, so you'll have my number," he said. "I have to go, but I'll be in touch."

"Thank you, Casey," Marguerite said.

Julio senior was speechless but patted his heart with his fist.

Casey smiled, returned the gesture, and left.

Chapter 32

WHEN CASEY ENTERED the conference room, his parents approached and hugged him.

"You've done it again," his mom said.

"What are you talking about?" Casey asked.

"Your father told me about the boy you met. You just keep impressing me, Casey," she answered.

"What did I do?"

"Your interaction with that boy was remarkable," Reid said.

"You guys would have done the same thing."

"Maybe so," his mother said. "But that's not the point. Just allow us to be proud of you, okay?"

"Fine. But, there is one more thing I want to do for him if it's okay with you guys."

"What's that?" his father asked.

"He's really sick, and they don't have much money, so if it's okay with you and Johnny, Sam, and Chelsea, I want to give them some of the reward money we received. And also, maybe we can fly him up to AllSport, to see if our doctors or trainers can help him."

"What is his condition?" Shane asked.

"Muscular Dystrophy."

"Oh, that's terrible," she said with a sigh. "I don't think there's a cure for that, is there?"

"No," Casey said. "But on the way up here, I read that physical therapy and swimming can help make him more comfortable. Massage therapy would probably be good too. He could do all that at AllSport. I really think it would make his life better. He's not going to live very long, so if we can help make whatever time he has a little better, then we should, right?"

"Well, we could, but it would depend on how his parents feel about it," Reid said.

"We could have them come too."

"And what about his sister?" Reid asked. "One of them needs to stay with her."

"Maybe she could come too," Casey said. "She could go to school on campus. She'd love it, and she'd probably get a better education. If not, we could fly his parents back and forth for a while and see how it works out."

"Casey, it sounds great, but it's a big change for them and an expensive one too," Shane said.

"It doesn't have to be. I mean, if you guys, or AllSport, can cover their room and board, we'll cover their flights."

"Who is we?" Reid asked.

"CAJOSACH Investigations."

"Wait a second," Shane said. "How much reward money did you guys get?"

"$175 thousand."

"What?" Shane and Reid said in unison, drawing the attention of everyone in the room.

Casey shrugged and quietly asked, "Is that a problem?"

Shane and Reid looked at each other.

"I don't know," Reid said with a shrug.

"Me neither," Shane said. "We better discuss it with Jay after the meeting."

"Yeah, and our accountant," Reid added with a chuckle. "C'mon, let's go sit." Reid put an arm around each of their shoulders and lead them to the three unoccupied chairs at the long conference table.

"Everything alright?" Jay asked.

"All good," Reid said. "We'll talk about it later. Sorry for the delay."

Jay nodded. Ice clinked as he took a quick drink from his glass of water. "Okay, folks, I have a lot to explain. We have a bunch of answers, but some issues will take more time to get to the bottom of."

He looked at his phone. "Here's what we know so far. Cartel bosses, Jose Camarillo and Pedro Abila have been fierce competitors for years. Abila fled immediately after we rescued the women and kids. Similar to Jose and probably every other cartel boss, he had an escape plan. It will probably be quite a while before he's found. But, we have his second in command, Rafael, in custody, and he is singing like a bird."

A few confused expressions around the table made Jay chuckle. "Sorry, it means he's telling us everything we need. Luckily for us, he was totally against abducting the women and children in the first place. He was pressing Abila to let them go. The more he pushed, the more irritated Abila became, and finally, after lots of arguing, Abila threatened to kill him. We caught Rafael when he returned to the hotel where we rescued the women and kids. He had come back to pick up cash he had stashed there so he could leave the country.

"Getting him to talk was easy. He said if he went to a local prison, Abila would have him killed in jail. He asked if we could lock him up where Abila can't find him. The truth is, I'm sure no matter where we put him, Abila will get him. But that's not our problem. His hands are just as dirty as Abila's, so he deserves whatever he gets. But offering him that safety was enough for him to give us the information we wanted."

"Where are you going to hide him?" Casey asked.

"Luckily, that's not my decision. It's a Colombian matter. Whether they put him in jail or not, I don't think he'll survive for long."

"That doesn't seem very fair," Chelsea said. "Shouldn't he at least be protected for giving us what we asked for?"

"Chelsea," Jay said sharply. "Just because he didn't agree with the abduction doesn't make him a good guy. He got rich by manufacturing and selling the addictive drugs that you always hear about on the news. The same drugs that kill tons of people every day. Do you really think he deserves protection?"

Chelsea shrunk in her chair. "No, I guess not."

"I'm sorry," Jay said. "I didn't mean to be harsh with you. I just get so mad when I think about the amount of illicit money these guys make and the lifestyle they live. They have so much blood on their hands, yet, they live like kings. It turns my stomach."

There were nods all around the table.

Jay took another swallow of water, cleared his throat, and continued, "Okay, let's get back on track. Rafael told us that years ago, the turf war between Abila and Jose had spread into Europe. Until recently, the Italian mafia was buying drugs equally from both men. Then, after one of Abila's shipments was delayed, they shifted all their business to Jose. Despite his repeated tries, Abila's attempts at negotiating fell on deaf ears, and his complaints were disregarded. The longer it continued, the more his fury festered. Regardless of the fact that even without the Italian business he still made more money than he could spend in a lifetime, he became consumed with the loss of revenue. His judgment became so clouded that he finally decided to threaten the mafia. He foolishly figured that if he could impose enough pain on the Italians, they would reward him with their business. How to inflict that pain became his obsession. He knew that, like himself, they feared little, if anything. In their business, one cannot be scared to die.

"Finally, after almost a year of lost business, his plan came together the minute he heard that Italy would be competing in the

World Cup Championship, practically in his backyard. He knew that Europeans are just as fanatical about their soccer teams as Central and South Americans are. Threatening mafia family members, and even murdering a mafia boss wouldn't be nearly as effective as causing Italy to lose the championship. He thought about kidnapping a player or two, but realized that would probably just delay the game. But, kidnapping the wife and child of one of Italy's top players could easily be used to influence that player to throw the game. And even if the player wasn't willing to lose intentionally, without his heart and soul in the game, Italy's chances of winning would be slim.

"The coincidence that both Marrese's and Sauro's wives and kids were together at the time of the kidnapping made the whole scheme even more powerful. Abila figured that since he had both players' families, it gave him even more leverage over the Italian mafia. Not only would he regain their business, but if he really pressured them, he might even become their sole supplier.

"He was so proud of his undertaking that he disregarded the possible repercussions it could bring. The abduction has created enemies for him everywhere. In Italy, he's got the mafia, the government, and almost the entire country after him. Most of Latin America wants to find him, too. He basically declared war on soccer fans throughout the world by putting his business gains ahead of their sacred championship game. Both the international kidnapping and the murdered guards will ensure jail time once he gets caught. The fact that he provoked so many powerful enemies will assure that his time behind bars will be extremely unpleasant and probably short-lived. I mean that literally. The big problem now is finding him. The longer he remains at large, the deeper underground he'll go.

"So, now comes our next issue. While we now know about Abila's and Rafael's involvement, we still do not know much about Jose. If everything Rafael has told us is true, then Jose had nothing to do with the kidnapping. While I had originally thought Abila and his crew went to the island, killed the guards, and took the women and children from Jose, it doesn't seem to be the case. Rafael said that Abila went to the island just looking to talk to Jose. He figured if he explained the abduction to Jose, face to face, that since Jose is such a big soccer fan, Abila could convince him to share the Italian drug business if he offered to let the women and children go. Rafael said that when he had tried to talk Abila out of the island visit, Abila was so wound up that he wasn't thinking clearly. Then, once they were on the island and realized that Jose wasn't even there, Abila got so mad he ordered his men to kill the two guards.

"Sorry to interrupt, but if Jose didn't have them locked up in his tunnels, how do you explain this?" Chelsea raised the troll doll they found under the pillow. She had been holding on to it since they found it.

"I asked Luna about that," Jay said. "She said that some of Jose's employees bring their kids to work when they are sick. The parents then sneak the children down to that room so they can sleep during their parent's shift. Chances are, a sick child left the doll there. At this point it doesn't matter anyway, because thanks to you kids, we saved the women and children. And, although I hope Abila gets caught, it's really not our problem.

"What I am concerned with now, is the safety of Luna, Marianna, Juan, Antonio, Carita, Tamara, and Diego. They all helped us work against Jose, and the problem is that we don't know if he can be trusted not to retaliate. So, the question is, if they want to get away from him, where do they go? I know Luna owns houses in other countries, but obviously, Jose knows about them too. I haven't mentioned this to anyone else yet, but they'd probably be safest living at AllSport, where my team can protect them.

"While the final decision would obviously be theirs, I wanted to run it by you all first. Are there any objections to inviting them to live at AllSport? They could stay in the dorms, or Luna could build a house or two on campus. I just think that for their safety, moving to AllSport would be best for them. The kids could go to school with you guys," he said, looking at Casey and Johnny. "Carita could work on campus, and Luna could too if she wants. If Tamara is as good as she says she is, she could train for the triathlon. Any thoughts?"

After a moment of silence, Cindy said, "I don't want to sound negative, but while bringing them to AllSport would probably be safer for them, it would also bring a degree of danger to the campus, wouldn't it?"

"I was thinking the same thing," Reid said.

Jay nodded. "I've thought about that too, and yes, it could bring problems. But, I wouldn't have suggested it unless I felt we could protect them along with everyone else on campus. Luna has plenty of money. She can pay for as many extra guards as needed to watch each of them around the clock. And, between her and Carita, I'm sure they have enough friends down here, including a few of Jose's guards, who would be willing to keep us informed of his whereabouts.

"We know where his planes and boats are kept, and we can watch them via satellite in case he decides to make a personal visit. But, if he's like most underworld bosses, he'll send others to do his dirty work."

"Yes," Tzlil spoke up. "But Jay, this will be different than most of his other issues. Since this is his family, it's personal for him. We've seen the difference it can make. It changes everything."

Sun nodded. "She's right. Chances are, once he finds out where they are, he'll come himself. Then, the only question will be whether it's a peaceful visit or not. All bets are off when high-end criminals or even terrorists are dealing with their own families. We've witnessed some extremely ruthless people who were compassionate and forgiving with their relatives. We've also seen those who had reputations of being soft and non-violent who turned merciless when it came to family members who turned on them."

Deep sighs emanated from around the table. Everyone was displaying their emotions one way or the other, except Casey. His arms were folded loosely, his head hung low, and he was slouching in his chair.

"Casey, are you okay?" Jay asked.

Casey slowly looked up. "No, not really. I'm kind of torn on this. I know you all are too. But for you guys, it's strictly about the safety of everyone on campus versus the safety of Luna's family. I'm thinking about that too, but there's more to it for me. I know most of you have noticed that Marianna and I have gotten kind of close during the last few days."

"Duh," Johnny said with a chuckle, sitting between Samantha and Chelsea.

"Shut up," Casey said as the girls simultaneously jabbed Johnny with their elbows.

"Ow. I'm sorry."

"Casey, please continue," his mom said.

Casey sighed. "This is kind of tough to put into words."

"Take your time, son," Reid said.

With a shrug, Casey continued, "I like her, but," he stopped for a moment, then continued, "but I hadn't thought about living with her. Wait, that came out wrong. You know what I mean."

"Of course we do," Jay said calmly.

Casey sighed again and lowered his chin to his chest. After a moment, he raised his head. "This sucks. I don't how to say it. I'm really confused."

"It okay, dude," Johnny said quietly. "We get it. It is confusing. I mean Samantha and I really like each other, but there's a comfort level because we live on opposite sides of the world. I mean, I wish we lived near each other, so we could really be boyfriend and girlfriend, but then, what if it didn't work out. We'd have to see each other every day, and that could get awkward. So for us, when we see each other, it's fun and all, but we always know it's for a short time. If Marianna lives on campus, it could be great for you two, or it might really suck. But here's the deal, if you go out with each other and then break up, it would be like any other couple our age doing the same thing. Think about Jimmy and Liz. We thought they'd be together forever, right? Then they broke up. They avoided each other for a while, but now they're okay with it. And now they are both are going out with different people. It's probably not easy, but you just move on and deal with it. But think about the other side. If it does work, you'll have like the hottest girlfriend ever."

"Wow, Johnny," Reid began.

Johnny raised his pointer finger. "Hold on, Uncle Reid, I'm not done."

Eyes opened wide all around the table. It wasn't like Johnny to be so assertive with adults.

"Sorry for interrupting," Reid said, making the gesture of zipping his mouth shut.

"That's okay. I just want to finish my thought." He turned back toward Casey. "So, here's my suggestion, take the plunge, dude. She's really cool, she's very smart, and she's totally hot. And we already know she can be a big help with CAJOSACH Investigations. And, above all that, it might also save her family's lives, or at least save them from whatever harm Jose might have in store for them."

Casey looked at Johnny for a minute, and his concerned look slowly broke into a smile. "You know what? You're right. I was just being selfish. We should bring them up to AllSport. In fact, if any of you are thinking that we shouldn't, because of the possible danger, you should think about what AllSport is really all about. It's about opportunity." Casey looked at his father. "Dad, you have never thought twice about recruiting a worthy athlete off the streets, no matter what his or her background was. How many of the AllSport athletes were in street gangs before coming to camp. How many gang issues have we dealt with on campus? You've never let that get in the way of bringing an athlete to camp, in fact, I remember hearing you and Uncle Buck saying that safety was half the benefit of AllSport. Giving kids a chance not only to succeed in their sport, but to have a better, safer life than they would have had on the streets, is what AllSport is about. So, while I'm just as surprised as you all are about Johnny being the one to set me straight, he did it. He made me realize that bringing them to AllSport isn't just the right thing to do, it's practically the definition of AllSport."

The following silence around the table was finally broken by Joel's quiet clapping, which slowly spread around the table until all had joined him.

"I'm amazed and really proud of you both, not for just thinking the way you do, but for helping us all see what's right," Casey's mother said.

Jay smiled and said, "Okay, everyone, unless there are any objections, I think we should ask Luna and the others to join us for dinner so we can make our offer. Agreed?"

"Absolutely," Reid said as the others nodded.

***

As coffee, tea, and after-dinner drinks were being served, Johnny and Samantha walked over to Casey and Marianna. "Do you guys want to come for a walk with us?" Johnny asked.

"No thanks," Casey answered. "We were about to do the same thing. Don't be offended. We just need some time to talk."

***

Casey and Marianna held hands as they walked at the water's edge on the beach.

"I'm going to miss you," Casey said.

"Me too," Marianna agreed. "I was so surprised when you guys offered to have us move to AllSport. It sounds like such a great place. I think my mom just needs some time to figure things out."

Casey nodded. "It's gotta be tough. Do you think your uncle is mad enough to hurt you guys?"

"No. He's a jerk, but I know he really loves us. The biggest thing, as you heard my mom tell everyone, is Diego. Uncle Jose would freak out if we took Diego that far from him. I mean he'd be really mad if the rest of us left, but if we took Diego, he'd make it his mission to find us, no matter where we went. I'm so glad my mom found that school. It'll be great for him, and it will get him away from Uncle Jose. The best thing for us all right now, is to stay here."

"Except for Tamara and Antonio, right?"

"Yes, I'm very happy for them. Getting an opportunity to train at AllSport will be amazing for them. I don't know about Tamara's potential, but Antonio is so good. With the right training, I know he'll become a pro. He's the captain of his local futbol club, and he outscores everyone in every game. His teammates will be devastated when he tells them he's leaving. Especially because they have a big tournament coming up."

"He should stay for the tournament and come to AllSport afterward. There's no rush, and he'll want time to say goodbye to his family and friends anyway. We can fly him up when he's ready."

Marianna smiled. "That will make him happy." She turned toward Casey and hugged him. "Thank you."

Casey put his arms around her and after a silent moment, said, "I wish you could come live at AllSport too."

"And I wish you could stay here."

"Well, at least now I know where I want to go on vacations, whenever my parents ask."

"Yeah, and I want to visit AllSport."

"Okay, so we'll visit each other, a lot! We'll have a long-distance relationship, like Johnny and Samantha. And, when we travel to big sporting events, you and Juan can meet us."

"Really? Juan too?"

"Three, four."

Marianna grinned. "Bad joke, but nice of you to include him."

"Well, he's part of our team, right? Maybe we'll call the business CAJOSACHMAJU."

She laughed. "That's ridiculous."

"Okay, how about CAJOSACHJUMA."

She laughed again. Then quietly said, "Will you please just shut up and kiss me."

The End

Acknowledgements:

As always when I think about what it took to bring this novel to fruition, I realize there are many people I need to thank for their extremely valuable critiques, insights and corrections.

First and foremost is my wife and best friend, Greer. The amount of times she read and reread this manuscript would make most people cringe. As with each of my previous novels, her input is invaluable. The details I often request of her as I work to keep the wording unique and fresh are enough to frustrate almost anyone. But she accepts the challenge every time I ask. Greer, my love, I truly cant thank you enough for all your yelp. You are a gem, luckily my gem, and I cherish you.

Another of my editors, Corey Cohn, plays a vital role critiquing and cleaning each manuscript I write. His work on this project made the story much more readable than my original drafts. Thank you, Corey!

Gracias to my friend, Deica Ruiz for your input on the Spanish edits.

After the first few edits, I'm lucky to have a wonderful group of Beta Readers to read and evaluate the manuscript. I would not publish any novel without the input, ideas, and thoughts of Beta Readers. Thank you for your help on this project Sheri Anderson,

Steven Peltz, Brian Summers, Kerry Lawrence, JoAnn Ferrigno, David Barnes, Michael Rooney, Harrison Mellow, Nicky Testaforte, and Jennifer Jenkins.

Finally, thank you to the team at Telemachus Press. Steve, Terri, Samantha, Mary Ann, and the rest of the team. You each make the publishing process seem so simple. I do know better, and for that, I thank you so much.

About the Author

Michael Balkind's novels *Sudden Death, Dead Ball, Gold Medal Threat* and *Stealing Gold* are endorsed by literary greats including James Patterson, Clive Cussler, John Feinstein, Andrew Gross, John Lescroart, Wendy Corsi Staub and Tim Green. He has appeared on ESPN's *The Pulse, Sportsnet's Daily News Live*, and has co-hosted *The Clubhouse* radio show. He is a member of Mystery Writers of America. Balkind's novel, *The Fix*, is co-authored with NBC Sports and Golf Channel Host, Ryan Burr. Balkind graduated from Syracuse University and resides in New York.

Balkind's website: www.balkindbooks.com
His author page on Facebook:
Michael Balkind—Mysteries & More
Follow him on Instagram and Twitter: @michaelbalkind

If you enjoyed *Kid-Napped in Cartagena*, be sure to
read Michael Balkind's other novels:

Visit Michael Balkind's Amazon Author Page: